Getting Old Is Murder

How can I describe this day? Everyone is on shpilkes. *Shpilkes*—an untranslatable word. It's like going crazy without going crazy.

At three o'clock, there are multiple knocks on my door. I can see four anxious faces through my kitchen window. Reluctantly, I let them in.

Evvie takes the floor. "We've made a decision. We're going to the movies."

"But first dinner," says Bella.

I look at them in horror. "Are you trying to say we shouldn't stay home and guard Esther? Have you all lost your minds? Who's going to be able to concentrate on a movie!"

"Me!" A unanimous chorus.

"So, tell me already." I can't believe I'm even asking. "What's playing?"

"*Sorry, Wrong Number,*" Evvie says. "With Barbara Stanwyck. And *No Way to Treat a Lady.*"

I am fairly salivating. Two great classics. What am I thinking? This is crazy!

Evvie pokes me. "Admit it, you want to go."

I am pacing now. Torn, and ashamed of myself. "We have a responsibility here!"

"To Miss Ungrateful?" Ida says. "Why should we care?"

"And how will you live with yourselves tomorrow if she's dead?"

That stops them for about a minute.

Getting Old Is
MURDER

Rita Lakin

A DELL BOOK

GETTING OLD IS MURDER
A Dell Book / November 2005

Published by Bantam Dell
A Division of Random House, Inc.
New York, New York

Map and ornament illustrations by Laura Hartman Maestro

Book design by Karin Batten

ISBN-13: 978-0-553-24258-1
ISBN-10: 0-440-24258-4

Printed in the United States of America
Published simultaneously in Canada

www.bantamdell.com

OPM   10 9 8 7 6 5 4 3

For

Who coulda, woulda, shoulda
been Gladdy Gold

and

Who inspired me all my life

You know that old trees just grow stronger
And old rivers grow wilder every day
But old people just grow lonesome
Waiting for someone to say,
"Hello in there. Hello."
Hello in There
BY JOHN PRINE

"Let's face it.
We all have the same five relatives."
Billy Crystal

If one life matters
Then all life matters
A Christian meditation

"The golden years have come at last
Well, the golden years can kiss my ass."
Hy Binder, taken from the Internet

Introduction to Our Characters

GLADDY & HER GLADIATORS

Gladys (Gladdy) Gold, 75 Our heroine, and her funny, adorable, sometimes impossible partners:

Evelyn (Evvie) Markowitz, 73 Gladdy's sister. Logical, a regular Sherlock Holmes

Ida Franz, 71 Stubborn, mean, great for in-your-face confrontation

Bella Fox, 83 "The shadow." She's so forgettable, she's perfect for surveillance, but smarter than you think

Sophie Meyerbeer, 80 Master of disguises, she lives for color-coordination

Francie Charles, 77 Always optimistic, Gladdy's best friend

YENTAS, KIBITZERS, SUFFERERS: THE INHABITANTS OF PHASE TWO

Hy Binder, 88 A man of a thousand jokes, all of them tasteless

Lola Binder, 78 His wife, who hasn't a thought in her head that he hasn't put there

Denny Ryan, 42 The handyman. Sweet, kind, mentally slow

Enya Slovak, 84 Survivor of "the camps" but never survived

Harriet Feder, 44 "Poor Harriet," stuck with caring for her mother

Esther Feder, 77 Harriet's mom in a wheelchair. What a nag

Tessie Hoffman, 56 Chubby, in mourning for her best friend

Millie Weiss, 80 Suffering with Alzheimer's, and

Irving Weiss, 86 Suffering because she's suffering

Mary Mueller, 60 and

John Mueller, 60 Nosy neighbors

ODDBALLS AND FRUITCAKES

The Canadians, 30ish Young, tan, and clueless

Leo (Mr. Sleaze) Slezak, 50 Smarmy real estate broker

Greta Kronk, 88 Crazy like a fox

Sol Spankowitz, 79 A lech after the ladies

THE COP AND THE COP'S POP

Morgan (Morrie) Langford, 35 Tall, lanky, sweet, and smart

Jack Langford, 75 Handsome and romantic

THE LIBRARY MAVENS

Conchetta Aguilar, 38 Her Cuban coffee could grow hair on your chest

Barney Schwartz, 27 Loves a good puzzle

AND

Yolanda Diaz, 22 Her English is bad, but her heart is good

Building Q-Quinsana

IDA 319 GLADDY 317 SOPHIE 314

TESSIE 216 SELMA 215

ESTHER & HARRIET 118

mailboxes & elevator

DENNY 119 IRV & MILLIE 114

ENYA 219 EVVIE 217 BELLA 216 HY & LOLA 214

GRETA 318 MARY & JOHN 314

mailboxes & elevator

Building P-Petunia
Lanai Gardens

Francie lives around the corner, in Building R.
Leo Slezak lives in Phase Four. Sol Spankowitz lives in Phase Three.
Jack Langford lives in Phase Six.

Gladdy's Glossary

Yiddish (meaning Jewish) came into being between the ninth and twelfth centuries in Germany as adaptation of German dialect to the special uses of Jewish religious life.

In the early twentieth century, Yiddish was spoken by eleven million Jews in Eastern Europe and the United States. Its use declined radically. However, lately there has been a renewed interest in embracing Yiddish once again as a connection to Jewish culture.

a choleria	a curse on you (get cholera)
a klog iz mi	woe is me
aleha ha-shalom	rest in peace
alter kuckers	lecherous old men
chozzerai	a lot of nonsense
dreck	dirt, filth
fahputzed	overly done
farbissener	embittered person
farblondjet	bewildered
gefilte fish	stuffed fish
geshrei	uproar
gonif	thief
Gott im Himmel	God in heaven

Kaddish	mourner's prayer
kasha	buckwheat groats
kasha varnishkas	groats & bowtie noodles
kibitz	someone offering unwanted advice
knish	meat or potato filled wonton
kreplach	like a wonton
kurveh	whore
kvetch	whining & complaining
maven	someone who knows everything
meeskite	ugly one
meshugeneh	crazy
mitzvah	a blessing
ongepatshket	overdone, cluttered
oy	an exclamation for emotions
oy gevalt	an anguished cry
pisher	a squirt, a nobody
putz	penis
rugallah	pastry with fillings
schlep	dragging a load
schmaltz	fat
schmear	to coat with butter or cream cheese

shayner boychik	darling boy
shayner kindlach	beautiful children
shikseh	non-Jewish girl
shmegegi	a fool
shnapps	whiskey
shpilkes	on pins and needles
vantz	bedbug
vay iz mir	woe is me
yenta	busybody

Getting Old Is

MURDER

Death by Delivery

The poison was in the pot roast.

In a few hours Selma Beller would be dead. This was regrettable because tomorrow was her birthday and she was so looking forward to it. Her husband, Ernie, had keeled over at seventy-nine. Having beaten him at gin rummy and shuffleboard, she had gleefully intended to beat him yet again, this time to the big eight-oh. Alas, poor Selma.

While she was waiting to die, Selma was dusting. Dust was her enemy. And she battled mightily. No fragile feather duster for her. And forget that sissy stuff like lemon Pledge. She used good old-fashioned Lysol, confident that neither dust nor germ escaped its lethal dose. Death to dust, she thought and then laughed, dust to dust.

Looking up, Selma glanced at the clock. Where had the afternoon gone? It was nearly dinnertime. Too bad her best (and only) friend, Tessie, was busy tonight with out-of-town visitors. She should have gone shopping this morning. Oh, well, there was always cottage cheese, with a piece of cut-up peach and some sour cream. She wrinkled up her nose. What she really craved was red meat. Bloody and rare.

There was a knock on the door.

Selma groped around for her glasses, misplaced, as usual. Giving up, she moved as quickly as she could manage toward the door, automatically straightening the doily on the arm of her emerald green recliner. Glancing toward the array of grand-children's photos on her foyer table, she blew a kiss at the smiling faces.

"Who is it?" she trilled. She would never open the door to a stranger.

"Delivery. Meals on Wheels."

Squinting through the peephole, Selma, though her vision was blurred, identified the familiar shopping bags with the Meals on Wheels logo. A volunteer wearing jeans, a windbreaker, a baseball cap, and sunglasses stood there, arms full.

"Wrong apartment," she said wistfully.

"Mrs. Beller? Apartment two-fifteen?"

"Yes, but I didn't order—"

"Happy birthday to you from Meals on Wheels. A special introductory order."

"Really?" Selma was feeling the beginnings of hope. "Something smells wonderful. What's in the bags?"

The volunteer consulted a piece of paper. "Pot roast. Stuffed cabbage rolls. Mushroom and barley soup, potato pancakes with sour cream, and apple strudel for dessert."

Practically drooling, Selma unlocked the deadbolt her son, Heshy, had installed, then the other two safety locks.

She squinted again as the volunteer entered with the packages. "Don't I know you? You look familiar...." But Selma was distracted as she sniffed the air in appreciation. "I can't wait," she said as she took the bags and carried them into her spotless kitchen. She quickly unwrapped the containers and began setting them out on her best Melmac dishes on her small white Formica dinette table.

"I just hope the soup isn't too salty. My blood pressure, you know."

A wrought-iron chair was pulled out for her. Smiling, she let herself be seated.

"At your service, Mrs. Beller."

"What a way to go." Selma giggled, tucking her napkin in.

Those were Selma Beller's final words. The last thing she saw as she was starting to lose consciousness was the logo on the Meals on Wheels shopping bags as the killer calmly refolded them, and her last fading thought was that the pot roast had been a little stringy....

1

Gladdy Gets Going

Hello. Let me introduce myself. I'm Gladdy Gold. Actually, Gladys. I'm a self-proclaimed P.I. That's right, a private eye. Operating out of Fort Lauderdale. When did I get into the P.I. biz? As we speak. My credentials? More than thirty years of reading mysteries. Miss Marple and Miss Silver are my heroines.

In case you were expecting someone like what's-her-name with her "A" is for this, "B" is for that—you know who I mean, working her way all the way to Z—well, that's not me. I'll be lucky if I make it to the end of this book. After all, I *am* seventy-five.

You think seventy-five is old? Maybe, if you're twenty, it's ancient, but if you're fifty, it doesn't seem as old as it used to. And if you're ninety, well, seventy-five seems like a kid. You ought to see those spry ninety-year-old *alter kuckers* trying to hit on me for a date. When I look in the mirror, I don't see that older, faded, wrinkled stranger who barely resembles someone I once knew. I see a gangly, pretty, eager seventeen-year-old, marvelously alert and alive with glistening brown hair and hazel eyes.

Did you know that when you get older, and the brain cells start to turn on you, the nouns are the first to go?

For example, "what's-her-name" I just threw at you. I meant Sue Grafton, and this time it only took about two minutes for my brain synapses to make the connection and pull her name out of the cobwebs of my mind. Sometimes it takes days. All the while, it was on the tip of my tongue. My poor tongue must be exhausted from all the information I keep stored there.

Hey, you young ones—laugh. Wait 'til you get to be my age. Then the laugh will be on you. You'll ask the same questions we all ask: Where did the years go? How did they go by so fast? And even worse—where did all the money go?

Enough with all the philosophy. The question for now is how did I get into this private-eye racket? Before I retired, I was a librarian, so if you say this is a strange career move, I would certainly agree.

I was minding my own business in Lanai Gardens, Phase Two, building Q, apartment 317 on West Oakland Park Boulevard, Lauderdale Lakes, when a few of my neighbors died suddenly. Considering that the youngest of us is seventy-one and the oldest eighty-six, this is not something unexpected. I mean, *everybody* is on the checkout line. For example, we used to have five tables of canasta: now we're down to one. The Men's Sports Club used to fill four cars on Sunday for their trip out to Hialeah: now the only members left are Irving Weiss and his pal, Sol, from Phase Three. Even the nags that broke the guys' wallets have gone to thorough-bred heaven.

As I started to say—I was beginning to suspect foul play.

I am convinced that these deaths to which I am referring are not natural. There is a killer stalking Lanai Gardens. Nobody believes me, certainly not the police, but I intend to prove it. But first you need to meet the rest of the gang.

2

Walking

It's seven A.M. on a beautiful, very typical Friday morning in paradise. As usual I wake up a minute before the alarm goes off. I start my coffee perking—a vice I will not give up. I take out my one slice of whole wheat bread, pop it in the toaster. Get out my one teaspoon of sugar and my one-percent low-fat milk and I am ready to "seize the day."

I allow myself twenty minutes to work on the unfinished Sunday crossword that never leaves my kitchen table. I used to do the puzzle, in ink, on the morning it arrived. Now, it can take as long as a week to dredge up answers from my disobedient brain. Frustrating, but you do not give up *anything* that affords you pleasure at this time in life.

Lanai Gardens is situated in one of the many sprawling apartment complexes in this part of southeast Florida. A lot of people think of Fort Lauderdale as this ritzy community on the water, or the place made famous by all those college kids who take their clothes off on Spring Break—but that's not where we live.

Our condo isn't fancy, but it's pretty nice with its peach stucco buildings (just beginning to peel), swaying palm trees (look out for the falling coconuts), well-tended lawns (when the gardener shows up), pools and Jacuzzis, shuffleboard courts, duck ponds (watch your step!), and recreation rooms.

Now, into a pair of sweats, and I'm ready to begin the morning workout, such as it is. It's eight A.M. and my fellow residents are coming to life.

We used to go to the air-conditioned malls for our morning stroll, but not after reading those articles in the newspapers about older women being killed. Now we've decided to exercise at home. Exercise? Fast walking, slow walking, shuffling, barely moving at all; whatever the body will endure.

I'm the first one out on the third-floor walkway to warm up. And that's the signal for all the others to rush out.

My sister, Evvie Markowitz, is always the next one out. While I am in the Q building (Q for Quinsana), she lives across the way in apartment 215 in P building (P for Petunia. The builders were big on flowers). She refers to herself as my kid sister. Seventy-three to my seventy-five. We don't look anything like each other. I am taller. She is heavier. (We're both shorter than we used to be.) Before we turned gray, she was a redhead; I, a brunette. I was the scholarly one; she the dynamic, dramatic one. I was the plain one; she was the beauty. This dictum came down from our well-meaning but unsophisticated immigrant mother who didn't understand what damage such labels could cause. It set the course for both our lives. We never really became friends until I moved down here.

Evvie starts her own warm-ups. She always says the same thing every morning, calling out to me over the tops of the cars parked between our buildings. "Glad, how did you sleep?"

"Pretty good," I call back.

"I only had to get up three times last night," she says.

"Don't complain. Five times for me!" This from Ida Franz, our whirling dervish, who pops out of apartment 319 in my building and fairly leaps into pace with me. Ida is seventy-one, with a body that's compact and wiry. Her salt-and-pepper hair is always in a tight bun which threatens to pull her face off her head. Her back is ramrod straight, which Evvie says is so she won't drop the chip on each shoulder. "And the last time was at three A.M. It didn't pay to go back to bed after that."

"So what did you do?" Evvie calls out from across the way, knowing full well what Ida will say.

"I called my son in L.A. He's still up at midnight."

Evvie makes a familiar disgusted gesture, flapping her arms. We are all used to Ida trying to make her children love her, a lost cause. She's the one who calls them; they never call her. And because her children make her crazy, Ida makes us crazy.

I hear what I hear every morning: Sophie, calling from her kitchen window. "Yoo-hoo, I'm coming. I'm coming. Wait for me!" Trust me. She'll be last one out.

Routine is very important to us. Ida, the perpetual wet blanket, says it's because we're all in our second childhood. Except for Sophie, who she insists never grew out of her first one.

Now the door to apartment 216 opens across the way in Evvie's building. Bella Fox, who is eighty-three, gingerly steps out.

"Good morning," she whispers.

The girls call Bella "the shadow" because she's forever trailing one step behind us. We are always afraid of losing her, because she is so forgettable. She's tiny, not even five feet, and she wears pale colors that add to her seeming invisibility. But I'm on to Bella. She may seem shy, but in her own timid little way she's not afraid to speak her piece. She says what she wants and she gets what she wants. "Hi, gang! Your personal trainer is here! Everybody ready?" This is from Francie Charles, calling up to us as she rounds the corner from her building.

Her arrival is the signal for all of us to go downstairs and meet on the ground floor. Then we walk together along a shady path that winds around the building.

Francie, who will be seventy-eight tomorrow, was a real beauty when she was young. Tall, elegant, and classy, a model in her younger New York days, she is still beautiful. She's our real athlete, the one who got us all started in this somewhat anemic form of exercise. "Something is better than nothing," she is always telling us. She is also our health nut, lecturing on the right way to eat, although no one really can, or wants to, change the bad habits of a lifetime. Francie's only weakness is advertised by her favorite sweatshirt, "Death by Chocolate," given to her by her adoring grandchildren. She is wearing it today.

"How is everyone?" she chirps. "Isn't it a glorious day? Aren't we all glad to be alive!" As grumpy as Ida is, that's how cheerful Francie is. The perpetual optimist. She makes every day a gift. If it wasn't for Francie, I'd have left Florida years ago.

Bella begins taking slow, mincing steps—her version of exercise—along the path, apologizing every time anyone passes her.

"Stop apologizing for living," Evvie is constantly telling her. But Bella, who is fairly deaf, either doesn't hear or chooses not to. We all love her, but she doesn't believe it.

We walk and talk. With plenty to say, as if we don't see one another every single day and night. Not to mention phoning one another a dozen or more times a day.

Our half-hour workout is just about over when Sophie Meyerbeer, our roly-poly eighty-year-old, finally steps out of the elevator, bandbox-perfect in her pink, color-coordinated, extra-tight jogging ensemble. Pink sweats, pink sneakers with matching pom-poms, and a pink flowered sun hat. I might mention that this month's hairdo is also pink. Champagne Pink.

When she finally catches up to us, Ida mock-applauds her arrival. "So happy you could make it, Princess."

Clueless, Sophie takes her sarcasm as a compliment. Being incapable of spontaneity, Sophie has to get all dressed up, including makeup (*fahputzed*, Evvie calls it), before she'll walk out her door. Her third husband, Stanley, who made a fortune in notions and novelties, spoiled her rotten. He babied her, never let her lift a finger. Insisted she dress like a Kewpie doll for him. (Boy, did we speculate on *their* sex life!) He left her well-off and impossible.

"We're just about finished," says Ida, cooling down by walking slower.

"Oh," Sophie says, pouting girlishly. "Well, I couldn't help it. I didn't sleep a wink last night. I had such a terrible nightmare."

Bella stops, glad for any excuse not to move. "Ooh, tell us." She sits down on a bench, fanning herself.

Sophie shudders. "I dreamed I had a heart attack!"

Bella gasps, fluttering her hands nervously. "Oy...just like Selma."

"Change the subject," Ida snaps. She is never comfortable talking about death.

"No, it's my dream," Sophie insists.

"Just because Selma had a heart attack doesn't mean you will," Francie says gently as she continues her stretches.

Evvie adds judgmentally, "Besides, she was overweight and never exercised."

"Yeah," Ida adds with a satisfied smirk, "she and her pal Tessie were both thrown out of Weight Watchers."

"Maybe something caused that heart attack," I say. "For example, you know how Selma waxed those floors?"

"Yeah," Sophie chirps, "you coulda gone ice skating on them."

"Maybe she slipped and fell. Or maybe something frightened her..." I continue.

"She was so scared of spiders," Bella chimes in,

happy to be able to contribute. "Remember that time she fainted when a teensie one crawled on her chair ... ?"

Ida puts her hands on her hips defiantly and glares at me. "So? Dead is dead. What difference does it make?"

"The point is nobody bothered to investigate," I say. "Nobody cared to find out what really happened. Maybe if she hadn't been alone, maybe if Tessie hadn't had company that weekend, maybe she wouldn't have died."

This gives everyone pause.

Ida's had enough, and starts for the elevator. "Well, I'm going to get my bathing suit on."

"Good idea," I say, sorry I even brought it up. What's the point in depressing them?

Francie puts a reassuring arm around me. "Hey, Ida called it." Mimicking her: "Dead is dead." She giggles and I join in.

The group disbands, each to her own building, to get ready for part two of the morning routine—the pool.

3

Swimming

Just as I'm ready to walk out the door and head for the pool, I look at the phone, count to three, and—it rings. I pick it up and say, "Yes, Sophie."

"Are we going to the pool?"

"Yes, dear."

"Can I walk down with you?"

"Only if you're ready."

"Well...I'll just be a minute."

Knowing Sophie's minute, I tell her as I always do, "I'll start down. You can catch up to me."

I hang up, but stay by the phone. I know my customers. It rings again. My daily double. "Yes, Bella," I say as I pick up.

"Are we going to Publix today?" she asks.

"We usually go shopping on Friday."

"Is it Friday?"

"Yes, dear. Now go knock on Evvie's door and she'll walk you down to the pool. Don't forget your towel."

"All right."

The phones. Umbilical cords. Lifelines. To keep connected. To counteract loneliness. God bless Bell South.

I walk down the three flights instead of taking the elevator, another small attempt to keep fit, and join the parade heading for the pool. Everyone's in bathing suits, sun hats, and thongs (not the kind worn by the young girls at Miami Beach, but the ones which adorn wrinkled feet) and carrying towels and small beach bags. Swimming time is also early in the morning—before it gets too hot to sit around the pool.

Francie is in the parking area chatting with Denny Ryan as he rakes up fallen palm fronds. He is a big six-footer, in his early forties, but you'd hardly know it. Perhaps being slightly slow-witted has kept him childlike. His mother, Maureen, died suddenly about seven years ago. Maybe it's cruel to say it, but he's better off. Even though she was his sole support and caretaker, she was a harridan. But there is a real sweetness to Denny, and we try to add to his small allowance from Social Security by giving him odd jobs around our apartments. He can and does fix everything.

It was poor Denny, just doing his job, who came up to Selma's apartment to fix a plumbing leak. He was the one who found her dead body, and he still hasn't gotten over it.

Francie and Denny have something in common: their love of gardening. Denny is very proud of the patch of ground the condo board gave him to raise flowers and vegetables. You should have seen the look of wonder on his face the first time a small shoot came up from a seed he planted.

"Good morning, Denny," I say.

"Hi, Mrs. Gold. Guess what Miss Francie gave me? A new plant." Denny will never address us by our first names. He feels it is impolite. Except for Francie, who is special to him. He squints down at the little identification tag, struggling with the Latin words. "Ge-nus of tu...tu...berous...herba..."

Francie and I exchange concerned glances. Her kind gesture is meant to help him get over his shock. "Forget the big words," she tells him. "Just call it dahlia."

"Dahlia," he says, smiling, committing it to memory. "Dahlia..."

"That's really pretty," I say.

Francie gets in step with me, and arm in arm we continue down the brick-tiled path toward the pool. In front of us, Ida is cursing our resident ducks as usual. They deposit their droppings right smack on our paths and it sends Ida into a tizzy.

The regulars are already at the pool. The seating arrangement is a tableau. Everyone has his or her designated place. And no one ever varies from it. Or there would be war.

At the farthest end of the pool, completely alone, sits Enya Slovak on a chaise longue. At eighty-four, she is a fragile remainder of a woman who was once very beautiful. She wears a big, floppy sun hat, but it's less to hide from the sun than from the rest of us. While her husband, Jacov, was still alive, he made her attend the various events we have in the clubhouse. The holidays were vitally important to him. Especially the group Passover dinner. Enya merely endured those celebrations. Now that he is gone, she has reverted to how she really wants to be. Alone. I say hello. She nods, then her head swivels back down to the book in her lap. Enya met her husband after they were released from Dachau at the end of the war. They had both lost their entire families. When I look into Enya's haunted eyes, I get the feeling she never fully left the camps.

Directly across the pool from Enya sits a small group who always congregate together. They are the snowbirds—the Canadians—renters and owners who fly in every winter to get away from the bitter weather up north. They're friendly but generally stick to themselves.

Moving clockwise from the snowbirds is another story and a half. Harriet Feder and her mother, Esther. Poor Harriet. Sometimes it sounds like it's already become part of her name: "Poor-Harriet." When Esther went into the wheelchair, Harriet gave up her Miami apartment and moved in with her. It's already four years. I swear that Esther, who looks like a sparrow and can out-eat anyone, is in better health than the whole bunch of us. But meanwhile, her daughter, Harriet, is stuck at age forty-four without much of a life. She's not bad looking, if she'd only use some makeup, maybe do a little something with her hair. . . . She's such a nice girl. Unfortunately for her, she grew up big-boned like her late father. And going to the gym every day . . . all those muscles . . . it doesn't help. Esther boasts that no one on her side of the family died before the age of ninety-five. And she is only seventy-seven. It's not that Esther is a bad person,

she's just so demanding. Get me this, get me that. . . .
Poor Harriet. See what I mean?

In the shallow end of the pool, by themselves,
holding hands and bobbing up and down like two
rosy apples in a barrel are "the Bobbsey twins" as
we call them behind their backs, Hyman and Lola
Binder—aka Hy and Lo, when we are playing cards,
but more about that later. Lola would be all right
away from Hy, but that's the point. She is never
away from his side. They've been married for sixty-
five years and she hasn't had a thought in her head
that he hasn't put there. They are still in love if you
call obsession love. Hy is short and chunky; Lola is
taller and much thinner. We decided that the happi-
est day in Hy's life was when the children grew up
and moved away. I once commented to Irving Weiss
that he and Hy were the only men left in our phase.
Irving, a man of very few words, shook his head and
said, "Then I'm alone."

I glance toward dear Irving, sitting next to his
Millie in the shade outside of the pool perimeter. His
life is hell these days, but he never utters a com-
plaint. Millie's Alzheimer's is getting worse, but do
not mention putting her into a hospital to Irving.
Not a chance. There she sits, totally unaware of all
her friends around her. She stares down at her sundress, picking at a thread, muttering to herself. We
all take turns helping Irving dress her and bathe her
and do the shopping and it is breaking our hearts to
see what has become of the funny, warm-hearted
Millie we once knew.

Denny Ryan walks up the path carrying a rose
from his garden. He reaches Millie and gives it to her.
He whispers to her and she seems to answer him.

Francie and I walk over to give her a kiss on the cheek. She stares up at us, vacantly. "Good morning, Millie," we say.

"Do you see them?" she says shrilly. Irving stiffens. Here she goes again. "Do you see the children? There! There, sitting on the fence. No! No! Don't let them see you looking! Don't make them mad!"

Francie and I are distraught by her hallucinations, but Denny, God bless him, joins in her fantasies. "Yes," he says, "I see ghosts, too."

"Do they scare you, Denny?" She always knows him, although she hardly recognizes the rest of us.

"Oh, yes," he says, "they scare me, too."

Millie shudders. "They're out to get us."

Irving puts his arms around her. "I'll protect you." She pulls away angrily, shouting. "No, you can't, they're too strong!" Everyone's watching, responding in their own private ways. Some with sadness, compassion, fear, and even terror. All with the unstated *There, but for the grace of God...* Irving helps her up from the bench. "We better go back in," he says.

Irving leads Millie away, Denny following behind, as if to shield them. There is silence, but the mood lifts. We have been living with Millie's deterioration for a long time.

Swimming is a euphemism for what we do in the pool. Except for Francie who really swims, the rest of us walk. Back and forth across the width of the pool, walking and talking.

Now Hy Binder slogs through the water toward us. "Look out," my sister Evvie whispers. "He's got a new joke."

I groan.

"Hey, Gladdy." I try to move out of his path, but I'm not fast enough. He punches my arm. He always punches my arm. He makes me black and blue. "Didja hear this one? Didja? I got it off the Internet on my e-mail. Six old guys"—they're always about old guys—"are sitting around the old folks home, smoking stogies and drinking schnapps when Sexy Sadie comes by batting her eyelashes at them. She holds up her pocketbook and says, 'If you guess what's in the purse you get free sex tonight.' One old guy says, 'Ya gotta elephant in there?' She bats her eyes again. 'Close enough.'"

Hy screams with laughter at his joke. "Didja get it, didja?" It's in incredibly bad taste. But then, so is Hy. I paddle away and he heads back to Lola, delighted with himself.

Evvie shakes her head. "Meshuggener. That man is an idiot."

I sigh. "But he's our idiot."

Francie points. "And here comes the other one."

"Hell-o, here I am." In yet another of her hundred color-coordinated garments—lemon yellow this time with a matching parasol to ward off that nasty sun—wiggles our beloved Sophie. Just in time for the rest of us to get out of the pool and head for the showers. . . .

Years ago, when a group of us were sitting around and kvetching about our troubles, wise old Irving said, "Go ahead, everyone put your pains on the table and pick up somebody else's. Believe me, you'll take back what belongs to you." When I look around at the denizens of our phase—Enya from the concentration camps; Millie with Alzheimer's, and Irving's anguish; Esther in a wheelchair; Harriet, lonely; and all the women, now widows, left to cope as best they can—Irving was right.

Little did we know the troubles soon to come would be shared by all of us.

4

The Designated Driver

I am in my apartment, showered and dressed and waiting for the others to get ready to go out for our typical late morning errands. And the phone rings.

"It's a matter of life and death. I have to get to Publix. I'm out of everything." This in a panicky whisper from Bella, she who has enough food in her pantry to feed all of Miami.

I reassure her, yet again that, yes, we will stop at Publix. I barely get the phone back on the hook when the next country is heard from.

Sophie, the fashion maven, sighs when I pick up. "Oy," she says, dropping one of her many philosophical malapropisms, "when did my wild oats turn to kasha?" I wait. She reveals that she has to drop off thirty or so garments at the cleaners. Of course I'm exaggerating. But only slightly.

Next. Evvie reminds me that she needs to deliver her latest review for the Lanai Gardens newspaper, which my sister started twenty years ago with a group of frustrated ex-New Yorkers who loved movies, plays, and all the arts. Everyone reads the *Free Press,* the pulse of Lanai Gardens, listing its Hadassah meetings, club activities, religious holidays, etc. The biggest draw is Evvie's famous movie reviews. We girls go to the movies every Saturday afternoon and afterwards Evvie goes home and dutifully comments on them. She has a big following.

Ida, cranky as usual, phones in, and in that imperious voice of hers, says she must go to the bank. Sometimes I think that tight bun of hers cuts off the air to her brain. She always goes to the bank on Fridays, and she knows I always make a stop there, but she will call to remind me—the Phone God must be served.

And *everyone* has to go to the drugstore for the usual assortment of prescriptions that have to be refilled. Not to mention vitamins and Dr. Scholl's foot pads and Ex-Lax. Francie has all of us on some herbs called Brain Pep. She swears that *Ginkgo biloba,* gotu kola, and Schizandra (I did not make this up) will save our memories. It obviously isn't working for me.

Gentle Irving now phones to ask that I please not forget the items on his shopping list. Things his Millie needs. As if I would forget.

"Everybody report in by now?" This is Francie calling to check up on whether everyone else checked in yet.

"All present and accounted for."

We both laugh at the daily absurdity of the phone calls. We know that before they even made these calls to me, they'd already talked to one another and gone through the exact same litany.

And why do they all call *me*? Because I'm the only one of the girls who can still drive and hasn't relinquished her car. Denny has his mother's old Ford Fairlane, which we use as a taxi occasionally. He also helps out by driving relatives to and from the airport—for a fee which we set for him, or he'd be too shy to ask. Hy Binder also drives, but no one in their right mind would get into a car with him, except Lola, who has no choice. God help her—he thinks he's racing the Daytona 500.

Harriet works; that lets her out. And Francie gave up her car when her car gave up on her.

"Well," Francie says, winding up, "enjoy your chores, Ms. Limo Driver."

"Sure you don't want to come along?" There actually is room for six in my old Chevy wagon, but it's a tight fit. "You can always sit on Ida's lap."

"What, and get stabbed by her quills!?"

"Sophie?"

"And get stabbed by her parasol?"

"Coward."

"Glutton for punishment."

"What can I do? They *neeeeed* me." As if we haven't enjoyed this conversation a hundred times.

"Read my lips." And we recite it, singsong, together. "Get a cab! Take a bus. Walk. Stay hooooome."

I smile as I hang up. I love that wonderful woman. She is my soul mate. What would I ever do without her?

5

Going into Town, Or Trying to

"Glad, can we please get going? I'm dying from the heat already." Evvie has a right to complain. We've been waiting forever, or so it seems, for everyone to get into my car. The pavement is burning our feet.

First, Bella, terrified of forgetting anything, left her shopping list on the kitchen table, so she went scampering back for it. Then Sophie, who would never let anyone break her record for lateness, went back for her sunblock even though we'd only be walking outside from the parking lot into the market.

"We can always leave them behind," I say.

"Then let's do it. Heckle and Jeckle are driving me up one wall and down the other," agrees Evvie, the impatient organizer.

"Bella! Sophie! Get down here already," screeches Ida, who has less patience than anyone.

Sophie waves gaily out her window. "I'm almost

ready. I got my head together, but the rest of me is falling apart."

Ida is in a bad mood anyway. As usual, her mailbox was empty this morning. She mailed an expensive birthday gift to one of her grandchildren. (She'd never admit it's bribery.) No one has bothered to thank her or even acknowledge receiving it.

I try not to open my mailbox when she is around. I feel guilty when I get so many wonderful letters from my grandchildren in New York. I'm truly blessed. And genuinely sorry for Ida.

Evvie is tapping her foot, a very bad sign. "I promised Meyer I'd get my copy over to the newspaper before noon. Now, he won't be there when I get there. I'm going to kill those two *shmegeggies*!"

She's furious; she's never late with her copy.

I've pulled the sunshade off the windshield, I've got all the windows and doors open, and I'll put the air on as soon as I see them coming. The car should be bearable enough to get in now. And we're still waiting.

Ida, trying to keep her temper in check, is now reading the notices on the bulletin board next to the elevator. "Did you see this, girls?" We turn.

"There's another flyer warning us about this guy who's killing older women. They say we should never go out alone at night, or go into bad neighborhoods."

"Well, we don't have to be concerned," Evvie says. "We're always asleep by nine o'clock and, anyway, we never leave our neighborhood."

"They're worried about us being followed home," I comment as I read over her shoulder. "This guy manages to get into women's apartments without breaking in."

"How can he do that?" Evvie asks. "You have to be pretty stupid to let in someone you don't know."

"Well, it happens all the time. My murder mysteries come up with tons of different ways. A guy carrying flowers poses as a delivery man. You'd open the door, wouldn't you? Or a telegram. Or someone in a cop's uniform? Or someone says your kids were in an accident and he's the good Samaritan they sent to get you...."

Ida and Evvie are silent for a moment. "I see what you mean," Ida says. "Who'd ever question any of those?"

I suddenly feel my blood run cold. "Is it possible," I say, thinking about Selma yet again, "maybe it wasn't a heart attack or an accident—?"

"Hey, dolls! Up here!"

Ida jumps, startled. We look up, to the second floor.

And guess who? It's our favorite pain-in-the-ass, Hy Binder, heading for the laundry room with a basket load of wash.

"We almost got away," Evvie moans.

"Didja hear this one?" he calls out to us. "What's the difference between a wife and a girlfriend?" Not bothering to wait for a response, he tells us. "Forty-five pounds."

"Get lost, Hy," Ida yells.

"What's it called when a woman is paralyzed from the waist down?" Pause, then a guffaw. "Marriage!"

There's no stopping him.

Evvie shrieks at him. "Why don't you go soak your head in the dryer?"

"Don't you mean washer?" Ida asks.

"Washer. Dryer. Who cares. Just get rid of him!"

Evvie starts to get into the car. "I'd rather melt than listen to his dreck!"

"Wait, but didja hear what happened real early this morning? No joke."

Lola comes out of their apartment with another basket of laundry. She continues it for Hy. "Guess who crazy Kronk got this time?"

"Who, now?" Evvie asks, changing her mind about the car in the face of a choice piece of gossip.

Greta and Armand Kronk lived here for many years. She was Spanish, he German. They hinted vaguely at being in "showbiz" and they would have nothing to do with any of us, although one year they did offer classes in flamenco. But they were so unpleasant, and their prices so expensive, very few people took their classes. Eventually Armand died and just about no one has seen Greta since. Food and liquor are delivered to her door. Especially liquor. A few years ago she started getting creepy, prowling the Dumpsters at night. First, she would smear garbage all over people's cars and front doors. Then she began scrawling juvenile kinds of poems on our front doors in greasepaint. Very short. To the point. And scary in their accuracy. No one can figure out how she knows so much about all of us. No one ever admits how close she comes to nailing us.

"The Muellers over us?" Hy comments. "I could hear them early this morning when John went out to pick up the newspaper. He woke us up with his yelling and Mary trying to quiet him. I looked out and he was pounding on Kronk's door, screaming, daring she should come out. So he can kill her!"

By now the two prima donnas have managed to come downstairs. And they want to know what's going on. Evvie shushes them.

"Wow!" says Ida. "What did she write this time?"

"Well, you wouldn't believe—" Lola begins.

Hy interrupts. "He got some soap and wiped it off the door real fast."

Sophie, the queen of pastels, tugs on Evvie, insists on knowing what she and Bella missed by being a teeny-weeny bit late. Evvie, annoyed, fills her in quickly.

"But before he finished wiping," Lola continues, "Mrs. Feder already read what Greta wrote."

"Wait just a minute," I say. "How did Esther Feder see from across the way on the first floor at the other end of the building to the Mueller's top floor at this end? What did she do, wheel her chair down the sidewalk?"

"She has binoculars," Hy announces, grinning. Hy is really getting a charge out of all this. "Well, old Feder told her darling Harriet. Harriet told Lola. Natch, Lola told me."

"I can't believe nobody blabbed about it by the pool this morning," Ida says, amazed.

"Not in front of the Canadians," says Lola.

We are always on our best behavior with our northern visitors.

Sophie, who reads the end of every novel first because she can't stand the suspense, pushes forward. "So, alright already, what did Kronk write?"

Hy beams from ear to ear, emoting dramatically.

" 'Mary, Mary, quite contrary. Kick him out. Your John's a fairy.' "

Conversation comes to an immediate halt.

Bella is the first to recover. In her own inimitable way of thinking, she's gleefully made a connection. She delicately wiggles her hand to get our attention. "Is that why he always wears pink?"

Back to my car. I jump in and quickly crank up the air. Ida gets in, and I wait to hear what she will say. She never disappoints me. "Glad, turn down the air! You want me to freeze?"

"Get in already," Evvie says. "I'm melting out here."

"Now where are you beauties off to?" a melodious voice wafts down the sidewalk towards us.

Oh, oh. From Hy's frying pan into Leo's fire. It's Mr. Leo Slezak, aka Mr. Sleaze, waving at us. That's mine and Evvie's name for this real-estate entrepreneur and slimeball. A not-too-bad-looking man, fifty-ish, if you like his type. Dapper in an oily sort of way. He favors creased white linen suits, Panama hats angled rakishly across his forehead. And a lot of gold chains.

He's standing with Tessie Hoffman, a hefty two-hundred-fifty-pounder, best friend of the deceased Selma Beller, and fellow Weight Watchers dropout. We all like Tessie because she can make fun of herself. If we ask what she's had for lunch, she'll say Shamu and fries. Like that. Selma's sudden death has devastated her.

Like a shot, the girls are out of the car again, ready to melt once more, but this time from Leo's baloney. Evvie and I cannot stand this man, but most of the other females in Phase Two think he is God's gift to women.

"Why are you here today, Leo?" Sophie gurgles.

"You, of course, know about Selma Beller. So sad. Well, her children gave me the listing and Tessie, here, is giving me the key to her apartment."

At the mention of Selma's name, Tessie's eyes tear up. She shakes her head and repeats her familiar litany. "She never even got to open her birthday present."

Smarmy Slezak pats her on the shoulder. "There, there," he says with his usual phony sentiment. He beams back at us. "I have a couple of hot prospects coming this afternoon."

I wonder how he gets those listings. Leo hasn't sold a condo in over a year. More than a dozen units just stand empty. He keeps moaning that business is bad. The snowbirds aren't buying much anymore. There are bigger and fancier condos going up all over the place, like the Wynmore or Hamilton House. If this keeps up, eventually we'll all have our choice of graveyards—Beth Israel, across town, or stay right here in our own apartments.

I swear if I didn't know better, I'd think he stands near the ambulance exit at the hospital and follows them when the sirens go off. One of us dies and that embossed card is out of his pocket and into the hands of a grieving relative faster than you can say "Escrow is closed."

"How do you ladies do it?" he says with that simpering lisp. "How do you keep so fresh and beautiful in all this heat?"

You don't want to hear their nauseatingly sweet answers. It would make your stomach turn.

Evvie leans over and honks the horn. "We have to go, girls."

Almost sighing, the three little twits begin backing away from Leo, the lady-killer. Like a magician, Leo whips a hand into his pocket and his cards instantly appear. His greatest fans take them lovingly. Evvie and I keep our hands folded. He reaches toward us.

"No, thanks. We already have a few dozen," Evvie says with ice in her voice. My sister does sarcasm very well.

Leo taps at the brim of his Panama and says what he always says: "Don't buy out the stores, ladies."

And we are off. Thank God. I have such a headache already. But as I drive through the wrought-iron gates out onto Oakland Park Boulevard, I think once more about Selma's death. It's the way she died that's beginning to nag at me. It reminds me of something. Someone I've seen before? But I can't drag it out of the cobwebs in my mind. Damn getting old and what it does to your memory!

6

Supermarket Shuffle

We have finally arrived at our local market. Picture a supermarket in any city in America. So, pardon me if I don't waste time describing where the cream cheese is.

But our Publix has one big difference: the customers. Shoppers under fifty-five are referred to as "the kids." The rest of us are seniors who live along Oakland Park Boulevard in the various condos, boardinghouses, apartment buildings, and retirement homes. The dress code? Canes. Walkers. Wheelchairs. The object? Shopping for food and surviving the experience. The secret agenda? Kill or maim everyone in your way. OK. Carts at the ready. Bracing ourselves, we take a deep breath, and start wheeling! Welcome to the Supermarket Shuffle!

Evvie and I watch as Ida, bun bobbing, teeth bared, relishing a chase, immediately dashes off on her own. Bella and Sophie, their four eager hands pushing one cart, meander their jolly way down the nearest aisle. And off Evvie and I go.

Aisle One. There goes Yetta Hoffman, ninety-seven, from our Phase Six, using her cane to dig into the back of eighty-eight-year-old Miltie Offenbach. He dares to block her view of the pickled herring specials. Move on. That cane is sharp.

Aisle Two. Look out for Moishe Maibaum, in fine fettle, using his walker like he used to fly his P51 Mustang fighter plane in World War II. "Oops, sorry, Mrs. Garcetti," he says, "just a flesh wound," as he knocks her against what was, only seconds ago, a tall pyramid of sugar peas.

Aisle Three. We are debating pineapple juice over prune.

Aisle Four. A store employee is giving out minuscule samples of lox on crackers the size of pinkie-nails and the line snakes around the perimeter of the entire store, punctuated by much pushing, shoving, and insulting.

"*Putz!*"

"Yenta!"

"*Meeskite!*"

"Lunatic!"

(Translation: Penis. Busybody. Ugly one and lunatic.)

A familiar announcement comes over on the loudspeaker. Cleanup on aisle seven. No, not some careless child, only a senior with palsy. A jar of Korean kimchi has smashed. You know what kimchi smells like?

Look out! Eleven o'clock, wheelchair bearing down on us. Jump! Breathlessly we grab for a couple of the hanging salamis and hold on for dear life. (Well, actually we just step out of the way.)

In aisle eight, a drama is taking place. Two women. Photographs. A letter. Tears. We reach for our items and move past quickly and quietly.

Meat and Poultry. A tug-of-war. Two sets of spindly arms hold tight to two equally spindly chicken wings. A fight to the finish. Move on. Forget making chicken soup. Get lamb chops instead.

One long hour later, our shopping is finally done. Evvie, Ida, and I have checked out, but we have to wait for Bella and Sophie. And here they come, Tweedledum and Tweedledumber, basket filled to the brim. I sigh. This will take forever.

The checkout stand. One needs the patience of Job. Fifteen minutes for the first customer; one tiny change purse filled with coins and the slowest fingers in the world eking them out.

Then the next customer and an argument over two cans of sardines. "They were cheaper last week. So how come the price is higher this week?"

"No, they're exactly the same price as last week."

"Listen, you little *pisher,* don't tell *me*! I'm old enough to be your great-grandmother."

Finally Bella and then Sophie.

Every item calls for a debate.

"How come the Bosc pears are so high?"

"How come the broccoli has no taste?"

"How come you don't carry the Del Monte peaches anymore? I mean the 'cling'?" Then there is the obligatory exchange of recipes. Complaints about the store. The attitude of the help. Local politics. World hunger.

Evvie taps her foot throughout, muttering obscenities, but that doesn't move them any faster.

When we're done, our clothes are rumpled and our faces are flushed and our pulses are beating just a little faster. All right. So I exaggerated. But, at our age, where else can we go to have this much fun?

7

No Rest for the Weary

Back home. At last. I'm beyond exhausted. Time to lie down and take our afternoon naps. I can't wait. We deliver Irving's groceries, then get our own packages out of the car and into the building's shopping carts. On the elevator, riding up, I hear this:

Bella: "Did we say we were eating in tonight or going out?"

Ida: "Out, we said OUT! Twenty times in the car."

Bella: "Oh, I didn't hear that."

Ida: "Well, if you wore your damned hearing aid—"

Sophie: "Not Chinese again. We ate that yesterday."

Evvie: "No, we didn't. That was *last* Friday."

Sophie: "So where did we eat last night?"

Evvie: "Home. We stayed home. It was canasta night."

Bella: "We played canasta?"

Sophie (the light bulb goes on): "Oh, that's right. I won."

Evvie: "No, I won. Didn't I, Glad?"

Me: "Who can remember?"

Sophie: "You won last week. I know I won."

Ida: "Who cares! When Sophie wins, it's by reason of insanity. She drives everybody nuts and we all give up!"

Evvie laughs. "Sore loser."

Ida: "Look who's talking. You almost filleted her with the cheese ball knife."

Evvie: "My finger slipped."

Bella: "I like Eleni's. Or Nona's. Can't we go there?"

"Next time. The birthday girl chose Continental. And," I remind them, "don't forget your presents."

We help Sophie in with her stuff from the cleaners, which took all of us to carry. We divide up the grocery bags from the shopping carts. Then Evvie starts to lead Bella back to the elevator, so they can take their things across the parking lot to their own building. Bella looks confused.

"Don't I live here?"

"No, dear, we live over there. We had to help Sophie."

"Oh." We once left Bella downstairs to wait while Evvie helped us carry, but she wandered away and it took us twenty minutes to find her, so now we just bring her up one building and down the other. Ida wants to put a bell around her neck.

Finally everyone is safely deposited in her own apartment. I turn up the air, start undressing. I head toward my bedroom, then remember. I rush to the phone. Too late. It rings. I wasn't fast enough to turn it off.

"Yes, Bella," I say.

"It's me, Sophie."

"Sorry. Yes, Sophie."

"So where did we say we were eating?"

"Continental," and I hang up before she can say another word. I quickly turn off the ringer.

Finally I am in my cool bed in my cool room looking forward to my nap with the utmost of pleasure. I might even get in a little reading later.

My eyes are closing and I feel myself letting go of consciousness when the doorbell rings. I try to ignore it, pulling my pillow over my head, but it doesn't stop. Finally, swearing and stumbling, I race to the door to find Sophie there.

"What!" I screech at her.

"There's something wrong with your phone. We got cut off, but when I rang again it didn't answer."

"No! *It* didn't answer, because *I* didn't answer! Go back to your apartment. *Now!*"

And Sophie scurries away wondering why I raised my voice at her. I want to bang my head against the door, but what did that door ever do to me?

8

Library and Liberation

Through the plate glass window, Conchetta Aguilar sees me staggering toward the entrance, carrying my usual load of returns. Grinning, she moves to the coffeemaker and pours me a cup full of her great Cuban coffee and hands it to me as soon as I put the stack of books down.

"Leaded? I hope."

"You betcha. I only needed one look at your face. Hard morning with the inmates?"

I nod, gulping the hot liquid down. "I left them in the clubhouse playing mah-jongg. I feel like I escaped Alcatraz."

Conchetta is head librarian for the Lauderdale Lakes branch. She's in her thirties, about five feet tall and just as round, and a lot of fun. When she found out I used to be a librarian in my New York days, she reached out as one professional to another. When she realized that the library is my one escape from Lanai Gardens, we became even closer.

Not only am I designated driver, but I am designated book chooser. This is no mean feat, since I have to carry around each girl's list of what she's read before. Heaven help me if I bring home a repeat. Bella reads only romances in large print. Evvie wants biographies of the stars. Ida likes the best-sellers, Sophie prefers the *Reader's Digest* condensations, and Francie reads cookbooks. Happily, nobody else wants to make the trip, so coming here is like a vacation for me.

"Come on, *muchacha*. Tell *mamacita* everything."

"What a day. Those girls are wearing me out. Publix was bad enough. Going to the cleaners was maddening. It was the bank that did me in."

Conchetta leans her arms against the counter, ready to listen. "Good. A bank story."

"The bank is always mobbed on Friday. Everyone has checks to cash. Ida, who hates waiting for anything, gets this brilliant idea. She sneaks in a slice of her famous pecan coffee cake and slips it to a teller who knows Ida's cakes. The bribe gets her to the front of the line. Neither one of them being subtle. And what a *geshrie* from everyone on line!"

"*Geshrie,* I guess, means an uproar."

"You got it. Wait 'til you hear what happened next. Harriet Feder, who's near the front of the line with her mother, lifts Ida up and carries her bodily, feet dangling, and drops her back at the end of the line where she belongs. All the while, Ida is hitting her with her purse, thus emptying the contents all over the floor. Everyone's hysterical. Ida is mortified. Knowing Ida, she will never forgive Harriet."

"And ... I can tell there's more...."

"Greta Kronk struck again."

"Barney, quick. Another Kronk episode."

A tall, skinny, and proud-to-be-a-nerd young man strides over. "Fantabulous," Barney Schwartz says. "Our Lady of the Garbage."

"Our what?"

"We're having a contest to give Greta a title worthy of her accomplishments," says Conchetta.

Barney adds, "I want to publish her poems. I already have the title of the book: *From Under the Belly of the Alligator.*"

I burst out laughing. "You guys are so bad!"

"I especially love 'Hy and Lo put on a show. They make me throw. Up.' Brilliant," says Barney.

Conchetta recites her favorites. " 'Tessie is fat. That's that.' And 'Esther's a pest and Harriet can't get no rest, yes.' "

"They've been benign up to now. Today took a different turn. She hit on a couple named John and Mary." I recite it for them and their eyes widen.

"Wow," says Conchetta. "I think her crazies are escalating."

"Is he?" asks Barney. "Gay?"

"I've always wondered, but how could Greta know?"

"That woman needs help."

"We've tried. But to no avail."

Conchetta is being beckoned. As she moves off to help a fellow book lover, she calls back, "Typical. The authorities are waiting for her to hurt somebody."

I head at last for the mystery section, perturbed by our exchange. But quickly my mood gentles. I am among my favorite things. Books.

A half hour later with a Virginia Lanier, a Barbara Neely, a Mary Willis Walker and a Ruth Rendell in hand (so many great women mystery writers these days), I have enough to keep me happy for a week. I pick out books for the girls. It's nearly dinnertime and I must gather up the lambs before they turn into lions.

Conchetta smiles at my customary stack as I check out. Then she picks up my Barbara Neely. "Like it so much you're gonna read it again after only two weeks?"

"What are you muttering about?" I pick up *Blanche Among the Talented Tenth.* "I didn't read this one. I read her first and third."

"Two weeks ago."

"Oh, yeah, smart stuff, what's this one about?"

"Blanche sends her kids to a snooty private school and they start getting attitude."

I smile sheepishly, and take it off my pile. "Well," I say, "if I ever get Alzheimer's, I'll only need one book from then on."

"And we'll be out of business."

I say my good-byes and *schlep* my books out to the car.

She knows I'll be back very soon. It's the way I stay sane. But all the way home I find myself thinking of Greta Kronk and what loneliness can do to people. But is Conchetta right? Is she dangerous? Would she do more than hurt someone? Would she kill?

9

Dinner at the Deli

The parking lot is already packed and the line outside the Continental deli winds clear around the perimeter of the minimall.

We're late, of course. Half past three is a shoo-in. Four o'clock is the right time. Four-thirty is pushing it and five is rush hour for the early-bird dinner ($6.50 for six courses plus coffee). It's now twenty-five minutes after five.

"I told you..." howls Evvie.

"Don't start," I caution my sister.

"The milk is spilled already," says Sophie, "so don't keep drinking."

Francie, the birthday girl, glances at Sophie and shakes her head. "I think she needs a translator."

"I think she needs a keeper," Ida snarls. "Why can't you say 'Don't cry over spilt milk' like everybody else?"

"That's what I said."

We get out of the car and head for the end of a very long line.

"Well, at least we can window-shop," Bella, our little ray of sunshine, says, eyeing the minimall with eagerness.

I keep time. Ten minutes stalled in front of Discount Linens. Fifteen in front of Klotz's Klassy Klothing. Sophie has disappeared into the deli to scope things out and now she returns with her report.

"The *kasha varnishkas* are already a dead duck. I told Dena to hide a plate of kreplach for us, there's only two left. If you were dreaming of the stuffed cabbage, wake up."

A few moans accompany the food report. Followed by a couple of I-told-you-so's.

Now a short wait in front of the prosthetics shop (a really cheerful window) and then the ninety-nine-cent store and finally we are in. It's ten after six and naturally everyone is starved.

The place is packed and we don't get our favorite waitress, Dena. Now you really hear groans. We get Lottie, she of the long, bushy black hair (a strand of which Ida swears gets in her soup every time we are stuck with her) and the very bad breath. She's so ugly and antagonistic, Francie swears she must be a relative. Who else would hire her?

As we sit down, she practically throws the pickle and sauerkraut appetizer dish at us, then hurries away like Hurricane Hannah, whirling from table to table, hurling dishes and insults with equal fervor.

The deli customers consist of a smattering of families, some couples, but mostly women sixty and up. We're all of us regulars here.

We study the menu avidly, as if we didn't know it by heart. Before we even get past the soups, there's Lottie, order book in hand. "What'll ya have, gals?"

"I don't know yet," Bella says warily, bracing herself for trouble.

"I don't got all day, so lemme hear something before I die on my feet."

Intimidated, Bella blurts out her choices, stringing them together like Jewish worry beads: pineapplejuice-saladwithThousandIsland-matzoballsoup-broiled-chicken-rice-spinach.

Ida, just to infuriate Lottie, goes into slow-motion mode. Every word takes forever to pass her lips. "Let...me...see. First...I might like the...tomato juice...with a piece of lemon...or maybe the grapefruit...."

Francie interrupts, trying to avoid trouble. She places her order quickly. "Tomato juice. Pot roast. Baked potato. Salad. French dressing." Evvie and I follow suit. We always get the same things, anyway.

"And...how...is...the kreplach soup this evening?" Ida's voice seems to get slower and sarcastically sweeter.

"It's the way it always is. In or out on the kreplach?"

"Well, I could say 'in.'"

"Say it!" we all shout.

"In. Alright already."

"And?!" Lottie is gritting her teeth.

"And...for my meat dish, I am simply torn between the sauerbraten and the sweetbreads."

"Don't be so torn, pick already!"

Ida looks her dead in the eye. "I do not like to be rushed. It is not good for my blood pressure."

"And I have six other tables to worry about. Think, dollink, I'll be back."

Lottie leaves and we all glare at Ida.

"Enough, already," I say.

"Why? I'm enjoying myself." She leans back, relaxed.

"Meanwhile, I'm starving," wails Sophie. She takes a bite of a sour pickle on the tray. "This is good."

"Then you should spit it out," says Bella, being bossy.

"Why?" Sophie asks mid-bite.

"My doctor says if it tastes good, then it's bad for you."

Evvie ignores this exchange and shakes a fist at Ida. "Why can't you behave? You are ruining Francie's birthday party."

"You certainly are," adds Francie, pretending annoyance.

Now that we've ordered, the bottles come out of the purses and the vitamins and the prescription drugs are lined up. Bella gasps. "I'm out of my Zantac. What should I do?"

"Tomorrow is another day," says our Sophie philosophically.

"I always take it before dinner."

Ida digs around in her purse. "I have some." She takes one out. As she hands it to Bella, "I'll take two dollars now, thank you."

Evvie swats her with her purse. "How can you! You would sell seltzer to a dying man in the desert!"

Ida is insulted. "My late husband, Murray, taught me that business is business. Supply and demand. Bella just demanded. I just supplied. I get paid. It's the American way."

Bella's eyes start to tear up. Francie takes a tissue from her purse and hands it to her. "Now you've done it."

"What did I say? I was talking about my Murray."

The tears flow harder, followed by pathetic little hiccups. Evvie rolls her eyes heavenward. "You said the *h* word. As in 'husband.' As in dead and not here anymore and we never go there! And furthermore, Zantac only costs a dollar seventy-five, you gonif!"

"Oh, if only my Abe, my angel, was here, things would be different." Bella was now going out on an old limb. Things would be different, all right, and not for the better. As the years pass, Abe's memory gets a whitewash. The mean-spirited, domineering Abe who often brought her to tears now brings her to tears because she's rewritten history. Now he's a saint!

Lottie is back. Ida sees five sets of steely eyes glaring at her. She shrugs. "I'm ready. Where were you? I'll have the noodle soup and it better be hot. Salad, oil and vinegar and no cucumbers. The steak rare and that doesn't mean well-done or medium or raw. Potatoes mashed and leave out your usual lumps. Oh, yes, and make sure we all have separate checks."

Lottie just stands there.

"What?" Ida asks, all innocence.

"Are you finished, Mrs. Have-it-your-way? I wouldn't want to miss something of vital importance."

Haughty now: "Yes, thank you. That will be all, my good woman."

"Oy," says Sophie, "I wish the food would get here so I can take home the leftovers."

And it goes downhill from there. Ida sends her soup back because it isn't hot enough. Bella chokes on a chicken bone. Ida pulls Bella's arms over her head and pounds on her back. Evvie makes her eat a piece of bread because that's supposed to prevent the bone from stabbing her. Francie makes her do special breathing. Sophie makes her blow her nose to free the passages. I am on standby in case we need the Heimlich, but finally, the bone is gone, and everyone takes credit for her method.

We give Francie her presents, apparently many minds with similar brainstorms. They all give her pretty soaps or bath salts. Francie good-naturedly wonders if we are trying to tell her something about her personal hygiene. I, of course, give her a book. A cookbook.

We all order dessert, but none of us eats it. We never do. There is always too much food to eat and dessert is taken home to be indulged in later. Naturally, Francie, the chocoholic, orders the chocolate cake with chocolate icing.

And finally the check comes. One check. Ida has a small fit, but there is nothing we can do but figure out who had what, which need I say takes another half an hour. Leaving the tip is one of the heavy decisions of eating out. Everyone is responsible for deciding her own. No one amount ever gets the same number of votes, with much debating on how fast the service was, how good, etc. But having

Lottie makes it easy. Everyone tips the minimum. Except Ida, who tips nothing.

We drive home with Evvie leading us in a medley of musical comedy tunes.

10

A Waltons' Good Night

Wearily we each trudge to our apartments, bloated as usual with too much food, carrying our little doggie bags. We watch one another, making sure we each get inside safely.

"Don't forget to double lock," Francie calls.

"Don't forget, movies tomorrow afternoon." This from our social director, Evvie.

"Don't forget, I have an early dentist's appointment," Ida reminds me.

"Good night, Bella."

"Good night, Ida."

"Good night, Glad."

"Good night, Evvie."

"Good night, Sophie."

"Good night, Francie. Happy Birthday."

I am the last one in and I know at least one of the girls is watching out for me through her kitchen window.

We said good night, but we didn't know we were saying good-bye.

11

Death by Chocolate

All lights were off, but one. Everyone was asleep before ten except Francie.

She was too excited.

Francie Charles was at her favorite pastime. Surrounded by her cookbooks, she paged through Gladdy's birthday present, a collection of the best desserts from Bon Appétit.

Naturally she was perusing the "fabulous cakes" section first. Her eyes glanced toward her doggie bag, still sitting on the kitchen counter. She was debating. Have it now or save it for tomorrow. She was practically drooling over the book's description of the double fudge cake with whipped cream. Or maybe she might try to make the triple mocha square first. It had been weeks since she'd baked anything. Maybe she'd surprise the girls tomorrow.

Happiness, she thought, is having a sweet tooth. She glanced up at the magnet on her fridge, last year's birthday present from her daughter-in-law,

Ilene. She always giggled when she passed it. "Men think the greatest thing in life is sex; women know it's a Hershey bar."

There was a soft knock on the door.

Surprised, she called out, "Who is it?" She was even more surprised when no one answered. Now she wasn't sure there had been a knock. But she went to the door anyway. "Anybody there?" No answer. She looked through the peephole. Nobody. Slowly, she unlocked the door and as she did, the package leaning against it fell onto the threshold. Francie picked it up and looked outside onto the balcony. She looked both ways, but there was no one there.

The package was a square white box tied with a pretty red bow. Something inside smelled wonderful. She reached for the note taped to the ribbon and opened it. In an almost immature hand it read, "Sweets to the sweet. Happy birthday." No signature. Inside the box was a vision of beauty. A thick slice of chocolate almond mousse with fresh raspberries and chocolate chantilly whipped cream! Francie was astonished. Where did it come from? Who could have found something as elegant as this in Fort Lauderdale? Her meager cake from Continental went into the fridge. She grabbed a fork and very gently dug into her gift to have her first taste. Heaven! Absolute heaven.

Now I can die happy, she thought, smiling.

Francie heard the turn of a key in her lock. Thank God, she thought, someone will save me. She lay on the floor, clutching her stomach. She had been in *pain for she didn't know how long, falling in and out of consciousness. She couldn't move. Her body was paralyzed and she knew she was dying. "Help me," she tried to cry out, but her tongue was also paralyzed.*

At that moment Francie realized three things: 1) There was no help coming. 2) The killer had returned to finish the job. And 3) she had forgotten to double lock her door after bringing in the gift that would poison her.

Francie's eyes were the only things that could move. They watched the betrayal, as someone she thought she knew so well moved about her apartment, cleaning up. The plate and fork were washed and put away. The remains of the cake dropped into a plastic carry-away bag. The note crushed and put in a pocket. The crumbs wiped off the counter into the sink.

Her body was dragged along the floor until she was positioned lying near the phone. Her hand was placed as if she had been reaching for it and failed. Her eyes looked into the eyes of her killer and she realized begging was useless. What she saw reflected was a coldness beyond compassion.

Francie's last thought was that she would never see her children and grandchildren again. And that was more unbearable than the pain.

12

Getting Old Is Murder

It's Saturday morning. The day is beautiful. Nothing is wrong, so why am I depressed? Must have been a bad dream brought on by something I ate at the deli last night.

I'm down at the mailbox as are a lot of my neighbors. It's a favorite meeting place, located to the left of the parking lot on the side of our building facing the elevator. Get the mail, see what's new on the bulletin board, touch base with the people who are about to get into their cars and out to do errands. And of course, take a copy of our free newspaper from the newly arrived stacks.

Everyone reads Evvie's review first.

KNISHES OR KNOCKS
GOING TO THE MOVIES WITH EVVIE
By
Evelyn Markowitz

Exclusive to:
THE LANAI GARDENS FREE PRESS

AFTER LIFE

OK, so it's a Japanese movie and who knows from Japanese? I love going to movies from other countries. You always see how the other half lives. Especially the French, ooh là là. My pet peeve against foreign movies is that they always put the subtitles on white backgrounds. So it isn't bad enough you miss most of what's going on in the movie while you're reading the long titles, but your head keeps jumping around trying to find them through all the white. Result: You haven't a clue what it was all about in the first place and end up needing an Alka-Seltzer.

When the video of this movie comes out, buy one—you'll be able to throw out your sleeping pills. Such a sleeper!

I liked the idea. When you die you come to this place and remember your favorite memory and you take it with you wherever it is you're going. But let me tell you, if where you're going is as dark and depressing as the place you're in in this movie, you shouldn't go anywhere with this crowd.

All that agonizing for two hours, and what memories do they come up with? Flying in a cloud. Reciting a really nothing poem. Sitting on a bench. It's bad enough they have to eat all that raw fish, do they have to live such boring

•

lives? They should make the director fall on a sword like they do in those other movies.

Now if my heroine, Barbra Streisand, was in this movie, she would have made them use the fluorescent lights like we have in the clubhouse so you wouldn't go blind trying to see what's on the screen. And she would have come up with a great memory, like finding this gorgeous hunk, James Brolin, for a husband after all those movies never getting the guy, and always being left alone, sad, but brave. And would that gorgeous Omar Sharif have been so bad? Too bad she couldn't keep both of them.

QUOTH THE MAVEN:

Enough already. I give it 1½ knishes. If this is all we have to look forward to after life, then as Hy Binder, in our phase, always says—I'm not going!

The End

Thank you, Evvie for another memorable movie interpretation. I shake my head. Just what I needed— an article about death in the mood I'm in.

Evvie's timing is always perfect. The celebrated editor-reporter-reviewer arrives downstairs for a round of kudos from everybody. And as always, she graciously takes the applause as her due.

"Loved it, just loved it," Mary Mueller gushes at her as she and her husband, John, get into their Buick on their way to the mall. John looks away, unable to face us these days because of what Kronk wrote on their door.

"Well, that's a movie we can miss, thanks for the warning," says Harriet Feder, as she installs her mother's wheelchair into the back of their van. "Off to another movie today?"

Evvie nods. "Every Saturday afternoon."

I chime in. "Harriet, why don't you join us?"

Harriet beams. "Why, I'd like that—"

"Allow me to say no, thanks, for my Harriet." Esther Feder's voice rings out from the passenger seat, where she is waiting. "We're already going to see a movie later."

"We are?" asks Harriet, puzzled.

"Yes, Harriet, darling, I just got this idea. After my doctor's appointment, we can pick up a tape from the video store and watch it when we get home. You know how we both love that sweet Fred Astaire. And maybe you'll make your mamma some microwave popcorn." Esther now directs herself at me. "That daughter of mine won't let me miss any pleasures just because the good Lord decided to make a cripple of me. Everyone should have such a good daughter."

"Poor Harriet," says Evvie as they drive off.

"I'm glad she didn't come with us," Ida says, still smarting from the way Harriet treated her at the bank.

Sophie giggles, remembering Ida's embarrassment. Ida pokes her in the ribs.

My eye is caught by the sight of Irving and his pal, Sol Spankowitz from Phase Three, sitting on a bench near his front door, foul smoke belching from their stogies. They are leaning over a newspaper, deep in concentration. The two friends are an odd couple, Irving being thin, almost frail and hunched over, quiet-spoken and polite, while Sol is chunky, pear-shaped, and bald, the only sign of hair his pencil-thin mustache. Sol is loud, brash, and as subtle as the butcher block he used when he was still working. I hurry over, Evvie on my heels, both of us thinking the same thing. Every Saturday morning we take turns sitting with Millie while Irving plays a little pinochle. And on Sunday afternoons in season, he and Sol go to Hialeah.

"I still like the six horse in the double," Sol says.

"Valenzuela's riding," cautions Irving.

"So, he's on a losing streak," Sol comments. "Maybe his winning streak will come back tomorrow."

"Who's with Millie?" I ask. "You didn't leave her alone?"

Irving's hands go up as if warding off any other words. His thumb motions toward the door. "Sleeping."

I smile. Irving, the ultimate cheapskate with words.

Many years ago, I once asked Irving why he didn't take a vacation in Europe. He could always go back to Poland and visit the place he was born. This was at a time all of us were still doing a lot of traveling. His answer to me was, "I been." And that was that. End of discussion. Short and sweet. Millie told us she thought the real reason Irving never went back is that he ran from the draft and was afraid the Poles were still looking for him.

"How are you, Evvie?" Sol asks, staring at her bosom. Sol has the habit of never looking any woman in the eye. Somehow he never gets past their breasts.

"I'm up here, Sol," Evvie says, pointing to her face.

Sol, startled, drags his eyes away and looks up into Evvie's eyes. She barely hides her irritation. "We are what our minds are, Mr. Sol Spankowitz. Our bodies are merely the vessels that carry our heads."

Sol doesn't understand a word she says, but he manages a brief, "Uh-huh."

Irving taps his watch, then nods at Evvie and me. "By eleven?"

"Have a nice card game," Evvie says.

They walk away, heading toward the clubhouse, with Sol still scanning the sports page. "What should we do in the trifecta, Irv?"

"Wheel the three horse," answers the expert.

I poke Evvie in the shoulder. "You've got a potential suitor there, sister. He's hot to trot."

"Let him trot down at the track. I'm not interested."

"Well. He *is* available. Not too many of those left."

"Big deal. He was a lech even when Clara was alive."

I always tease Evvie about Sol, but somehow my heart isn't quite in it today. "Well, he's good for a nice dinner now and then."

"I can buy my own dinners, thank you. Besides, I still have dear old Joe hanging around, now that the broad from Miami dumped him. Besides, I like my freedom." She stops, seeing the amused expression on my face.

"Gotcha."

"And what about you? You are so busy fixing me up, how about your love life?"

"Let's change the subject."

Evvie smirks. She is about to open Irving's door when we hear another door open right above our heads and angry voices arguing.

From where we are hidden by a straggly ficus tree, we see Hy Binder hurrying down the second floor walkway, and Lola grabbing his arm trying to stop him. Evvie and I exchange glances. The Bobbsey twins fighting? This we gotta hear.

"But I got the lawyer hanging on the line." Lola sounds frantic.

"He can hang forever." Hy is really angry.

"You gotta talk to him sometime."

"When hell freezes over. Twice."

"But our kids will kill one another over the money."

"Let them."

"Please, Hy, the man wants to tell you about a living trust."

"The only trust I care about is the one I wear for my prostate."

"That's a truss. Not a trust. Stubborn man! Everybody has to make out a will."

Hy turns just as he starts down the stairs.

"I told you a hundred times. I don't need a will. I'm not going!"

With that he rushes past us, giving us dirty looks, gets into his car, and careens off. Lola, crying now, runs back into the apartment and slams the door after her.

Evvie erupts with laughter. She looks at me. "What?" she says. "Why aren't you laughing?"

I shrug. "I know it's funny, but it's also depressing, Hy being afraid to plan for death."

"Boy, are you grouchy today," Evvie says as she opens Irving's door. We walk in quietly, hearing nothing.

Millie is indeed sleeping, curled up on the couch in the sunroom. We also call it the Florida room, this screened-in porch. I remember when Millie decorated it with wild, brightly colored pillows and rattan furniture, how delighted she was with how it looked. She told me it made her think she was in a Bette Davis movie. "She looks so peaceful," I whisper.

"Like she's off in some other world," Evvie says.

We sit quietly for a few moments. What a day. My mood just keeps getting darker and I can't shake it. Millie's eyes open. She seems restless. Evvie reaches for the pitcher on the side table and pours her a glass of water. Millie grabs the glass and drinks the water down greedily. Then she flings the glass to the floor. Not a problem: We started using plastic dishes a long time ago. Evvie tries to take her hand. Millie shoves her away. Now, she tries to put a shawl around her shoulder, but Millie hurls that away, too.

"Ev, stop!" I say. It breaks my heart to see how hard my sister tries.

"I feel so helpless."

"I know dear, we all do."

I'm suddenly aware of shouting outside. "Glad! Evvie, are you in there!?" Then pounding on the door.

We both jump up. "That sounds like Sophie," Evvie says. "What's going on?"

I unlock the door. Sophie stands there. And

Denny. And Bella. All of them ashen-faced. Behind them I see other people standing around too, watching. For a moment everything is frozen. I am aware of half of Sophie's hair covered with curlers, the other half limp and wet. Denny has keys in his hands and his hands are shaking. Bella is moaning.

It must be bad. I shiver. "Who is it?"

Sophie sobs. "Francie..."

I shake my head violently as if to throw the word off. My mind refuses to accept this. Please, God, not Francie! I can hear Evvie gasp and I feel her grab my arm.

As much as I don't want to hear it, I need this to be over with. "Tell me..." My voice is a croak.

Sophie begins to hyperventilate and Bella's eyes lose focus. Denny tries. "I went up...the air-conditioning didn't work good...the air comes out warm it's supposed to be cold...I promised in the morning...She said come up, but not too early...She didn't answer, so I thought she went out...so I opened the door with my key...."

He quits. This is all he can manage.

"Denny, tell me, how bad is she hurt?! Did you call nine-one-one?"

He looks at Sophie plaintively for help. "I went to get you, but you weren't home. So, I went to Mrs. Meyerbeer...."

I wait for the miracle I know won't come. Too late to plea-bargain with God...Too late...

Sophie can't stand it anymore. She screams. "She's dead! Francie's dead!"

Evvie gasps, starting to slide down. I clutch her arm and pull her back up.

"Bella." I try to get her attention. I touch her

hand. She finally manages to focus and look at me. "Bella, please stay with Millie."

She doesn't answer. She goes inside. And I start running, pulling Evvie with me. Sophie and Denny follow right behind us. Denny and Sophie are both crying. Stupidly, I wonder where Ida is, and then I remember dropping her at the dentist this morning. I am dimly aware of people everywhere. Standing in the street, or on their balconies. Whispering. Crying. Shaking their heads in disbelief. Bad news travels fast.

Francie is dead. Francie is dead. . . . How can I go on without her?

13

Funerals on the Run

"Where are we now?" I ask for the hundredth time, or does it only seem that way?

"On four-forty-one and passing Twelfth Street," Evvie reports. As always she sits in the front seat next to me. The upper half of the opened map covers her side of the windshield, and the lower half is spread across both our laps. And she still doesn't have a clue as to where we are.

"It can't be," I tell her, once again pushing the map out of my line of sight. "We passed that corner five minutes ago."

"I told you we were lost!" wails Ida. "We already passed Fuddruckers twice!"

Bella is keening, "Oh, God . . . Oh, God . . . We shoulda been there half an hour ago."

"I knew we shoulda taken University. This traffic is killing us!" Ida's voice is sharp.

"Shoulda, coulda, woulda," singsongs Sophie for the third time in fifteen minutes.

All our voices are shrill. We are beyond our boiling points. Today, of all days, the air conditioner isn't working. Even Ida is hot, which should give you an idea of how bad it is. The windows are all open, and between the dirt flying in and the deafening noise of the trucks rumbling past us—I am not coping well. And naturally we are all dressed up in clothes that feel way too tight after living day after day in loose sundresses and bathing suits. We are sweating and miserable.

"We're so late, we're so late. . . ." Bella, who is in tears, sounds like a demented Alice, only this is no tea party we're going to.

Ida is now shouting. "Of course we're late. Because Sophie wasn't ready." She elbows her in her stomach. "How could you be late for Francie's funeral!"

"Stop already with the blame," Sophie says defensively. "You're a broken record, play another."

"I'll stop when you stop being impossible!" We have been driving around aimlessly for forty minutes and Ida has lost it by now. I think we all have.

"I knew we should have hired a car," Evvie says.

"Woulda, coulda, shoulda," says Sophie yet again.

"You say that once more, and I'll throw you out the door!" Ida's hand moves across Sophie's lap toward the door handle. Sophie shuts right up.

But Evvie is right. I should never have offered to drive to the cemetery. I am much too upset about Francie. I can't think straight, and I'm making mistakes.

Evvie grabs my arm, jerking the steering wheel.

"Don't ever do that!" I shout at her, trying to avoid a pedestrian crossing the street in front of me.

"Turn right! This is where we were supposed to turn right. On Davie Boulevard."

"No," I insist. "I did that last time and that's why we're right back where we started. Davie and Twelfth are the same street. It's left."

"No, right. You turned left last time."

"Gladdy's right, it's left, not right," says Ida, digging her fingers into the upholstery behind my back.

I know I'm driving erratically. Now I narrowly miss a Holsum's White Bread truck as I turn onto Stirling.

"Oh, no," Evvie gasps.

"What! What is it?" I ask, in a state of total panic.

"Look. Look where we are." She points across the street and everyone stares out the window.

"No!" Ida says. "It can't be! We're at bingo!"

Sophie is so excited she is jumping up and down in her seat, her black wide-brimmed hat, with tiny red rosettes, bobbing. "Yes! And today's pick-a-pet day!"

And sure enough we've arrived at a spot that is very familiar to all of us: the Seminole tribe reservation where we go every week to play bingo.

I pull over to the curb and stop the car. I throw my arms across the steering wheel and lean my head on my hands. I am laughing and I am crying and I am laughing...I'm hysterical.

"What's so damn funny?" Ida asks.

"Pppick-a-ppppet day." I can't stop laughing.

"So? What's so funny about picking out a

stuffed animal full of money when you win at Bingo?"

Evvie is beside herself. "You're babbling on about winning a stuffed animal and they're burying Francie!"

"I just realized," I say through hiccuping sobs. "We've been to so many funerals at Beth Israel Park Cemetery and we go to bingo every week and I never realized it before. The cemetery is on the same street as bingo."

Evvie starts to laugh, too. "If you go left you play, if you go right you die."

Ida and Sophie are stone-faced. "I don't see what's funny about that," Ida says, crossing her arms.

"You wouldn't," Evvie says.

By now my laughing has turned into sobbing. I bang my fists on the steering wheel. I just can't stop. "Francie is dead! Francie is dead and gone and we'll never see her again! And I can't find the damned cemetery!"

Good old Bella joins in with me. She hasn't stopped crying anyway, since she got in the car. Now her sobs escalate. A moment later, Evvie is crying, too, and leaning her head on my shoulder. And like falling dominos, Sophie and Ida grab onto one another as they erupt into tears.

If anyone driving by looked in our windows, what a sight they would see.

We all needed a cry. I finally compose myself. The others pull themselves together. I check the map one more time.

"OK, now I've got my bearings. We are directly

east on Stirling Road. I know how to get there now. We're only about six blocks away."

"Thank God," Bella says.

I make an illegal U-turn, ignoring the honking horns and squealing brakes, and we are finally headed in the right direction.

We drive through the ornate cemetery gates, and I pull up to the main information office. Evvie jumps out to get directions as Ida yells for her to hurry. The rest of us climb out of the car and try to stretch our aching muscles, at the same time peeling our sticky clothes away from our bodies.

Evvie rushes out again waving at us a paper with a lot of small black-and-white boxes on it.

"Oh, no," says Ida, "not another map."

"Come on, we have to follow it. Look for row twelve."

"Aren't we taking the car?" Sophie wants to know.

"It'll be faster if we cut across," Evvie shouts.

We all race after her as best we can.

"Cut across what?" Bella asks with trepidation.

"Across the stones."

Bella stops in her tracks. "You mean walk over all those graves?" she says in horror, looking down at the seemingly endless rows of flat stone markers. "With all the people I know under there?"

Now everyone has stopped.

"All right!" Evvie says, exasperated. "So, walk on the grass around the stones."

"But they're still graves."

"Bella. Come on!" says Sophie.

"I can't. It's not right. I'll walk along the outside."

"Forget it," Ida says. "That'll take forever."

"Don't be ridiculous, Bella. You've been to plenty of other funerals here and you walked on the stones," Evvie says.

"I don't remember that."

Evvie is moving briskly along. "Here's aisle twelve, now we need to find plot two-eleven...."

Ida grabs Bella by the hand and starts pulling her. Bella digs her heels into the ground. But with one good yank, Ida dislodges her. "One more word out of you and I'm throwing you into the next open grave!"

We follow Evvie, moving briskly along. Except for Bella who is trying to walk on her tiptoes and keeping up a litany of *Oh, God*s.

Sophie keeps looking down at the grave markers. "Keep your eyes open for six forty-two."

I ask why.

"Because I changed my plot. I wanted one with a corner view and I wanna make sure I got it."

Bella utters a small screech.

"What is it now!?" Evvie calls without looking back.

"I've stepped on my cousin, Sarah! Oh, God..."

"Over there!" Sophie points. And sure enough, not thirty feet away, I can see our neighbors and friends from Lanai Gardens. And in an instant, I know this is not good news. They are not facing in the right direction. They're turned away from the graveside. In fact, they are all walking toward us.

We meet them halfway.

"Such a lovely service," says Mrs. Fein from Phase Three.

"How could you miss it?" asks Hy Binder.

"It was inspirational," says Lola.

"It's over?" Evvie says, totally dejected.

"By five minutes. Where were you girls?"

"Don't ask," says Ida.

I watch in misery as Francie's son, Jerry, and his wife, Ilene, and the grandchildren pass by, heads down, unable to see or talk to anyone. Denny is there, in a suit much too small for him, probably the last suit his mother ever picked out for him. He is sobbing uncontrollably. Harriet struggles as she pushes her mother's wheelchair over the uneven ground. Irving, with the help of his pal, Sol, is supporting Millie, who has no idea where she is or why. Tessie Hoffman passes us muttering something about another death so soon after her dear Selma. Enya, as always, walks alone. Even Conchetta and Barney have taken time off from the library to pay their respects. I recognize a few of our Canadians. And—no surprise—there's Leo Slezak with a few of his cohorts from the Sunrise-Sunset Real Estate office. The Sleaze, being what he is, is slowly sidling up to Francie's family, his hand in the pocket where he keeps his damned cards.

Evvie looks at me and I look at her. We are despondent.

We nod and watch mutely as everyone passes us on the path. We wait until every last person is gone and then the five of us walk up the knoll and over to where Francie's casket sits on an elevated hoist.

We stand there silent and bemused.

Bella looks to me for help. "Say good-bye," I tell her.

"How?" Without the rabbi, she doesn't know what to do.

"Any way you like, Bella, dear. She'll know."

And each of us in our own way quietly says our last words to Francie.

"Thank you for always being nice to me," Bella says.

"I'll miss you," Sophie says, "especially your baking." She stamps her formal black orthopedic sneakers, annoyed. "Oh, that's a stupid thing to say. I don't know what to say to a dead person."

Ida turns away. She chokes up, shakes her head. For once the words won't come. She picks up a stone and places it on the casket.

"Thank you for your friendship," Evvie says, sobbing. "There will never be anyone like you again."

I can't speak. I silently tell my beloved friend what is in my heart. What do I do now, Francie? You're the only reason I stayed down here. Because we shared the same interests and laughed at all the same things. Because we were intellectual snobs at heart and we knew we really didn't belong down here, but going back was too hard, so we made it work for both of us. Because we knew what the other was thinking before we ever said it. Because home is where the person you love resides. And that person was you and I no longer have a home—

"Glad?" Evvie interrupts my reverie. "Remember how I first met Francie?"

I smile. None of can remember what we ate for breakfast, but ask about the distant past, and it seems like only yesterday.

"I don't think I ever heard that story," says Ida.

"It was a couple of years before you got here."

"It was just after I arrived," I comment.

"I was here," Bella says, "but I forgot."

"So, tell us," says Sophie as she sits on the bench next to the plot. Bella immediately joins her. Ida and I sit on the bench opposite.

"Actually, we met Al first. It was twenty-five years ago, when the buildings were new and people were first starting to move down here. Millie and I are standing on the balcony with our laundry, gossiping, when we see this nice-looking man walking up and down in front of our building. He keeps walking, then he disappears around the corner and then here he is again. Then a few minutes later, we see this beautiful woman doing the same thing. We finally figure out they are looking for each other, but keep missing each other. Soon, I hear him calling 'Francie, where are you,' and then we hear, 'Al, where are you?' Millie and I start laughing. Finally Millie can't stand it and she calls down, 'Hey, Francie, if that's who you are, stand still!' She is so surprised she stops in her tracks. A minute later Al appears and they run to one another hugging and kissing. 'I thought I'd never see you again,' he says.

"Everybody used to get lost at first. This place seemed so big, and all the buildings looked exactly the same. But we all became good friends after that."

We sit quietly for a few minutes. Behind us a half dozen graceful flamingos meander by, unmindful of our presence. "That was a nice story," Bella says.

"Now what?" a very subdued Ida asks. All of us stare at this tiny piece of ground where Francie will stay forever. At least she is with her beloved Al once again.

"Now what, what?" Evvie asks in return.

"Are we going to the get-together? Everybody said they were going after the services," says Bella.

"Do we have to? I'm afraid to look anybody in the eye after missing it. We'll be the laughing-stocking of Lanai Gardens," says Sophie, Queen of Malapropisms.

"Well, I don't care. We'll get to talk to Jerry and Ilene and the kids. It's the least we can do," says Ida.

"I agree," Evvie adds.

"All right," I say. "Where are they having it?" The incredible silence that follows says it all.

"Nobody took down the name of the restaurant? Or the address?" I say, gritting my teeth.

"I think it starts with an *M*," Sophie contributes.

"You mean like meshugeneh, like all of you?" I say to them. "I can't believe this is happening. Why do I have to be responsible for everything? I left one thing up to you to take care of..." I sigh. "Is it at any of the places we usually go? Everybody *think*!"

"No," Ida says. "I remember saying to someone I never heard of that restaurant before."

"It's someplace in Margate, or maybe Tamarac," says Sophie.

"It could even be Boca Raton," says Bella.

"Well, that's that," says Evvie.

Another long silence.

"I can't do it!" Bella cries.

"Do what?" I ask.

"Just go home and do nothing. I won't be able to stand it."

"Me, too. I don't want to be alone," says Sophie. "I'll just keep crying."

"We can go somewhere for lunch by ourselves. I

could eat." Ida says this with no conviction whatsoever. It gets the silence it deserves.

I walk over to Francie's coffin, sitting out here in the hot sun waiting for the groundskeepers to come and slowly lower it into that horrifying gaping hole.

I bend toward it, cupping my ear as if listening. "What? What's that you say?" The others turn and gawk. Finally I straighten up. "Well, it's peculiar, but if that's what you want, Francie."

I start walking away. The girls look at one another, befuddled. I call over my shoulder. "Francie told me what she wants us to do. Come on."

They just stand there. "Come *on*, girls."

They run after me, puzzled but obedient, as Bella says, "Oh, not again over those dead bodies!" And Ida calls back to the casket, "Rest in peace, Francie, you hear!"

Five minutes later I pull into the parking lot of the Seminole Indian Bingo Hall and Casino. They are staring at me incredulously, and I tell them as I park the car, "Francie said that we should win the pick-a-pet for her!"

I open the trunk where all our bingo gear is always at the ready. Before they start grabbing for them, I raise my hand in warning. I tell them that they are never, never, under penalty of torture, to tell anybody where we went after Francie's funeral.

I had to think of something to save this godawful day. And knowing Francie, if she could have whispered anything at all to me, she would have said, "*Carpe Diem,* babe—seize the day. What the hell—PLAY BINGO!"

14

Murder Will Out

The quiet is deafening, if that makes any sense. Since Francie's funeral last week, a pall has fallen over Lanai Gardens. Our friends and neighbors go about their day's activities very quietly. When people speak, they speak in whispers. There are none of the usual complaints about the weather. Francie made a difference in our lives and her loss is beyond measure. And maybe because it is Francie, we think about our own mortality. Especially we who live by ourselves. It brings an icy feeling to the back of the neck to think about dying all alone.

Francie's family went back to New Jersey after Evvie and I offered to take care of disposing of the rest of her things. Their instructions were: Take something to remember her by, and give everything else to charity.

Now Evvie and I are in Francie's apartment early in the morning. The first twenty minutes, we do nothing but just sit here and think of Francie in this place she loved. Her apartment reflects the bright and cheerful person she was. Her fabric colors are lemon, coral, and avocado green; her furniture style, light and airy wicker.

"Let's do the bedroom first," I say, to make a start. As we get up, Sophie flings open the front door and hurries in.

"Your coffee and bagels," she announces.

"Thanks, Soph," Evvie says. "Just leave them on the sink."

We start working on the closets, but are aware that Sophie hasn't left. We hear her clattering about.

"What are you doing, Soph?" I call out.

"You work, don't worry about me. I'll just kibitz."

Evvie and I exchange glances. Does that mean she plans to keep talking and drive us crazy?

We box Francie's clothes, and what a painful task it is. Remembering when she wore what. Remembering her laughter. And how she made everything fun.

Sophie's head pops into the doorway. "She did have aspirin," she says as if continuing some earlier discussion.

"Why?" asks Evvie. "Do you have a headache?"

"I read somewhere that if you're having a heart attack, someone should give you an aspirin. It could have saved Francie." She looks at us, eager to share her knowledge.

Exasperated, Evvie says, "But she was *alone*, Sophie."

"Well, maybe we should all carry aspirin all over our bodies from now on." She waits for a response.

"Thank you for sharing that. Don't you have someplace to go?"

"Not 'til two when we play cards." She disappears back into the kitchen-living room area.

Evvie holds up a beautiful peach organza cocktail gown. "Remember?" she asks.

"Jerry and Ilene's wedding."

Evvie nods and folds it away carefully. She opens the next drawer. "Oh," she cries out.

"What?" I pull my head out of the closet.

Evvie is holding up Francie's favorite sweatshirt, the one that says "Death by Chocolate." "She loved this crazy shirt." With that she starts to cry.

"We can't keep doing this. We'll never get done," I say as gently as I can.

"That's just it! I don't ever want to get done, because that will be the last we have of her."

We hear more noise from the kitchen. Sophie calls out, "You know how neat and clean she was. If Francie could see the crumbs in her sink, she'd die!"

"I'm going to wring her neck," Evvie says through gritted teeth.

I laugh. Everyone should have some comic relief in their lives. "Just leave it, Soph, we'll get someone in to clean."

The doorbell rings. "I'll get it," Sophie calls. As she opens the door, we hear her voice turn all sugary. "Well, hello there. Please do come in."

"Bet you five dollars." Evvie smirks.

"No bet. It can only be—" I call out, "Is that you, Mr. Slezak?"

Evvie and I return to the living room and there he is—gold chains gleaming.

"Good morning, beautiful ladies," he says, saluting us with his dirty white Panama hat as he snoops around. "I see by your hard work you are earning stars in your crown."

Evvie snarls at him, "Jews don't get stars in crowns!"

"Well, so call it a mitzvah, this good deed."

"My Stanley used to say, 'One mitzvah could change the world, two could make you tired,'" Sophie adds.

"Why are you here, Mr. Slezak?" I ask.

"*Leo,* why do you fight calling me Leo?"

"So, *Mr. Slezak,*" Evvie says deliberately, "tell us what you want."

"I need a set of keys. The family, such nice people, gave me the listing."

Evvie groans. We forgot to warn Jerry.

"Grave robber," Evvie mutters.

"You'll leave the furniture for a while? A property always shows better with a little interior décor."

"What difference will that make," Evvie says, losing her patience. "You'll never sell it anyway."

"How can you show such cruelty?" He pleads, "Don't I live here, too, among you? Am I not one of us?"

Evvie smirks at his pathetic parody of *The Merchant of Venice.*

"I work my buns off for you ladies. And why haven't you taken advantage of my 'Save Your Family Grief' program? A little rider added to the will about disposal of assets—"

"*I* have," chirps Sophie.

"We've already saved our families from grief,

thank you," I inform him. "We have it in our wills to give our apartments to the first homeless people they see, rather than let Sunrise-Sunset Real Estate get their paws on it."

Leo shrugs. He tried.

Evvie unclasps an extra key from her key ring and tosses it at him. "Don't slam the door on your way out."

"I'll walk you," Sophie says, almost drooling as she clutches at his arm and apologizes for our rudeness.

An hour goes swiftly by and we are making good progress. The refrigerator is almost emptied when a familiar doggie bag catches my eye. "Evvie, look. From dinner... our last dinner together. Remember, Francie took home the chocolate cake. She never ate it."

"That's not like her."

"Maybe she never got the chance." We look at each other considering what that means. For a moment I hesitate, and then I say what's been on my mind. "There's something I want to discuss with you. Something really serious."

Evvie looks at me, alarmed.

"Coincidences. I've been thinking there have been too many. Selma and Francie."

"What are you talking about?" Evvie asks, now more puzzled than alarmed.

"The birthdays for starters. Selma and Francie both died on the night before their birthday. Both were very healthy. Both died suddenly of heart attacks. With no history of heart attacks that we know of. They both died alone. Both were trying to reach for the phone. And there's something about that damn phone that's driving me up the wall and I can't remember what it is."

"But isn't it possible? Couldn't it have happened like that?"

"Yes. However, Miss Marple and I agree—we don't believe in coincidences."

"Oh, you and your mystery books—"

"I learn a lot from them. What it's beginning to sound like is an M.O."

"Again from the mysteries?"

"As in 'modus operandi,' the method used in a crime."

"A crime?" Now the worry lines appear on her face.

"As in murder—"

The doorbell rings and we both jump.

"Later," I say as I go to answer, hoping it isn't Sophie again.

Surprisingly, it is Harriet Feder, carrying a small basket.

"Come on in," Evvie calls out warmly.

"I hope I'm not interrupting. I took the day off, and I thought maybe I could help in some way." She indicates the basket. "A snack for the hard workers."

"Thanks, Harriet, that's really very thoughtful. You're not sick . . . ?"

"No. I just can't get over Francie. . . . I started to go to work and then I said the hell with it. The hospital can manage without me for a day or two. Considering how low the pay is, anyway. Then I sat around the apartment feeling depressed. I need to do *something*."

"We'll take all the help we can get," Evvie says.

"We're just about to start on the dishes," I tell her.

"I'll pass them down, you put them in the cartons," I say as I head towards the kitchen cabinets.

"OK. Keeping busy will help."

"How's your mother?" Evvie asks.

"She's fine. The usual aches and pains. I just wish I could find a way to make her accept being in that chair. She was always such an independent person."

Evvie and I exchange glances. To us, Esther Feder seems quite happy in that chair as long as she can boss everyone around. Especially Harriet.

We all work quietly for a while, then Harriet starts to clear the knickknacks off a corner shelf. She picks up one of many birthday cards that still linger there as a silent reminder. "This must be from Denny. He always sends such sweet, simple cards." She looks inside and smiles. "How does he always remember? I know the cards he sends me are always on time."

"That's easy," Evvie says. "About five years ago, we had a crafts class in the rec room and Denny attended. He made this birthday reminder calendar and it got him so excited, he went to each and every person in Phase Two and got them to mark down their dates."

"That's right. I remember when Mother and I moved in, he came and asked for ours. What a sweet boy." She smiles wryly. "Not a boy. He's actually about my age. The poor dear. He must be suffering terribly right now. Wasn't he the one who found both Selma and Francie's bodies?"

Evvie says, "Now that you mention it, you're right. Both times he was on his way up to fix something..." She turns to me as she says meaningfully, "What a coincidence."

"Thank God he has keys to all our apartments. Who knows how long poor Francie would have lain there, if he hadn't gone in." Harriet stops, aware of our tension.

Just then there is a knock at the open kitchen window. It's Ida. "Harriet," she calls in a snippy voice, "your mom wants you." She still hasn't forgiven her for the bank.

"Oh," says Harriet, looking at her watch. "She must be waiting for her lunch. Call me later." She leaves.

"I forgot the board gave Denny those keys. Another coincidence?" Evvie asks.

"Speaking of lunch," says Ida through the window. "I have it ready and waiting in my apartment. Take a break."

"Maybe we should," Evvie says. "Right now, I need to get a breath of air. But somehow I lost my appetite."

Suddenly a comment Sophie made jogs at my memory. "Go on ahead. I'll be with you after I lock up."

Alone in the apartment now, I am in a turmoil of emotion. I hurry to the kitchen sink. Sophie, in her dithering, talked about it being dirty. Crumbs, she said. I see tiny bits of debris. I touch them. They are soft, like the texture of cake. Brown cake crumbs. I pick them up and smell them. It's chocolate. I know it is.

Two thoughts pop into my head. 1) Sophie's right. Francie would never leave a dirty sink. 2) If she didn't eat the chocolate cake from Continental, where did these crumbs come from? And now I keep hearing words repeating in my head. *Death by chocolate. Death by chocolate.*

15

Making a Decision

I am waiting for Evvie in her apartment. She's getting ready for swimming. We had dinner together last night and breakfast this morning because she wanted to talk about the bombshell I threw at her yesterday, and we are still talking. If you call going around in circles talking.

"I'm almost ready," she calls from the bedroom.

"No hurry," I call back. I am on her sunporch skimming through one of her many movie magazines. While my apartment is a study in simplicity with a few nice antiques, a small collection of prints, and too many books, Evvie's place is a cluttered tribute to showbiz. If my sister "missed the boat," as she is fond of saying, she has certainly kept up with the ebbs and tides of her lost profession. Evvie wanted to be Doris Day. But Doris Day didn't have Joe Markowitz for a husband, who insisted she stay home and be a proper wife and cook and clean and care for the children. She had her one-week shot as a torch singer, performing in a small club in Jersey, and she was pretty good. (She swears Doris sang there, but I doubt that.) But then the war ended, and the guy she had met and married on a romantic weekend, before he shipped out for Korea, came home. That was the end of her career.

But the memories and dreams live on in her movie posters and recordings of Doris Day.

"I still don't think it was murder," she says as she comes out, rubbing on suntan lotion. She's only said that eleven times by my last count.

"But it is a possibility," I say, feeling like a broken record myself.

"It can't be anyone who lives here."

"I didn't say it was. I only said it might be."

We walk out her door and head down the stairs.

"I refuse to accept the possibility it could be Denny!"

"I never said it was."

"But he does have all the keys and he was the one who found them both."

"It could be a coincidence—"

"Which you don't believe in."

"But it could be."

We say our usual hellos to the usual gang and make our way down the path, passing our ducks in their pond, carefully avoiding the poop on the path.

"Look." Evvie grabs me. "There's Denny in his garden."

"So? He's usually in his garden at some time or other during the day." Denny sees us and waves.

"Does he look like he could kill anyone?"

"No, Ev, I don't think he could. But the truth is,

anyone is capable of murder if provoked, or if they believe they have a strong enough motive."

"Or is crazy."

"He's retarded, Ev, not crazy."

"The Kronk is crazy."

"We don't know that she's crazy. Maybe she's just eccentric." Evvie has forced me into this role of devil's advocate and now she's driving *me* crazy.

"Is she dangerous? Is she capable of murder?"

"Who knows? Nobody has even seen her in years."

"But she might be. She could be a raving maniac by now."

We arrive at the pool. I shush her. "Quiet. Drop the subject now. I don't want anyone else to know what we're talking about."

We greet everyone, drop our towels and pool shoes, and wade into the pool. I'm glad I didn't tell Evvie about the chocolate crumbs. I'd never hear the end of that discussion. But I do feel I have to do something about my suspicions.

"Hey, girls, c'm'ere, I've got another great joke," calls Hy as he and Lola bounce up and down together at three feet deep.

Evvie whispers to me as she starts to get in. "Well, if the murderer has to be one of us, I hope it's Hy. I would love to see him in Alcatraz."

"Alcatraz is closed."

"Whatever."

Of course Hy has to "playfully" splash us before he begins his joke. "There's these three guys standing in a bar boasting of how great they are in the sack. The Eye-talian says he rubs olive oil on his wife before sex and she screams with pleasure for an hour. The Frenchie says he pats butter on his wife and she screams for two hours. The Jew says he schmears chicken schmaltz on his wife and she screams for *six* hours. The Eye-talian and the Frenchie are impressed. 'How did you get your wife to scream for six hours?' 'Easy,' he says, 'I wiped my hands on the drapes!' Didya get it, didja?"

A few of us actually laugh.

I glance over at Enya sitting in her usual place. When Hy is most vulgar I look at her, hoping she isn't listening to him. She seems oblivious.

Tessie swims by me. Chubby as she is, in water she's as buoyant as a sponge. She does her usual laps. I get an idea. I wait until she is through and I follow her out to where her chaise is parked between the Feders and the Canadians.

I speak very softly. "Listen," I say, "you cleaned out Selma's apartment after she died, didn't you?"

She responds to my seriousness. "Yes, I did. Why?"

"I'm just curious about something. Do you recall seeing anything at all that was odd or unusual in the apartment?"

"Not that I can remember." She pauses. "You think there's something wrong?"

"I'm not sure, but I do want you to give this some serious thought. We'll talk later."

As I pass Harriet, she gives me the smallest of nods and an OK sign as if she guessed what I said to Tessie and was giving me her approval. I start to walk toward her, then stop. Esther is tugging at Harriet's arm.

"Sweetheart," she says, "I think I need more lotion." Since she is covered up to the neck, this seems unnecessary, but Harriet gets out the cream and works it into her mother's face.

"No," she says, "on my shoulders. I feel the sun through my robe, pull it down."

"Mom," Harriet says with a patience beyond Job's, "you can't get a burn through clothes."

Esther looks toward me, slyly. "You don't want them to see the marks." Harriet throws me a weary look over her mother's head. Her glance says, *See what I put up with.* Mine says, *You have my deepest sympathy.* I change my mind about approaching. She has enough to deal with. "Talk to you later," I tell her and jump back into the pool.

Evvie paddles over to me. "What was that all about?"

"Later," I say to her, too. I am putting everyone on hold until I can figure out what to do.

Evvie says, "Irving didn't bring Millie down today. I think we better check."

"Good idea," and we both leave the pool.

"So, where are you going?" Ida calls after us.

"We're gonna look in on Millie."

"OK."

You may have noticed by now that everybody keeps tabs on everybody else. The Lanai Gardens FBI is always on the alert; God forbid somebody should miss something. Especially since our behavior is so predictable that any small deviation is cause for complete attention by a mob of people—especially the girls.

We arrive at Millie's. When we walk in we immediately see how frazzled Irving looks. He is sitting at the dining room table, the remains of breakfast still there, his head in his hands.

"What's wrong?" I ask.

"She had a bad night. I was up until maybe four A.M."

"What was she doing?"

Irving looks embarrassed. "She was yelling at the children."

Poor Irving. He's been living with Millie's hallucinations so long, he talks about them as if they were real. They're real to Millie, so he goes along.

"Why was she yelling?" Evvie asks.

Irving shakes his head, and turns red.

"They want to do disgusting things with him and I won't let them." Millie shambles into the living room, her hair disheveled, her robe a mess. Looking coy one moment and furious the next, she bends over her husband. "Don't they, lover boy?" She runs her fingers wildly through the few strands of his hair.

Irving has always been a very shy man. Millie used to tell us funny stories about how he would undress in the closet when they were first married. He's never used a curse word in his life and now his demented wife is talking unashamedly about sex in front of other people.

"The children like to fuck!"

Irving pulls away from her and hurries out to the kitchen, holding his hands over his ears. Millie laughs as she watches him go. It is more like a cackle. Alzheimer's is a horrible disease. The Millie we are looking at bears no resemblance to our old friend.

Then once again, that peculiar symptom—suddenly, the light goes out in her mind and the catatonia returns. She starts to fall down, but Evvie catches her. Balancing her between us, we walk her back to bed and tuck her in.

We join Irving in the kitchen. He is standing at the stove with a tepid cup of tea.

I start carefully. We've been down this road before and he always cuts us off at the pass. "Irving. Maybe it's time—"

"No."

"Maybe you need someone to come in during the days."

"You all help...."

"You need more. You have to be able to sleep. You can't watch her twenty-four hours."

He says what he always says. "I'll think on it."

We start for the door. "We'll get one of the girls to come and spell you, so you can take a nap," I say.

He nods and we leave.

"I can do it," Evvie volunteers.

"No," I tell her. "I have other plans for us."

16

Keystone Kops and Nosy Neighbors

Do you think we can make our getaway without anybody noticing?" Evvie is whispering, as if that would help.

We are walking very quietly down the stairs from my apartment on the third floor. "Ha ha," I say, "fat chance."

Ida's door flings open and she steps out onto the walkway. She sees us round the second floor stairwell and calls down to us over the banister. "Where are the Siamese twins off to now? First it was dinner, then breakfast. Now out to lunch I suppose?"

"Here we go," I say. "Send in the clowns!"

Evvie sighs. "If three-nineteen is out, can three-fourteen be far behind?"

And sure enough, Sophie's head pops out of her kitchen window. "So where is everybody off to?" she calls out.

"Maybe if we don't answer..." Evvie says softly.

"Dream on," I say.

From across the parking area, Bella's third-floor door opens and she peers out. "Am I missing something?" she calls out in her whispery little voice.

Evvie and I are now on the ground floor tiptoeing to the car. God bless them—they may be half deaf and half blind and well on their way to senility, but they don't miss a trick.

Now we pass the Feder apartment, 119, which is two doors away from my parking spot. Esther Feder is at her usual post, sitting in the doorway behind the screen, so the bugs won't get her. Which is actually a bizarre sight if you think about how she looks with her head pressed against the dark mesh partition. She raps at the screen to get our attention. "Where are you girls going in all this heat?"

Ida, the acrobat, now hangs over the balcony. "So, what's the big hurry?"

Sophie trills, "If you're stopping at Publix, maybe you'll bring me a pint of sour cream? I'll pay you back later." Which is a joke. Sophie borrows money from all of us, and we've yet to get a penny back. Ida calls that the lifestyle of the rich and disgusting.

The three-ring chorus is getting louder.

"We can't just ignore them. We have to tell them something," Evvie says.

"You're the writer. Make something up." I open the door and turn on the air so I can cool off the car.

"We're going out on blind dates," she calls out.

"That's the best you can come up with?" I say.

"Oh, yeah? They'd have to be desperate to want *you* old ladies." And now dear Hy, the snake charmer, comes out of his apartment carrying the garbage, adding his two bits.

All the clowns are laughing. The idea of us having dates is just too funny.

Ida especially loves this. "Who's your matchmaker, Yentl Frankenstein?"

Esther, excited, now pushes her screen door open so she can see better. "You got dates? Maybe you can fix my Harriet up?"

There is a loud clatter from inside the kitchen and Harriet appears quickly, wiping her hands on her apron. "Oh, Mom," she says, embarrassed. "Please!"

"Well, you told me to sit in the door and spy on them."

Harriet turns red in the face. "That's not funny!" She spins her mother's wheelchair around sharply. "Go inside now! Eat your lunch. You know I have no time for this. I have to get back to the hospital!"

"I didn't mean anything. Don't hit me." Esther wheels herself in quickly.

Harriet looks at us. "I'm sorry," she says. "Sometimes Mom can be so difficult." Then she smiles and leans in toward us and whispers. "You really have dates?"

Evvie whispers back. "Of course not. We're going to the police station and we don't want anybody to know. You know what yentas they all are."

"Evvie!" I say sharply. "My sister, queen of the yentas."

Harriet joins in the conspiracy. "I knew it! You do think there's a connection between their deaths. Don't worry, I won't say a word. Good luck. Let me know how it goes."

We get into the car and make our escape, leaving a lot of disappointed faces peering after us.

"I'm sorry," Evvie says. "I didn't think it mattered if I told Harriet."

"I just didn't want anyone to know until we were sure there was a crime. You know how rumors spread."

"Yeah, like cream cheese on bagels," she says with a sigh.

We leave Lanai Gardens and I make our turn onto Oakland Park Boulevard, and I can finally breathe a sigh of relief.

"Come to think of it," Evvie says, "when was the last time you and I had some time alone away from the gang?"

"When you had to cover that speech by that Israeli fund-raiser. No one else wanted to go. If I hadn't had to drive you, neither would I."

"Oh, yeah. He lectured on 'Is Israel In Trouble?'"

"Which YOU slept through. Though I did love your review."

Evvie bristles, ready to be insulted. "Why, what was wrong with it?"

"Nothing, because it was so..." I stop. "A senior moment. What's the word that means 'short and sweet'?"

"I don't know. What's wrong with 'short and sweet'?"

"Because I can't stand it when I can't think of the word that won't come out of my mouth when I want it."

"Good? Was the word good? My review was good?"

"That's not the word. Never mind."

"My review wasn't good?"

"That's not the point. I am talking about my loss of memory."

"Now you've got me not remembering. I don't remember what I wrote in that review."

"You said, 'Yes. Israel is always in trouble.'"

"That was it?"

"Yes. It was pithy." Now I get excited. "That was the word—pithy!"

Evvie points. "There it is. The police station."

As I make the right turn from Oakland Park Boulevard into the parking area, I say as sternly as I can, "Evvie, promise me you'll let me do all the talking."

"Mum's the word."

We are finally shown into the office of Detective Morgan Langford, and I'm already exhausted. The waiting seems endless. The paperwork, too. The sergeant at the front desk would not let us go any further until we first explained to him what we wanted. I held my ground. I would only speak to someone in Homicide. Why should I waste my time going through it twice? Finally, I used the "age card" and pretended senility. He was glad to be rid of me. But, I think, as punishment, he sent me to Detective Langford.

It's amazing that in all my seventy-five years, I have never really seen or been in a police station. In movies, in books, but not in reality. I have to admit to a little shiver of excitement. I want to yell out, "Hey, Agatha, look at me!"

Evvie is also all a-twitter in her first police station appearance, but she is off in another art form. She is preparing to become the actress she should have been. Suddenly she has an attitude. She is trying to look sophisticated and worldly. I just hope she doesn't decide to sing.

Detective Langford is busy reading the very little information I grudgingly filled in while waiting. This gives me a chance to study him. He's in his thirties, very, very tall, and skinny. His clothes hang on him. He seems to favor loud checks and plaids. He is very relaxed. Maybe too relaxed.

"So," he says, "you insisted on talking to Homicide. Are you planning one, reporting one, or looking for one?"

And cynical.

Before I can stop her, Sarah Bernhardt begins to emote. "We are here to report two murders. They are Selma Beller, who kept a very clean house, and Francie Charles, who was the best pastry maker in Fort Lauderdale."

"When did these murders occur?" asks long and lanky, trying to keep a straight face.

"Evvie..." I growl, but she ignores me.

"One month ago and one week ago."

"How come they haven't been reported?"

"Because nobody knows they were murdered. Everybody says they had heart attacks, but we know better. Only my sister, who is an expert in murder mysteries, and myself, a writer for the Lanai Gardens *Free Press,* know the truth."

"Are you finished yet?" I hiss at her. I notice she doesn't mention that the *"Press"* is a throwaway.

"Would you like to add to this, Mrs. Markowitz?"

"I'm Gold, she's Markowitz, my blabbermouth sister. I know this may sound far-fetched to you, but two women did die in our buildings. But their deaths..."

Evvie obviously can't stand my slow, logical pace. "Too many coincidences. Agatha Christie doesn't believe in them and neither do we!" Pleased with her pronouncement, she folds her hands, waiting for the detective to take over the case.

"And what are these coincidences?"

Evvie blabs, "Tell him about the cake Francie never ate and that the girls both died on the night before their birthdays and that Denny had keys to their apartments and they both died reaching for the phone."

Hearing the way my sister lays out our case, I could just about imagine Langford's opinion of us. He is drumming those long bony fingers impatiently on the desk.

"And these are the devastating facts that make you suspect murder?"

Evvie, totally missing his sarcasm, blathers on. She gets a brainstorm. "What about the serial killer? He kills old women. What's his M.O.? That means his method," she explains to the Homicide detective.

If his tongue was any farther back in his cheek, he'd choke. He asks dramatically, "Interested in the M.O.'s, are we? Well, our killer sneaks into apartments of women who live alone. Late at night, he creeps up on them when they are sleeping and strangles his victims. Were your victims strangled?"

"They didn't look strangled. But then, we're no experts," Evvie grandly admits.

I've had it. I reach over and smack my hand over Evvie's mouth. Evvie, eyes widening, looks at me, horrified. She tries to speak, but I keep my hand firmly pressed on her mouth. I turn to Langford. "Listen. I know none of this sounds incriminating—

but there is something wrong with their deaths. Can't you give it a little time and investigate?"

Langford gets up—rather, it's more like unfurling himself—and he is an awesome six foot six or so. Evvie gasps in pleasure amidst her pain. He is moving toward the door, which is his way of moving us to the door—and out.

"I really would like an autopsy," I say in desperation.

"You wouldn't like it. It hurts like hell," he says and roars with laughter.

As firmly as I can, I make my last-ditch stand. "I think they were poisoned. I am a reasonable, rational woman, unlike my sister here." With that I let go of her, and glaring at her, I dare her to make a sound. "Please do not condescend to me with bad jokes. I do not make such statements lightly. These women were murdered. In my heart I know I'm right."

He opens the door. "Well, thanks for dropping in." And we are dismissed.

As we head for the door, Evvie, oblivious, punches my arm, delighted with her premiere. "How'd we do, sis?" she asks.

I tell her she deserves an Academy Award. And I deserve what I got for taking her along.

All the way home, I simmer. The detective wouldn't take me seriously because I'm old in his eyes. Well, I'll show him, that snotty string bean.

I wake up suddenly, look at the clock. It's nearly eleven. I must have fallen asleep reading. The light is still on. Suddenly I am jumping out of bed, throwing my robe and slippers on. Scrambling through my junk drawer for my flashlight. I grab my keys and I'm out the door. I don't want to do this. I don't want to walk around alone at night, but this can't wait until morning.

Maybe I should wake Evvie. No. Coward. It's not the middle of the night. What am I afraid of?

I know what I'm afraid of.

I truly believe there is a killer loose around here.

It's a beautiful night with a wild, full moon. The kind of moon that once upon a time meant romance, not terror. I walk down the stairs. I tell myself, *See, there are a few people still up.* I can see the flickering of TV sets. Then I giggle. Maybe I'll run into Greta Kronk. Maybe she'll tell me what's so great about digging around in Dumpsters in the middle of the night.

So far so good. Now I have to walk around the corner. It seems darker as I make the turn, but that's silly. Between the moon and the streetlights, I can see what's ahead. But then again, I can also be seen.

I curse the memory lapses that come with getting old. Two wasted days to remember what should have clicked the instant I saw it. And now I'm walking around in the dark.

I jump, startled, then realize it's a stupid palm tree swaying and what I saw was its shadow. But, finally, I'm at Francie's apartment. I curse the key. I curse my hands that won't stop shaking. When the lock finally gives, I go straight for the kitchen. I don't even turn the lights on, the flashlight will be good enough.

The proof is in the pudding, I think, giggling with relief that I got here safely. The poison will be in the chocolate. I will bring it to Detective Langford and say, "Here's your proof." He'll have to listen to me!

I flash the light over the sink. Even as I see it, my mind refuses to accept it. No!!! Damn it, no! The chocolate crumbs are gone! Someone has scrubbed the sink clean.

I crumple into Francie's favorite armchair and start to cry. In my mind the heroes and heroines of every murder mystery I have ever read are wagging their fingers at me, shaking their heads ruefully. *We taught you so much and you learned nothing. Failure. You had it and you lost it. You old woman, you old failure.*

Whatever courage got me here is gone now. I sit in the armchair all night, just an old lady waiting, trusting in the safety of daylight.

17

Canasta

It's Sophie's turn to host the weekly canasta game. Not my favorite place to play cards. First of all, Sophie's apartment is enough to give me a headache even before we play. Her decor is what Ida calls Early *Ongepatshket*. This is almost untranslatable, but the closest meaning would be overdone to the max. If there is an empty space, something must be put in it. And something is never enough. Too much is never enough. Why one doily on a couch, when five would be better? If you get my drift.

In everyone else's apartment, we get served some nuts and raisins, tea and maybe sponge cake. Not in the home of Sophie, the bountiful. A huge bowl of fruit. Boxes of candy. Later on, coffee and three kinds of pie. Bella calls her generous. Ida calls her a show-off.

Ida is not here yet. But when she arrives, the battle of the air conditioner will begin. Sophie will want

subarctic temperatures. Ida will want the tropics.
Speak of the devil. Here she is.

"Turn down the goddamn air," she announces
before even getting through the door.

Sophie folds her arms. "No. My house, my
rules. In your house we sweat like pigs!"

Bella, the pacifist, says meekly. "Put on your
sweater, Ida dear."

The card game begins.

"So how much do we need to open?" Bella asks.

"It's one-twenty. It's always one-twenty!" Ida
snaps at her.

"I forget."

Evvie asks Bella, "Did you bring your hearing
aid?"

"What?" she asks.

"Never mind."

"So, partner, are you ready to open?" Ida asks
Evvie.

"Already, they're starting. This is a card game,
not a discussion group." Sophie glares at them.

"I'm close," Evvie says, ignoring Sophie.

It is my turn to sit out the game. We play a
round robin, alternating who gets to play. Bella
would prefer never to touch a card since there are
already four of us, but the two sadists insist she
can't just sit and watch. She hates to play as much as
they hate playing with her. What can I tell you? This
is the way it is. I'm glad I'm sitting out. I don't think
I could concentrate.

It's Ida's turn. She looks at Evvie. Evvie comments ever so lightly, "Have you seen *Hy* lately?"

"Yes, indeed I have," says Ida, putting down a
jack. Evvie blows her a kiss.

Sophie glares. She knows what they're up to. "Cheater," she mutters. "As if you give a hoot about Hy Binder!"

Ida stands up. "How dare you!"

Sophie says, getting surly, "Next time it'll be 'and how is dear old *Lo*' and you'll give her a *low* card—"

Evvie throws her cards down on the table. "That's it! You have some nerve!"

Bella looks from one to the other thoroughly confused.

War is about to begin.

"Girls," I say, "we need to talk. Girls!"

They take one look at my face and know something is up. Reluctantly, they throw their cards into the middle of the table, still simmering, except for Bella, who is relieved.

It takes a few minutes for them to calm down and plump up pillows and generally get comfortable. Finally I have their attention.

"You all wondered where Evvie and I went the other afternoon, I'm sure."

Ida answers huffily. "We certainly did."

I drop my bombshell. "We went to the police station. To report the murders of Francie and Selma."

For maybe three seconds there is a stunned silence. Then they are all talking at once in a barrage of words. *Murder? Francie? Selma? Not possible. Oy gevalt! What are you talking about? You're kidding, right? Police, really the police? What did you say? What did they say?*

Finally Evvie bangs on the table. "Shah! Be quiet and you might learn something!"

Slowly they settle down, all eyes glued on me in horror and excitement.

Bella looks confused. "You mean you didn't have dates?"

I say, "No, Bella, no dates."

Evvie, of course, jumps in. "Gladdy thinks they were both murdered but that cop wouldn't believe her!"

"After he just dismissed us as crackpots, I tried to forget about it, but Francie won't let me. I keep hearing her in my head: *Find out who did it. You have to.* It was the crumbs that convinced me."

A chorus of "What crumbs?" follows.

Evvie looks at me suspiciously. "You never mentioned crumbs."

"I know," I say guiltily. "It was the crumbs that Sophie found in Francie's sink. Chocolate cake crumbs. If Francie didn't eat the cake she brought home from Continental, where did they come from?"

Evvie is hurt. "You didn't tell me."

"I'm sorry."

"I told you Francie wouldn't leave a dirty sink! I knew it!" Sophie is delighted with herself.

"Maybe she didn't like the cake from Continental," says Bella. "Maybe she baked a new one." Then gleefully, "From her new cookbook." Bella is pleased with her theory.

"And ate an entire cake herself? Puleeze," says Evvie disdainfully. "Our health nut who eats tiny portions?" Evvie realizes what she just said. "Who *used* to eat . . ." She stops, on the verge of tears.

"I don't understand," Ida says. "Who would want to kill them? They didn't have enemies."

"And why? Why would anyone hurt them? They never hurt a fleabag," Sophie insists.

"It was the coincidences," my sidekick informs them. Evvie proceeds to list my suspicions.

"If it wasn't heart attacks," Sophie asks me, "what made them dead?"

"I think poison."

There is a group gasp at this as each of the girls tries to absorb this momentous information.

"I went back to Francie's apartment. I went to get those chocolate crumbs. It could have been the proof we needed...."

Evvie gets it first. "Oh, no. The cleaning girl was there after we left."

"Gone," I say. But was it the cleaning girl? Or did the killer get there first?

"Why are you telling us this?" Ida asks softly.

"I want you all to help me find the killer."

There is a long moment as they digest the earth-shattering things I have been saying. Bella and Sophie reach out and hold hands. Ida jumps up, needing to move around.

Bella sighs. "How can we? A killer could be anywhere."

"Yeah," says Ida, "maybe he's the serial killer."

"The serial killer is a strangler, the cops told us," Evvie informs them.

"You're not saying..." Sophie begins.

"I am saying. I think the killer lives here or comes here, somebody we probably know or have seen hanging around."

"*A choleria!* A plague on him! I can't believe such a thing," Sophie cries out.

"I'm never going out of my apartment again," wails Bella.

"They were both killed *in* their apartments," Ida says with evil relish.

"*Vay iz mir*, I'm dying!" Bella is in tears.

Sophie screeches, "Whose birthday is next?"

"Does anybody know when it's my birthday? I can't remember," asks Bella plaintively.

"We don't know for sure if that means anything," I say, trying to calm them.

Evvie takes a stronger tack. "Snap out of it!" she says, the movie critic paying homage to *Moonstruck*.

"I really do need help," I say. "I want us to go around and talk to everybody. Find out if they saw anything unusual the nights of the murders."

Again, silence as this is absorbed. Finally Sophie sighs. "*Oy*, I wish I were only seventy-eight again!"

Ida pats her on the back. "Don't worry, Princess, you'll find the strength. We all will, for Francie's sake."

"I don't know," Sophie says. "Maybe we're opening up a can of snakes."

Bella whimpers. "Maybe you'll make the killer mad and he'll come after us."

"God forbid," Evvie says.

"I'm more worried we'll scare a lot of people, but it has to be done," I reply. More silence.

"Everybody in?" I ask.

I get a chorus of "in's."

"Then, hopefully, we'll get real information, so the cops will believe us and take over."

The girls get up and start clearing the cards off the table. We always help the hostess clean up.

"You should have told me about the crumbs," Evvie says accusingly.

"I know," I tell her. "I know."

"*I* would have remembered!"

"I know! Don't keep rubbing it in!"

Suddenly we hear sirens very close. Ida runs and flings open the door. "Police cars! Coming in here!"

"Murder! Another murder!" Sophie screams.

And Bella faints.

I feel very guilty. What have I unleashed?

18

Old-Timer's Disease

We don't even wait for the elevator. In spite of our age, and the possible damage we can do to our bodies, we are running down the three flights of stairs and across the parking area to where two policemen, and a small group of our neighbors in a varied assortment of sleepwear, are gathering. The flashing lights from the police car zigzag across the watchers like strobe lights at a "happening." Something is happening all right and we are terrified.

All the activity is centered at Millie and Irving's apartment. The police are pounding at their door. Thoughts crowd my head. Making assessments. It's after nine P.M. They must be asleep. It's not an ambulance, thank God, so Irving didn't call the paramedics. So, why are the police here? Please, God, don't let anyone be hurt. The officers keep hammering. No one is answering.

We arrive at the door, hearts throbbing with fear

and overexertion. Throwing questions at them, although we are so out of breath we can barely speak.

"What is it?"

"Why are you here?"

"What's wrong?"

"Please talk to us. We're their friends."

The taller policeman with an orange mustache tells us they got a 911 call.

The short, stubby one says, "The woman was screaming that she was being raped and someone was trying to kill her."

The girls breathe a collective sigh of relief. "Boy, have you got the wrong address," Evvie informs them.

By now the group is beginning to look like a crowd. Hy and Lola, in matching robes, peer over the balcony right above our heads. Peripherally, I am aware of Harriet, tying her robe, as she hurries across the parking area. Tessie is not far behind her.

On this side of the building, Denny pokes his head out of his apartment. He looks disheveled, wild-eyed.... When he sees me looking at him, he turns and scurries back in. The expression on his face is pure fright. Poor thing. After having discovered both Selma's and Francie's bodies, I don't blame him for not wanting to be witness to yet another fearful situation.

All eyes turn as the door squeaks open to just the barest sliver. "Who is it?" Irving whispers.

"Open up. Police." Orange mustache is very forceful.

The door opens slightly farther. Irving is in his pajamas, his eyes sleep-encrusted and barely open, still not really awake. I sigh in relief. He looks at his visiting assemblage with alarm. "What is it? What's wrong?"

"We're here on a nine-one-one. Did you phone the police?"

"No," he says, still befuddled.

"I did," says a raspy voice behind him. The door is flung wide open.

How can I describe what Millie looks like? We all stare in awe. She can hardly move because she is wearing so many layers of clothes. I would guess she tried to put on everything in her closet and finally stopped when no more would fit. After the eye has absorbed that, the real horror seeps in. Millie has a huge pair of scissors in her hand which then makes you notice that most of her clothes have been mutilated. I hear someone moaning behind me.

Then there is the makeup. Millie's face is layered with cosmetics. And her hair! There are ribbons wildly tied to every possible strand. As I wonder where she got ribbons from, I realize they are the cut portions of her clothes.

Millie hits Irving on the back with her fist. "Rapist!" she shrieks. "Sodomist!" Where did she ever learn that word? "Assassin!" Irving freezes, mortified, standing there letting the blows fall on his bent shoulders.

I am vaguely aware of someone quite tall pushing his way forward through the growing crowd. But I can't take my eyes off Millie and Irving.

"She's ill," I finally say to the two policemen. "She doesn't know what she's doing."

"Irving wouldn't hurt a hair on her head," I hear Sophie say behind me.

"This is all a terrible mistake," Evvie says.

The short one speaks kindly to us. "Can you handle it from here, or do you need our help?"

"We'll manage," Ida says.

Millie's fit is already lessening. She now leans her head on Irving's shoulders, dropping the scissors as she does. He reaches behind and holds onto her. Taking charge, Ida hurries in to help him.

As Ida closes the door, the crowd begins to disperse. The patrolmen walk to their cars, but stop to greet someone. "Detective," I hear one say, and I wheel about. And there's Morgan Langford.

I hurry over to him, Evvie following right after me, with Sophie clutching her arm.

"What are you doing here?" I ask.

He bends as if in greeting and smiles. "Mrs. Gold. Mrs. Markowitz."

"Such a good memory," Evvie marvels.

"Just call *me* Sophie," Sophie says, pushing her way in front of Evvie.

By now Harriet has joined us and she introduces herself as well. Evvie pointedly explains to Sophie and Harriet, "This is the cop we talked to, the one who wouldn't believe us when we told him about our murders."

"Enough, Ev," I say. "He's here now."

"I heard the police call," Detective Langford says. "I thought I'd check it out."

"Then you did believe me!" I am feeling vindicated.

"I didn't say that," he answers mildly, bursting my balloon.

"Morrie!" I hear an excited voice coming up behind me.

To my astonishment, there's Bella, obviously

recovered from where we left her resting, hurrying
over as fast as she is able. And then, standing as high
as she can on her toes (all four foot eleven of her),
which still only brings her up to his belt buckle, she
reaches up (as Langford leans way down to accom-
modate her) and gives Detective Morgan Langford a
big, gushy kiss. Good thing he didn't pick Bella up,
she could have gotten a nosebleed.

Morrie?

"You know him?" Evvie asks, beating me to it.

Bella grins. "This is Jack Langford's son from
Phase Six. You remember, I was in Hadassah with
his mother, Faye, until she passed, aleha ha-shalom,
may she rest in peace."

Langford smiles way down at her. "So, you're
one of these troublemakers, are you?" Bella looks
confused.

Ida rushes up to join us, worried she is missing
something. "Millie's back in bed," she reports.
"And who is this tall, handsome stranger?" she
gushes. Next she'll start to bat her eyes.

Evvie fills her in. Ida, being Ida, immediately
leaps in where fools would fear to. "How dare you
not believe Gladdy!"

"Hey, whoa. Easy, ladies."

"Lay off," I growl at Ida. Making an enemy of
Detective Langford is not smart.

"Look," he says to me, "just find me a shred of
something to go on, then I promise to get involved."

"Fair enough," I say, thinking guiltily of the
cake crumbs I let get away.

"But, Mrs. Gold, be very careful. If there really
is a killer, he's smart. He hasn't made any mistakes.

That makes him very dangerous. Do not, I repeat, do anything foolish. If anything comes up, call me!"

Langford leaves and everyone voices an opinion.

"Gorgeous," breathes Ida.

"Ooh, so tall," says Sophie.

"Wow!" says Harriet. "Next time take *me* to the police station.

"I'm reserving judgment," says Evvie.

"Such a *shayner boychick,*" says Bella. "I know him since he was this tall." Her hand moves up and down trying to measure the man as boy. If we believe Bella, Lanky was six feet tall at two years old.

I smile. So, he's Jewish? Well, what do you know!

You've heard of the immovable object and the irresistible force.... Well, that's stubborn us seated in a row in the Weiss living room, facing even more stubborn Irving. After all the excitement, we went back to check on Millie and found Irving in tears.

"Enough, Irving," I say. "No more discussion. Things have to change."

"I never heard her get up."

"It could have been worse," Evvie says, shuddering. I know she is thinking about the scissors.

"All right. I'll unplug the phone. I'll hide it before I go to sleep."

"She'll think of something else," Ida says. "Remember how she got out of the apartment that night and wandered down to Oakland Park."

"I put double locks on the doors. I hide the keys. She doesn't get out any more."

"No, she calls the cops in," says Bella.

"No more putting off, Irving," says Sophie. "If you're in a hole, you better start digging."

"It's time to get real help. Full-time help," I say.

"Around the clock," adds Evvie.

"No," Irving says. "I have no room for a stranger to sleep."

"You can't stay up all night and watch her."

"I'll nap during the day if someone is here."

"Irving," Ida says carefully. "You know she'd be better off in managed care."

Irving puts his hands over his ears. "No! I won't hear this."

I get up. I feel so weary and so helpless. Through the bedroom door, I can hear Millie softly snoring. "All right, dear. We'll try hiring someone. But if that doesn't work . . ."

Irving turns his back on us.

We all tiptoe into the bedroom and take a look in at Millie. She is curled up with her thumb in her mouth. She looks almost young lying there, as though the Alzheimer's has made her face soften as she gives up her worldly cares. Her eyes open and she smiles slyly at us. Almost like she knows what havoc she causes and it tickles her.

We take turns kissing her good night. Suddenly Millie says pleadingly, "Where's Francie? Why doesn't she visit me anymore?"

My precocious granddaughter, Lindsay, when she was younger, mispronounced Millie's illness as old-timer's disease. As we watch Millie's suffering and try to remember happier days to offset our reality, maybe that's a gentler way to put it.

19

Gladdy's Gladiators

It is Sunday afternoon and we are sitting in the clubhouse, our chosen headquarters, strategizing. Now we are six. Since Harriet met that cute Morrie Langford the other night, she has begged to be allowed to join our merry band of private eyes. Ida, naturally, is not thrilled. She still hasn't forgiven Harriet, even though Harriet apologized for the bank incident.

We have a chalkboard and chairs. What more do we need? Except that the PA system keeps spewing out songs of the thirties and forties so loud we have to shout to be heard. The stereo music is supposed to play outside around the pool. Manuel, our groundskeeper, turns it on and up every morning before he heads out to do his landscaping chores. However, he didn't do it today. The music is inside and blaring at us instead. None of us knows how to figure out the complicated panel, so Evvie is on her hands and knees (not easy with arthritis) searching every wall, looking for the plug to shut the whole thing off. With no success. Hopefully, Manuel will be back soon, or those of us who aren't deaf will be.

The first half hour is spent wasting time with general nonsense, all at the top of our lungs. Sophie suggests we give ourselves a name.

Ida informs her this isn't bingo, this is not a club, it's very serious business.

Bella, not hearing her, suggests "Gladdy's Girls."

Ida says, "No names, dammit!"

Sophie, always happy to spite Ida, says, "How about 'Gladdy *and* her Girls'?"

Bella says, "I like 'Gladdy's Gladiators' better."

"Where did you come up with that?" Evvie says from somewhere under one of those industrial-type tables.

"Gladiator is like Gladdy, and Florida has alligators."

"That has a certain logic, I think," says Harriet.

She's even beginning to make sense to me and that's scary. "Thanks for all the credit," I say. "But maybe we should get down to business."

"It'll look good on T-shirts," says Sophie.

"No T-shirts!" screeches Ida.

"With our names maybe on the pockets," says Bella.

"No, I don't like pockets," Sophie adds.

Ida picks up her copy of the Broward *Jewish Journal* and swats them both. "I'll give you a T-shirt, you meshugenehs! What has seventy-five balls and kills idiots like you!"

"I give up," Evvie says, getting up from the floor and brushing off her clothes. "I can't find the switch and somebody should really sweep better in here."

"Is it time to take our coffee break?" Bella asks.

"We haven't started yet," Ida says with disgust, "and she wants a break."

"I brought rugallah. Raspberry." She offers up a handful sweetly. This activates the bringing out of other plastic Baggies.

Another fifteen minutes are spent dividing up our coffee and tea and Danish and cinnamon rolls and all the other various goodies everyone brought, "so no one should go hungry until lunch in two hours."

As everyone eats and chats, I look at the dozens of group photos lining the walls. I can feel the spirits of twenty-five years surrounding me. This building could tell some stories!

Ida sees me glancing around.

"Ghosts," I say.

Ida nods. "So many people gone. But what good times."

"Tell me," Harriet says.

"Such parties," Ida says. "We'd use anything as an excuse to celebrate. Besides having all the real holidays and the Jewish holidays, there were birthdays and anniversaries and welcoming new arrivals and the births of grandchildren. . . ."

Evvie laughs. "Harriet, you should have seen us in the beginning, fresh from New York. The men had all retired and we came here planning to do nothing but have a good time."

Ida says, "Correction. Murray retired, I never got to retire. I still had to cook and clean and shop. . . ."

Evvie cuts her off. "At first, in winter, everybody wore their fur stoles and wool dresses. Until we wised up and dumped them for shorts and sun-dresses and muumuus."

"You shoulda seen the pool in those days, not like the ghost town it is today," Ida says. "Standing room only. Every lounge chair was spoken for. You would put a towel down to reserve your seat, turn your back, your lounge was gone. We had to bring chairs down from the apartments. All the kids came visiting at the beginning. With all the grandchildren. So much giggling and laughing..."

"Don't forget the weekends in Miami Beach," says Evvie.

"The New Year's Eve parties were the best," says Sophie. "Everybody got snockered and a little *farblondjet.*"

"Evvie jumped into the pool naked one year!" says Bella, giggling.

"I told you a thousand times, I was wearing a body stocking!"

"You couldn't tell from where I was standing, dearie," says Ida. "You shoulda seen the men's eyes bugging out."

"I got drunk. That was when I knew Joe was going to dump me for that blonde. He dumps me the week before New Year's Eve, that bastard."

"Everybody was alive and healthy then...." says Bella. "My Abe looked like Valentino in a tux." The tears start to well up.

"Remember, Evvie, how your choir used to sing for us?" This from Sophie.

Evvie shakes her head. "Gone. All of them gone."

"Now the pool is always empty. None of the

kids come down anymore," says Ida bitterly. "We're lucky if we even get a letter."

"We only got each other," Bella says.

Uh-oh, I think, this trip down memory lane is taking us up the garden path. I pick up a piece of chalk and tap it sharply on the board. "OK, my gladiators, enough with the food and gabbing. Time to get down to business. For Francie's and Selma's sakes." With the rustling of the cleaning up of packages and such, and a few last sniffles, they pull themselves back into the present.

I draw a diagram on the chalkboard dividing up the six buildings in our phase. Each building has thirty-six apartments, so that's a lot of ground to cover. I suggest we each pick a building and go by ourselves, but Bella says she's too scared to go alone, so she insists on going with Sophie and that's OK.

We agree on what to ask. We are looking for any suspicious behavior. Or any people seen hanging around who don't belong here. Especially anyone seen near Francie's or Selma's apartment on the days they died. A discussion evolves about what to tell people as to why we are asking.

I say we should tell the truth.

Sophie is afraid of scaring everybody. And she has a point.

Ida believes in being devious. "Let's tell them we're thinking of hiring a security guard and we want to find out if we need one. Like if we've seen any weird characters around."

Harriet is afraid that will backfire and I think she is right.

Bella is nervous. "We can't just out-and-out say we think Selma and Francie were offed."

We all stare at her. She giggles. "I heard that on the TV last night."

Evvie, who loves lawyer shows, says it should be on a "need to know" basis. "We'll say we're doing a survey, but if they ask, we tell them more. If they don't, we don't."

Harriet agrees, but is dubious. "Evvie has a point, but suppose someone should want to get into it? What do we say is the motive? Who would kill them and why? And how? You think poison. How can we be sure? We have no proof. We have nothing. We don't want to make fools of ourselves."

Evvie speaks. "Listen, my sister Glad has intuition. I remember when we were kids, once she was out shopping with our mother and she insisted they rush home. And there I was lying on the floor sick as a dog. Glad just knew!"

"That sounds more like ESP," says Ida.

"Whatever," says Evvie. "I trust it. And we have to start somewhere." Evvie puts her arm around me to show her support.

I thank her. "I'm hoping we'll get lucky and someone will have seen or heard something. For now, let's agree to try what we've been talking about and see how that works."

Evvie and I volunteer to start with the P building, her building.

Harriet volunteers to take Q, the building where we live.

Ida volunteers the R (for Rose) building around the corner where Francie lived. Since Selma lived in Q, these two are the key buildings, and we want to tackle them first.

Sophie and Bella will tackle S (Sweet William)

across from where Francie lived. That way, we are dealing with all the apartments closest to the murder scenes.

"Do you think anybody will talk to us?" Bella worries.

"Everyone but crazy Kronk," says Ida. "She never opens the door to anyone."

"Probably Enya won't talk to us, either," says Harriet.

"Well, do the best you can," I say. "But I have to impress upon you very strongly what Detective Langford said. We have to be very careful. We are playing with matches here. Stay cool and calm and don't do anything foolish."

There is a knock on the door. I quickly turn the chalkboard around. It has a lot of our ideas written on it. Evvie goes to unlock the door. Hy is standing there in a bathing suit and a towel around his neck. Like some fierce bantam cock, he struts aggressively into the room.

"So, what's with the locked doors and secret meeting? You girls planning a revolution?"

"Yeah," says Ida, "we're planning to get rid of the few men who are left. Especially those who tell stupid jokes."

"Geez," he shouts, "it's loud in here. Why don't you turn down the hi-fi?"

"Because we don't know how to work the PA, Mr. Know-it-all," says Evvie.

Hy looks around the room briefly, then walks over to the panel, selects a switch, and turns it to Off. There is silence. Glorious silence. He shrugs and starts singing, "Oh, it's nice to have a man around the house...." wiggling his butt as he does.

"Didja hear the news this morning?" Hy asks.

"No," we chorus. "And not interested."

"CNN announced that senior citizens are the leading carriers of aids."

"What!" Ida hollers. "You nutcase!"

"Yup. Carriers of hearing aids, Band-Aids, Rolaids, walking aids, medical aids, government aids, and especially monetary aids to their children!"

Evvie picks up a volleyball and throws it at him. "Get out, you *vantz*... you bedbug, you!"

He grins, covering his head with his arms. "I'm going, I'm going." He runs out the door. A moment later he's back. "I forgot. I came to deliver a message. Glad and Evvie are wanted at Irving's. He's interviewing and needs your help. Hey, so don't kill the messenger!"

Hy starts out the door again.

"Hey, Hy," Evvie calls, "you make out your will yet?"

He gives her a dirty look. "None of your business, yenta."

"Yeah, right, we know—you're not going."

"I'd be glad to help you go," says Ida maliciously, lifting up a heavy ashtray.

Sophie joins in. "You're so ugly now, I hate to think what you'll look like when you're a hundred and fifty."

"Yeah, you and Mel Brooks, the thousand-year-old man," says Evvie nastily.

Hy gives us all the finger and walks out again. Everybody laughs.

I quickly erase the board. "Meeting adjourned," I say as Evvie and I hurry to the door.

20

Job Descriptions

We can see them as far away as the path to the pool. A sizeable group of women milling about the Weiss apartment. The ad we wrote must have been better than I thought, or a lot of people need work. Even from where we are, I can see they are quite an assortment of ages. Different heights. Different skin tones. The few seats on the bench are taken; the others either stand or lean against the wall. Most of them carry worn purses, shopping bags, or lunch sacks.

We hear shouting from inside the apartment and we quicken our pace.

In the living room, three people sit rigidly, not looking at one another. Irving is sitting ramrod-straight on a dining room chair, staring into space, his face red from anxiety. A thin woman who looks fortyish also sits on a dining room chair. She is speaking very gently to Millie, who is on the couch, her fingers tearing away at a bit of thread on the hem of her sundress and her head turned toward the window. Millie is shouting, "No, no, go away. I hate you."

The woman must be from Haiti. She speaks in that wonderful lilting way, trying to calm Millie.

"But I don't hate you, hon. Not at all. You and me, we could be friends."

"Never," screams Millie. "You make the children angry."

The woman smiles at us when we come in. "I must have said something to anger her, but I don't know what."

"It's just her sickness," Evvie says.

"Maybe she'll get used to me?"

"No. No—get out." Millie, with little strength, manages to pick up a pillow and weakly throws it at the woman. The woman gets up.

"I think maybe she won't," she says, and starts out. "Good luck to you, Mr. Weiss."

Irving can't speak so we say his good-byes for him.

"What's going on out there?" I ask. "Didn't you set different appointment times when they called?"

Irving shrugs. "I just said come."

Millie tosses another pillow to protest this conversation.

"I thought maybe she'd watch TV in the sunroom..." Again he shrugs helplessly.

Millie cackles. "Trying to put one over me, heh, old man? Millie is too fast for the old man."

"This won't work," he says. "Tell them to go home."

We attempt to get Millie to go into the bedroom to take a nap, but she sits as if glued to the couch.

She knows what's going on and no one is going to get any job without her approval. My heart sinks. She isn't going to approve of anyone.

The afternoon drags on with painful slowness. One after another the women come in, give their resumes, and try to enchant the little princess who behaves more like the wicked queen. Haughtily the petitioners are each and every one rejected. The "children" whisper in Millie's ear, goading her into shamefully cruel comments.

Evvie and I exchange glances. We are getting nowhere, fast. Irving left us six women ago to take a nap. "You pick," he said, turning the thankless job over to us.

Finally, the last woman is gone. Millie has defeated us. She seems to be dozing on the couch by now.

Evvie whispers to me. "Next time we do this upstairs."

I start gathering up the paper cups from the many coffee and water offerings and bring them into the kitchen. Evvie goes off to the bathroom.

I think back on that god-awful day when we all faced Millie's doctor together and heard for the first time what we suspected anyway. Millie started to tell the doctor how terrified she was of the possibility of having Alzheimer's. This doctor, who, I suspect, along with too many others, came down to Florida to suck the money out of the elderly, didn't even bother to look at her. "What are you worried about, lady? It takes about ten years for Alzheimer's to kill you. You'll be dead long before that, anyway."

We were all too shocked to say anything.

Later, I cursed him and hoped *he'd* die horribly and soon.

I'm pulled out of my reverie. "Come in, come in," says a high, pleasant voice. "Don't be a stranger." I turn, startled to see Millie through the kitchen pass-through window, beckoning to someone at the front door. I turn again and there is a very young Hispanic woman standing uncertainly on the threshold.

Millie walks to her with ease and graciously reaches out to shake hands. The princess has returned. The young woman smiles a wide, gold-toothed, lopsided grin. Millie pulls her into the living room and whirls her around. Then she proceeds to do a right-on-target parody of husband and two closest friends. Evvie returns to my side and we both watch this bizarre scene. Millie has our voices down pat.

"And my dear, do you have experience? No, never mind, I don't care about that. The important thing is can you dance?"

The woman, by now introduced as Yolanda Diaz, is enchanted by Millie and says, pretending insult, *"Qué mujer de Guadalajara no puede bailer?"*

"La rumba? Cha-cha? Lambada? Tango?" asks this expert of the salsa scene.

"Naturalmente," says Yolanda.

"Perfecto," says Millie, who has never before uttered a word in Spanish. With that, she drags Yolanda by the hand over to the ancient hi-fi, which hasn't been used since Millie took sick years ago. She tosses records every which way until she comes up with an old Pérez Prado album. Millie pulls it out

of its sleeve, dusts it off by blowing on it and unerringly manages to get it onto the record player.

Evvie and I are beyond dumbfounded.

And then, there they are, the usually catatonic eighty-year-old woman doing a mean rumba with this very young, puzzled, yet willing applicant, to "Cherry Pink and Apple Blossom White."

Irving comes out of the bedroom in his stocking feet, rubbing the sleep from his eyes. "What's this racket?" he asks.

"Irv, come meet Yolanda," Evvie says, smiling. "We just hired her." With that, Millie collapses to the floor and falls asleep.

21

Kronk Strikes Again

Yolanda—the Spanish dancer, as Irving refers to her—seems to be working out. Sort of. Millie is thrilled with her. Irving is less than thrilled. He is finding all kinds of things to nitpick about. Too many taco-and-refried-bean dinners instead of his favorite cholesterol killers, steak and potatoes. Too much hot salsa in everything. Suddenly Millie, who never ate Hispanic food in her life, is scarfing down any food whose name has an *a* or *o* at the end of it. Irving now lives on Tums. I try to calm him, promising I will give Yolanda a weekly menu to follow. "But, isn't it worth it? Millie is better than she's been in a long time."

"Ulcers, I'm getting," Irving whines.

He grudgingly agrees, but he doesn't understand why he is upset. Suddenly Yolanda is telling him to go outside and get some air and smoke his cigars, or go play cards, she'll watch Millie. So used to being tense every moment of every day, how can he let down his guard?

We all like Yolanda. She smiles a lot and hums when she works. And takes time to talk to Millie. She doesn't speak much English, so her communication skills are part Spanish, part English, part pointing, and part miming. Millie thinks this is all being done to entertain her. Yolanda makes her laugh. We haven't heard Millie laugh in a long time. Millie was right to make her own choice.

The Gladiators are hard at work. Carrying their newly bought clipboards with attached pens, they are canvassing the buildings. Dutifully making notes when people aren't home, so they'll remember to call back. In protest, because we wouldn't let them have T-shirts, Sophie and Bella are wearing their bingo shirts.

So much for the lecture on keeping cool. Pandemonium has struck. Everyone wants to know everything. The suggestion of two murders churns up all the neighbors, either with fear or excitement, and everyone is comparing birthdays, wondering who will be next—even though we try to assure them that probably no one will be next. I think we are spreading hysteria more than gathering information. Eileen O'Connor in the R building is having a birthday next week. She has suddenly decided to leave tomorrow for a visit to her sister in Boca Raton. She has not made any plans for returning.

Esther Feder's birthday is in two weeks. She has been quoted as saying, "I have only one word to say to that killer—he better not mess with me!"

More and more, I feel guilt-ridden about having opened this Pandora's box. We haven't seen this much excitement since the uproarious Florida election of 2000.

"Who could forget?" Ida comments. "It took thirty-seven days! We got a president, and by then, who cared?"

Sophie scowls. "They didn't have to insult us in the newspapers." She mimics: "If you think we can't vote, wait 'til you see us *drive*!"

"I never did get what 'electile dysfunction' means." Bella says, mutilating the pronunciation.

Evvie puts an arm around her. "Don't even ask!"

I am sitting in the kitchen doing my least favorite chore—the monthly bills—before going outside for our morning workout. It already feels like another scorcher. Suddenly I hear a piercing shriek and my heart starts pounding. I remember Detective Langford's warning. Has our snooping forced the killer to strike again? Running out onto the walkway I see Ida, first one out, leaning over the rail and pointing, her hand shaking. Following its direction, I see my car. Its windows are covered in soap.

As Ida and I hurry downstairs, the other girls are not far behind us.

"That damned crazy Kronk!" swears Evvie.

I sigh. I guess it was finally my turn.

We stare at the words that are soaped on the windshield. *You know. I know two.*

"I'll get water and a rag," Sophie volunteers, hurrying back to the elevator.

"That miserable pain in the neck. When will we ever get rid of her?!" Evvie asks angrily. "I'm taking it up at the next board meeting again. Enough is enough!"

"Oh, hell." The others react to the tone of my voice. I am looking down at my front right tire. It's been slashed. Too late, I remember needing to replace the faulty spare.

"What does she mean?" Ida says, trying to decipher this latest Kronk poetry-in-code. " 'You know'? Know what?"

Sophie adds, "Maybe crazy Kronk's really the killer and she's confessing. Like 'I killed two.' "

"How come no one ever sees her!" Bella cries, stamping her feet in frustration.

When the tow truck arrives, I convince the girls that since there is only room for one person alongside the driver, I'll go alone. I decide that since I'm taking the car in, besides buying a new tire, I might as well get it lubed and attend to all the other things I've neglected to fix. Maybe I'll even splurge and detail it.

"Who did that to your windows?" the driver asks after practically ripping my arms out of their sockets as he pulls me up into the seat next to him.

"It's a very long story," I tell him.

The girls wave as we head out.

In all the excitement I didn't give any thought to the meaning of Greta's scribblings on my car. I would be very sorry later.

Ye Olde Curiosity Shoppe

The repair department said give them a couple of hours. Usually I have a book in the trunk. All I need is a coffee shop and the time will fly by. Hmm. No book. I guess I forgot to leave one.

So, I decide to walk. Even though this is an industrial area, maybe I'll find something of interest. I find myself relaxing. A few hours to myself. What a luxury. To my surprise, I see a bookstore sign up ahead and that gets my attention.

A huge red banner announces the Grand Opening Today: J. Marley's For Mysteries. The proclamation under it defiantly states "Who's afraid of Barnes & Noble?" I move closer to read all the captivating information splashed across the window in Day-Glo paints. Party! Free! Exciting Panel Discussion! Special Famous Mystery Guests! Come as your favorite sleuth! And indeed, cheerful partici-pants are crowding in wearing a wide array of costumes. Apparently I'm just in time and I join the throng.

A jovial and diminutive gent, dressed in a costume right out of a Dickens novel and wearing a name tag—J. Marley, Proprietor—stands at the doorway waving us in.

Once inside, I admire this charming little shop, done up as a classic Victorian English gentleman's library with wonderfully uncomfortable horsehair sofas and high-backed wing chairs slipcovered with hunting scenes. A drop-leaf oak side table set up in front of the small gaslit fireplace holds the makings of a proper English tea—crumpets, cucumber sandwiches, scones, trifle—all of it looking delicious. I look closer. Alas, not real.

Seats are being set up for the panel discussion in a large adjoining conference room and I am lucky to get one of the last chairs. There is much friendly banter as strangers get acquainted by guessing one another's identities. I sigh happily. How lucky to have accidentally found this place. I am prepared to have a very good time.

J. Marley moves up to the front podium. He makes a delightful welcoming speech which not only lauds his own bravery for opening up an independent shop, but also the courage of those who come here willing to pay retail! "Those megawarehouses that call themselves bookstores don't scare me. True book lovers will gather where others of their ilk assemble, and you here today are proof of that." This gets a round of applause. He grins mischievously. "I do hope you're not only here for the free punch and entertainment. You *will* buy something."

Marley now turns to the group seated onstage.

"Today's guest speakers, the world's greatest detectives, will address the intriguing subject of 'How To Solve A Murder.' And allow me to admit what trouble it was getting them here, since they all exist only in the febrile imaginations of some of the greatest mystery writers of all time."

There is a nice round of applause.

"How fortunate I was to find this amazing group of players who swear they are being channeled by their literary originals."

Marley indicates a delicate elderly lady in a modest print dress and very sensible black laced shoes, who all the while has been attending to her knitting. With a flourish he introduces, "Miss Jane Marple!"

Miss Marple smiles primly. "I bring you a message of regards from St. Mary Mead."

"And now, Monsieur Hercule Poirot," says Marley with vivacity.

Poirot stands up, tips his bowler and bows stiffly. "*Bonjour.* I, too, wish to extend salutations. From Hastings and, of course, Miss Lemon."

Miss Lucy Pym is next and she is all atwitter. "Oh, I do appreciate the applause. It's because of my new book, isn't it? You readers do want some new thing, don't you?" With that she quickly sits back down, blushing.

"Mr. Sherlock Holmes."

"Yes, yes," he says intolerantly, "if we must exchange these tiresome greetings, then I shall, of course, mention Dr. Watson, who even as we speak is chasing my deerstalker hat which the winds blew from my head." This brings much laughter and Holmes sneers nicely at it.

"Last, but not least, Lord Peter Wimsey."

Lord Peter wipes his monocle, then smiles. "Regards, of course, from her ladyship, the former Harriet Vane. And Bunter would be sorely tried if I neglected to mention him. A pleasure to be here in the Colonies again."

The discussion begins with amusing questions from the floor, answered wittily by the sleuths. But I hear nothing because of the roaring in my ears as I listen to person after person chat about murder.

A pathetically weak voice calls out, "I have a question."

To my astonishment, I am rising, and although I don't recall doing it, I am the one who spoke. I stand transfixed. What am I doing? All eyes are on me. I can hear my own breathing, and suddenly, I blurt out: "I'm investigating a *real* murder! Two murders, actually. And I desperately need help!"

The audience holds its silence for a moment before bursting into appreciative applause. Marley, chortling, says, "And what a clever opening gambit from the lady sitting next to Charlie Chan."

It's as if everything that has been troubling me has surfaced without my permission. To my horror, I am the center of attention.

Miss Pym pipes up. "Well, best left to the police, dear, I always say."

"But they don't believe me. And I think the murderer lives among us."

"Madam. Don't let's shilly-shally here. Where is your proof?" Holmes says with disdain.

"That's just it. I don't have any."

"Dastardly clever, the killer, eh, what?" comments Lord Peter.

"Yes. He hasn't made any mistakes yet."

"He will eventually. They all do," says Miss Marple sagely, not even missing a stitch.

"You must use the little gray cells, Madame, and all will be revealed." Hercule Poirot plays with his thin, waxed mustache.

"Suspects. Who are the suspects? Do not waste our time with frivolity!" Holmes bullies me.

"Well, there's Denny, our handyman..." I say hesitantly.

There is a burst of rude laughter from both audience and panel.

"Yeah, and he lives in the Bates Motel!" screams someone from the audience.

"And his dead mother done it," howls another.

"You better not take a shower, lady," shouts another.

"Order. Order," says Marley, clapping his hands to calm the waves of laughter.

Holmes tamps down the tobacco in his pipe, chortling. "He's as much a cliché as the 'butler who done it.'"

I try to keep my voice steady. "There's also the real-estate man who goes after the property of the deceased."

Miss Marple tut-tuts. "Quite nearly as bad as the janitor person."

"Is there a redheaded man on a bicycle?" asks Holmes snidely.

"No."

"Perhaps a vicar who's had a bit too much port?" asks Miss Marple.

"Of course not."

"A headmaster who has absconded with school funds?" asks Miss Pym.

"No. No. No."

"I say—surely the bloke left a weapon? A croquet mallet? A spade? A lead cosh?" Lord Peter winks at me.

Now everybody is hooting with appreciation for what they think is my impassioned playacting.

I stand up, furious. "Stop it. This is real!"

"But *they* aren't," snickers someone in the audience.

"But did the dog bark?" adds another wag in the crowd.

I can't believe it; I'm actually starting to cry.

Marley wipes his tears, too—of laughter. However, he decides that I have taken up enough of the panel's time. He interrupts, making an assumption. "Well, good luck with your novel, lady. Any other questions?"

I am briefly applauded and then forgotten. The panel continues on.

I look around befuddled. I run out of the conference room and back into the quiet library section and throw myself down into one of the armchairs.

Shaking and crying, I just sit there unable to move. Whatever got into me to do that!

I am handed a handkerchief. I look up to see a tall man peering down at me. He's in his seventies, with a full head of hair, the colors of iron and steel, and a lovely smile.

"I believed you," he says.

"Why? No one else did!"

I use his handkerchief gratefully.

"May I?" he asks indicating the chair next to me.

He has a gentle, deep voice with just the faintest touch of an English accent. Still snuffling, I nod.

"I'm sorry they upset you," he says. "But I don't think they were making fun of you."

"I know. It was all a game and I was spoiling it." I look up into his eyes. Such twinkling blue eyes. "What am I going to do about my murders? Someone has to find the killer."

He takes my hands and holds them gently. "If I were a mystery writer, I'd suggest that you look for someone who is behaving out of character. Who is behaving in a way that is alien to his or her personality?"

The man smiles at me, and for a moment I think I know him. "Thank you," I whisper gratefully.

"And don't forget," he says, now grinning, "the killer is always the one least suspected. As Holmes would say, 'It's elementary.'"

I get up, and return his handkerchief, then head for the door.

"Gladdy?" the velvety voice calls after me.

I turn, startled. How does he know my name?

"It is Gladdy Gold, I presume? May I buy you a cup of coffee?"

23

Lust in the Heat

Don't you just love the name Fuddruckers?" I say. "Works for me," says my mystery man.

We have just been seated in this overly bright popular hamburger hangout and the stranger has promised he'll tell all once we get our coffee. We drove around in his spiffy 1985 Cadillac 'til we found this place, and all the while he remained stoically quiet. I can hardly wait.

He smiles benignly at me as I study him while pretending to read the menu.

Dignified comes to mind. Built like a teddy bear, the way I like them. What *am* I thinking? Who *is* he and why am I blathering on like this? I feel rattled, and skittish.

The coffee is served by someone who looks young enough to be my great-granddaughter. Good, I think, now we can get started.

"Do I know you?" I decide to get the old ball rolling. And he does look familiar.

He takes a sip of his coffee. "We met briefly fourteen years ago. At a New Year's Eve party at Lanai Gardens. We were all standing around the pool in Phase Five drinking the obligatory inexpensive champagne in paper cups."

"Fourteen years ago and not since?"

"Unfortunately, no. But under the circumstances..."

Unfortunately? Interesting, that. Now I'm beginning to realize I am unconsciously mimicking his British accent. "Should I apologize for not remembering you?"

"Nonsense. I was just one in a dreadfully large group of people, but you—you were unique. You wore this lovely pink flowery dress and a matching hat with ribbons. Roses, I believe. I remember thinking you looked simply fetching."

"Did your wife mind that you thought me fetching?" I might have been fetching then, but I am fishing now.

He smiles. "I belong to the Jimmy Carter school of adultery. I lust only in my heart. And rarely. You were one of those rare occasions. You were sitting alone on a bench, sipping your bubbly and looking rather pensive. There was an aura about you...."

With a sharp pain, I remember now. It wasn't me being pensive it was me responding to bone-chilling sadness. It was the anniversary of my husband, Jack's, death. No matter how many years had gone by, that date would always remain devastating for me. I would never get over it. How could I? Now here I was, uprooted, trying to get through my first New Year's Eve in a place far from home. I felt totally lost and adrift.

I had been at loose ends when Evvie had called me from Florida, begging me to fly down from New York and stay with her. Joe had left her and she was threatening suicide. I forced myself to stop thinking about myself and focus on her. Came down for a visit and never left. But that night was hell.

"Jack," I murmur aloud. Moaning in memory of my beloved. It's been so long since I've allowed myself to think of him.

"So, you do remember," he says, delighted.

"What?" I am having trouble pulling myself back into the present. "What did you say?"

"I never thought you'd remember my name. It was long ago and our meeting so brief. I'm awfully flattered. Funny we should meet like this. Just the other day, my son Morrie happened to mention your name. You know, the police officer?"

I quickly put it together. "Your name is Jack," I say, looking closer at this tall, tall man. "Of course. Jack Langford." The recently widowed Jack Langford, or so I'd heard. But where? And from whom? The final click. Bella. Who knew his wife in Hadassah.

He almost blushes. He's that pleased.

He reaches his hand out across the table and we shake formally.

"It's hard to believe, isn't it," Jack Langford says, "that we've lived in the same place fourteen or so years and have never occasioned upon each other."

"Well...Phase Two and Phase Six...We *are* separated by Three, Four, and Five." I sound positively idiotic.

"And speaking of Phase Two, that which you implied in the bookstore—your friends were murdered?"

We were on safer ground than talking about early lust. If safer is the right word when dealing with murder. "I'm afraid so."

"And Morrie doesn't believe you?"

I quickly come to his son's defense. "I have no way to prove my suspicions. It sounded far-fetched to him."

"He always was stubborn. Takes after his father."

"Well, you gave me good advice. I'm going to look at everybody and see who's behaving differently."

Jack senses that he is upsetting me and changes the subject. He begins to ask me all sorts of lovely questions about myself, and I have a lot to ask him, too.

We have all these years of catching up to do and we talk and talk until I finally realize just how long I've been away. The girls must be worried.

Even my car feels better after a day away from—dare I admit it?—the girls. The new tire makes me feel like I'm driving on air. C'mon, who's kidding whom?

And just because Jack Langford said hello. No, he didn't *just* say hello; he said he lusted after me. Had been attracted to me. Intimating that if he hadn't had a wife, he would have made a pass. Never mind it was fourteen years ago. Very flattering. Alas, wasted, since I never even knew it. And I was a mere sixty-one then. Truth? When's the last time *any* man looked at me? As a woman. At what age did I become invisible? I think this is one of the hardest things to deal with when getting old. Men no longer look. Not in that same way. That sly I-can't-wait-to-get-into-your-pants look. Gone forever. I'll never again feel that extraordinary wild passion of reckless youth. That's the true unfairness of age. No matter how old, you still remember it, but you can't have it anymore. Youth belongs to the young. And what a waste. They don't appreciate how tenuous is this gift, and how carelessly they abuse it.

So, I'm attracted to someone! I thought I packed that emotion away in mothballs with my winter coats.

I think about what Jack said to me when he dropped me off at the garage. "After all, I might have been sprightly back then, but now I'm just an elderly gentleman. Surely you couldn't be interested?"

"And what am I—a spring chicken?" That was the pathetic retort I was able to come up with to hide my absolute amazement. I wanted to jump up and down and say you bet I'm interested, you cuddly darling, you. But sanity prevailed. Good breeding prevailed.

"Call me!" I shouted after him as he drove away. I could see him grinning as he *vroomed* off like a teenager in a hot rod.

"You'd be proud of me and Harriet. We partnered and together we came up with our first clue." Evvie is jabbering at me even before I get out of my car.

"Really? Sounds like you girls were busy."

"We talked to Tessie and she remembered something she found in Selma's apartment when she cleaned up."

"This could be important!"

"She said she found a little piece of wrapper stuck to the bottom of the dining room chair. She recognized it as a piece of bag the Meals on Wheels people use to deliver. She didn't think anything of it at the time. But, now she wondered. She couldn't remember Selma ever being a customer of Meals."

This was something real. At last. "Then we've got to call them! They'd have a record of the food going out on that date and who delivered it to her."

"Way ahead of you, sis. Harriet called. Nobody remembered anything."

I'm disappointed. But it would explain why Selma would open her door. The murderer must have knocked and offered her a delicious meal. I was beginning to see a pattern. Someone offered Selma food. Selma, who dearly loved to eat. Someone offered Francie chocolate cake. Someone who knew she loved chocolate. This someone knows us very well. I shiver as if he just walked over my grave.

And what did Greta's soaped message on my car mean, if anything at all? Or were they just the ravings of a poor lost soul?

At dinner I tell the girls about the unusual party at the bookstore. But I do not say one word about Jack Langford.

24

Death by Dumpster

The first blazing rays of Florida sun were about to light up the sky. But in those few moments while Dawn played coy, a hand scribbled erratically in a whitewash paint: I SAW YOU KILL 2—YOU DEVIL YOU.

Anxiously, Greta Kronk skittered away from the door, the small paint can wobbling from her bony wrist. Her heart was pounding because she knew what a terrible chance she had taken. She pushed her wild black hair back into the fiercely colored magenta scarf that encircled her face, and pulled her voluminous lavender dancing skirts and petticoats around her knees. Were it not for her deceptive clothes, Greta would look like the emaciated wraith she was. She glanced up at the sky and feared she had waited too long, that the light would betray her.

Holding her breath, she moved as quickly as the clumsy skirts allowed her, around the corner to the far end of Q building. Again she looked around. It *was all right. This was a wall without windows. She could breathe. Quickly she hid the paint can deep in the first Dumpster. Now she would attend to her regular early morning business—searching all the Dumpsters for treasures. She opened her gunny sack, eager to plunder the riches this morning's trash would provide. The first thing she found was a twisted soup strainer. Good, she thought, this I can use.*

The killer opened the door of the apartment. With a few quick strokes of a rag, the damning words were washed away. The killer also looked around, not really concerned. It was still much too early for anyone to be up.

Greta was so pleased with her take—a slightly bent set of plastic dinnerware and a wonderful black wig—that she wasn't aware she was no longer alone.

She gasped as the killer loomed over her.

"What you want?" she said, trying not to show her fear. "This my stuff, get your own fluff." Talking was hard for her. It had been so long since she had spoken to anyone.

"I don't want your stuff, you fool—"

"Then go 'way. Don't want play."

"It's not nice to paint on people's doors."

Greta stared, worried, because the killer's hands were hidden.

"I ain't got paint...." But her eyes betrayed her as she instinctively looked toward the Dumpster where she had hidden the can.

"Wanna see what's behind my back?" The hands came out with nothing in them. Greta looked confused. Her eyesight was not good. She didn't notice the thin, colorless latex gloves.

"What did you see, Greta? Tell me!"

Greta moved backwards, but the killer kept pace. Her eyes looked into eyes that showed no sympathy. She knew she was doomed.

"You know what you're gonna see now?" The killer pulled her by her hair and dragged her back to the Dumpster. Greta tried to run, but her feet were pedaling in air.

"I don't tell...I not told. I not be so bold...." she said, gasping.

"Bad news, Greta. No pot roast for you. No chocolate cake. You love garbage, now eat your last meal!"

The killer pulled a rancid onion from the trash can and forced it down her throat. "You like your salad? Sorry, no dressing." Greta gagged, and the food was retched out, but the killer pushed it in again and held her mouth shut until it went down. "Ready for your main course?" Her eyes widened and teared as horrible remnants of foul-smelling food were shoved into her mouth. In her terror, she was not aware of the powdery substance that was forced in along with a slimy strand of what had once been spinach.

For a few more minutes she coughed and dry-heaved. Finally, she stopped struggling—paralysis began to set in. Her body sank to the ground, as the voluminous skirts cushioned her.

The killer took a moment to retrieve the paint can from where Greta had hidden it. At the corner of the building the killer turned and smiled.

"Too bad, Greta, you're about to miss your greatest literary masterpiece."

Greta's last thought before she lost conscious-

ness was of a doll she had had as a child in the old country. A gypsy dancer she could gently fold up into its beautiful gown. Its eyes would close and the doll would go to sleep. She, too, would now go to sleep at last. She hoped Armand would be waiting for her and would forgive her for taking so long.

25

Sing Gypsy, Cry Gypsy,
Die Gypsy

I come home from my early dentist appointment and I know immediately something is wrong. Too many people are hovering about outside, most still in robes, moving every which way. An ambulance and a police car are parked near the side of my building. Oh, God, I think hysterically, who is it now?

I don't stop to ask. I head where the flashing red lights beckon.

The girls are there. Quickly I count them off. Bella. Sophie. Ida. Where's Evvie? Oh, no, where—? There she is, thank God. Standing with Harriet and Esther, who is seated in her wheelchair. Hy and Lola stand next to them, clutching one another for support.

The girls see me as I approach and they all grab at me, crying, all talking at once.

From Ida: "Hy went out to the Dumpster—"

Then Bella: "He was schlepping this big carton

from a new TV, though I don't know what was wrong with the old one—"

And Sophie interrupting her. "He saw a nightmare in the daytime and then he ran around the corner yelling—"

I am trying to see who the paramedics are bending over, but I can't tell who it is.

"This all happened a couple of minutes ago," Evvie tells me.

"We only just came downstairs," Sophie adds.

"Tell me already!" I can't stand it. "Who is it?"

"The Kronk!" they say in unison.

"Greta?" I ask incredulously. I turn to Hy. "Tell me what you saw!"

He shrugs. Clears his throat. Hitches up his inevitably loud-patterned shorts. Clearly he's told his tale a few times already. "First I don't see nothing. The TV box is bulky and I can hardly see my way around it. I'm just about to lay it down and start to stomp on it so it'll fit in the Dumpster and I see a bunch of what looks like colored rags. Then I go closer and it's a body laying inside of them rags. I don't even recognize her. It's maybe five years since I even laid eyes on her."

Hy, always loving the spotlight, is determined to squeeze out every ounce of drama. And Lola, truly in shock, for once is not interrupting him. "At first I think it's a stranger, but, no, she looks familiar. I know it's nobody else, because everybody else I would recognize, so logic tells me it's Greta Kronk. All I know for sure, she doesn't look sick. She looks dead. So I run for somebody to call the nine-one-one."

His audience is rapt. Hy always did know how to tell a story. But this one was no joke.

"Could you tell what killed her?" I ask.

"I don't see no blood, so I figure she died of old age, or from eating that putrid garbage. Her mouth was full of that crap."

Everyone responds with horror, making gagging and gasping noises. Bella, turning pale, leans against the wall that separates us from Phase Three, for support.

A policeman comes toward us, his notebook at the ready. It's orange mustache again. I remember him from the infamous night Millie called 911. "Does Mrs. Kronk have any relatives?"

"Nobody," we all chorus.

"Do *you* know what killed her, Officer?" I have to ask.

He shakes his head. "Maybe her heart gave out. Looks like she just keeled over."

I move closer and watch as the ambulance attendants lift her onto the gurney. It's the first time any of us have seen Greta in years. She looks so thin. She must have been starving herself. I remember the dress she's wearing. It was the gypsy costume she wore when she gave dancing lessons that one year and very few people showed up. In those days, she was buxom and she filled out that dress pretty good. This body lying here is like a skeleton. Now I can see Greta's face clearly, and I jump back, startled. Her face! My God, her face! She looks terrified. As if something frightened her to death.

Sol Spankowitz ambles over. "Did you see what she wrote?"

I stare at him, puzzled.

"That crazy broad wrote another poem. On her own door. Like she wrote it to put on her gravestone. Weird. Come take a look."

The girls and I follow Sol around the corner, and now I realize what people were staring at when I arrived: Greta's front door on the third floor of P building.

"What does it say?" Bella asks tugging at me.

"I don't know. It's hard to read from down here."

Mary and John Mueller, her neighbors, are up there with a few other people from the building. They hear me and they all look down from the balcony. John calls to us. "It says, 'Get fed. Get dead.'" His voice is bitter. "Well, that's the last nasty poem *she'll* ever write."

His wife, Mary, turns away, embarrassed. Who can forget the cheap shot Greta took at John's masculinity?

We finally end up in Evvie's apartment, drinking tea. Needless to say, this is accompanied by a plate full of cheese Danish. As is typical, we are seated at the dining table in our usual card-playing seats. Harriet has pulled up an extra chair to join us.

I sigh. "Now I'll never get a chance to ask her why she wrote what she did on my car."

"Poor, sad lady," Harriet says as she reaches for another pastry. "What a way to die. All alone like that."

"And we were trying to get her thrown out." Bella sighs. "I feel so guilty."

Sophie giggles behind her hand. "Look at you,"

she says pointing at Harriet. "You're eating all the Danish."

Harriet laughs nervously. "Just neurotic eating," she explains. "From all the excitement. I better start working out at the gym more often. By the way, did I tell you I'm starting my vacation? Maybe I better spend it exercising."

Considering what good condition her body is in, she doesn't have to worry about working it off. We should be in such good shape.

"How many heart attacks are we gonna have around here?" Sophie demands to know.

"*Another* heart attack?" I ask pointedly.

Evvie looks at me. "*Another* coincidence?" We exchange glances. She knows what I am thinking.

"That was only a guess the officer made. He couldn't know for sure," says Ida. "Maybe she's been sick for who knows how long and she just happened to die right then and there."

"What are you saying, Glad?" Harriet asks.

"Now a third woman dies suddenly for no apparent reason? All having just eaten food that came to them oddly?"

"Garbage is eating?" sniffs Sophie.

Bella jumps up, spilling her tea on her lap. "You think she was poisoned, too!"

"You are turning into a one-track train," says Sophie.

"How could that be?" Ida asks me. "How could the killer know she was going to eat garbage?"

"You mean he had to put poison in all the garbage cans?" Bella surmises.

"Every day until she picks the right can to eat out of? Nonsense!" Ida shakes her head vehemently.

"No," I say, grossing myself out even as I suggest it, "but what if he forces the poisoned food down her throat?"

"How could he make her eat it?" Sophie says. "I, personally, would clamp my mouth shut."

"I wish you would," says Ida, glaring at her.

"A gun. He had a gun! Oy, a gun in Lanai Gardens. That I should live to see the day!" Bella is getting hysterical.

"Bella, dear. He didn't need a gun. She was undernourished and very weak. It wouldn't take much to overwhelm her," I say quietly.

"Why would anyone want to kill that poor pathetic creature?" Harriet asks.

Bella asks shrilly, "Was it her birthday? Does anybody know?"

"I don't think so," Evvie says, musing. "April comes to mind."

Sophie gets up and starts pacing, wringing her hands as she does. "You wanna know why!!! I'll tell you why! Because he's a serial killer, that's why. He's gonna kill us all before he's through! Eating us to death with our favorite food!"

Bella fans herself furiously with a paper napkin. "Garbage was her favorite food?"

"Please, everybody calm down," I say.

"Yeah," says Evvie, "before we all really get heart attacks."

Bella is shaking her head agitatedly.

"What?!" Ida demands.

"I'll never eat gefilte fish again," Bella says wistfully of her favorite food.

"Fool!" Ida mutters under her breath.

26

Death of a Poet

It's mid-afternoon and Lanai Gardens is at rest. Nap time. *La siesta.*

I'm too overwrought to sleep. I sneak out of the apartment building under cover of silence.

Now that Kronk is gone, Marion Martini, who has been hiding her car around the corner from U building, has driven it back. She's been secreting it there since the night the Kronk smeared raspberry juice all over her new upholstery. And all the other car owners who've had to wipe garbage off their windshields won't miss her, either. How sad. No one cares that she's gone.

I drive to my place of refuge, the library.

"So," says Barney with mock seriousness, "what's been going on at Lanai Gardens? This last week, the library has been recipient of a thousand rumors. Everybody has a different story."

"Ten people have died, we've been told," says Conchetta, hardly able to keep a straight face, "but maybe it's four, or maybe two. They've been stran-gled, poisoned, knifed, and put under Haitian voodoo spells."

I laugh in spite of my sorrow.

"And you," says Barney, "are the inciter of said rumors. You are now a private eye?"

Conchetta grins. "That's what you get from reading too many murder mysteries. So, give us the real enchilada."

And I fill them in on what has happened up until today.

My friends silently absorb what I'm saying. For a few moments the only sound in the room is the minute hand ticking its way around the big old maple library clock.

Barney whistles. "Whew. That's heavy. No won-der you haven't been around."

"Too many coincidences," says Conchetta.

"My point exactly."

Barney asks, "Did you really go to the police? I love that the rumors escalated to the FBI and the CIA. Someone even mentioned that you might go into the witness protection program. That's my favorite."

"Oh, boy," I say, "there's Pandora's box and then there is a Jewish Pandora's box. . . . Yes, I did go to the police, but they didn't believe me. And now there's been another death. This morning."

"No!" Conchetta stifles a cry.

"Who?" asks Barney.

"Greta Kronk," I say. The two of them stare at me, dumbfounded.

It's quiet today in the library. Few people choose to battle the midday heat, and wisely stay home. In almost complete privacy, we three move over to one of the reading tables and sit down with the inevitable cups of Conchetta's Cuban coffee.

"How?" they both ask.

"She died next to the Dumpster behind my building. Her mouth was stuffed with rotten food—"

"Madre mia!" Conchetta says, "How awful! And I thought she would be the one who would hurt somebody."

"Now, I'll never get a chance to meet her," says Barney wistfully. "I'll miss her rhymes."

"There was one left on her door," I tell them.

"What did it say?" asks Barney, barely able to contain his excitement.

I recite. " 'Get fed. Get dead.' " That quote will be engraved forever in my mind.

For a moment neither of my friends speaks.

"Wow...." Barney finally whispers in awe. "But how could she have written 'get dead' after she died? She certainly wouldn't have done it before."

"Exactly. I finally figured out that was the killer's idea of a sick joke. Trying to make it look like Greta wrote the poem."

A lone straggler comes out from behind the stacks and brings his books to the checkout counter. We wait until Conchetta returns.

We tip our cups in memoriam for the poet who gave us such memorable rhymes as "Tessie is fat and that's that."

Conchetta says, "I especially loved 'Sophie shop til she drop.' "

Barney adds his favorite: " 'Leo buys. Leo sells. Leo tells. Lies.' "

"It's the recklessness of the killer this time that puzzles me." I say. "Considering that the other two murders were conceived and carried out with icy meticulousness, this time he had to have forced the food down her throat. And to attack in daylight. What a chance he took."

"Was it her birthday, too?" asks Conchetta. She pours us some more of her coffee, but I can't drink it. My stomach feels like acid is eating my insides.

I am suddenly sick to my stomach. "No!" I say, as realization kicks in. "Damn it!" I am so angry at myself, so angry that once again my slow memory synapses have failed me.

I am shaking with the frustration I feel. "Greta wasn't on the murderer's list! She knew that he had killed. Twice! She knew that and tried to tell me by soaping the words on my car, and I just didn't make the connection! If I had only realized she was proba- bly a witness to the crimes, I could have saved her life! And found out who the killer was."

Conchetta comes to my side and puts her arm around my shoulder.

I am distraught. "What am I going to do?"

"Go see that detective again, and this time you'll be able to convince him," Conchetta says.

As I drive home I think that maybe the killer finally made a mistake. Please, God, let it be true.

27

Digging up the Dirt?

I'm practically living by my phone. Maybe one of these days I'll give in to progress and get an answering machine. But who knows. One thing could lead to another. I might get tempted to buy a car phone, then a beeper or cable TV or, God forbid, a computer. I've managed to live this long keeping life simple.... Ignore me, I'm rambling. This waiting is driving me crazy. I've been trying to get an appointment with Detective Langford but he's been away for two days at some cop conference in Miami. I know he's back today. I've already left three messages.

Speaking of the phone, it hasn't been ringing off the hook as is usual. Where are the girls? I'm grateful, because I would have to get them off the line pronto. And they'd insist on knowing why. And if I tell them, Evvie especially would demand to go with me, and there is no way I'll put myself through *that* again. But what are they up to? I wonder. Mah-jongg is over by now. Curious.

The phone rings. It's Langford at last. I beg to see him as quickly as possible. Can't I tell him over the phone? No, I insist. It's too important. I can hear the weariness in his lethargic voice. Too many mai tais on the beach? Too many blond shiksas around the piano bar? Miami Beach can be a dangerous place. Reluctantly, he tells me if I can get over there in five minutes, he'll fit me in. Beggars can't be you-know-what. I'm out the door as fast as I can grab my car keys.

As I start to pull out of my parking space, I catch a glimpse of movement across the way in P building. Bella is tiptoeing into Greta Kronk's apartment behind Sophie. Can the others be far in front? Now I recall hearing something about Evvie, as a member of our condominium board, giving herself the authority to look through Greta's papers. Since there aren't any relatives that we know of, maybe there's a will, or something. Evvie tells me this has never happened before, that there isn't some person to contact. So yes, we do need to do something. About her remains, for one, poor thing. And the apartment and her possessions. Having just seen what she looked like, I shudder to think what her apartment looks like.

Naturally, the gang isn't about to be left out of that juicy adventure, so I see she's taken them along and I can imagine them drooling over the prospect of uncovering Greta's secrets. Four yentas in search of dirt. What a concept! Or five. I think Harriet has started her vacation today. Now I know why they didn't call. They don't want me spoiling their fun by being the voice of their consciences.

Morrie (I can't think of him as Morgan anymore) Langford is a man of his word. He doesn't keep me waiting, but the fact that he stands in the middle of his office tells me he intends to make this short. And I intend to be there as long as it takes to convince him. So I sit down.

I go through it all, Selma to Francie to Greta, step by step. I am proud of my logical presentation. Finally, *he* sits down.

"Wait a minute." He stops me. He rifles through the papers on his desk. "I have the officers' report on Mrs. Kronk."

"Save your eyesight," I tell him. "It will say probably natural causes." Now I'm behind him, reading over his shoulder. "But note where he says there was food in her mouth—"

Langford moves away from my prying eyes. "Do you mind?"

"Sorry."

"The police do not make assumptions on how a person died. They merely report what they see. If violence has obviously occurred, it becomes a crime scene and they call it in. If nothing looks suspicious, their job is over after the body is picked up by the coroner's office." He sees my frustration. "Look. She could have been hungry."

"Nobody's that hungry. She had money for food."

"You know that for a fact?"

"She had money for rent, for condo fees, for gas,

electric. . . . Those things I know for a fact. And besides, she had delivery people bringing her bags of groceries."

"What is it you want?"

"Once you speak to the coroner, you'll see that I'm right. I want to know what the autopsy said. I tried calling them but they wouldn't give out that information. I need you to call up for me."

"What makes you think they did an autopsy?"

"Don't they always?"

"Not if the death seems natural." He looks at the report again. "The woman is what—in her eighties? Seemingly emaciated?"

"The woman was found near a Dumpster, for God's sake. Isn't that suspicious enough? Please call."

"Being found near a Dumpster, rather than in it, may not necessarily seem suspicious."

He looks at me for a long moment.

"In your board members' many earlier complaints to the police department about Mrs. Kronk harassing people, they refer to her as a possible mental case."

Boy, is he thorough. The man has done his homework. Over the last five years, as Greta's behavior escalated, we complained plenty. But, funny, he doesn't mention how many times we were ignored. Bring proof, they demanded of a spirit that moved invisibly in the night. Call us if she hurts somebody. Yeah. Right. When it will be too late. Well, now somebody hurt *her*. Permanently. I pull myself out of my dark thoughts.

"Crazy people might eat garbage," he insists.

"Then again, they might not."

"Her death might be considered bizarre, but there's nothing—"

I don't let him finish. "The poem on the door—wasn't that bizarre?"

"It doesn't prove that whoever wrote the poem killed her. You say she alienated just about everybody in your buildings with her nasty poems. Somebody could have seen her dead body and then written the poem as a mean prank."

"Puleeze. It would mean reacting to the fact she was dead, getting this cruel idea very quickly, and then finding her paint can and rushing up to her third floor apartment and composing the poem in her style and painting the poem, returning the paint can to the Dumpster, and then getting away without being seen. Two things come to mind. Do you know how many people live right there in those two buildings? Who are forever snooping out their windows? Besides, eighty percent of them are way too old to be able to move that fast. For a prank? Not likely."

"But possible."

"Not probable. C'mon, Morrie. Excuse me. Detective Langford. The only person vicious, devious, and fast enough to do all that has to be the killer. Please call. They must have finished the autopsy by now."

Langford picks up the phone and dials a number. I hold my breath. He gives them the relevant information and waits. I can hardly sit still. I feel like I'm jumping out of my skin. He thanks them and looks at me.

"Well? Well!" I shout. "What's with the suspense? Tell me what they found."

He takes a deep breath. "Do you have any idea

how many dead bodies show up at the morgue every day?"

I'm beginning to get a bad feeling about this. "I don't know and I don't care. I only want to hear about Greta."

"They signed her death certificate and she's been released to a mortuary. Natural causes, Mrs. Gold."

Befuddled, I ask, "You mean the autopsy didn't find any poison?"

"I mean they didn't see any need for an autopsy."

I cannot believe this. I cannot! "Detective Langford. Hasn't anything I've said to you today given you cause to believe there is at least the possibility of foul play? Come on!"

"Let me give this some thought."

"Think fast. Please. Before she's plowed under and you'll have to dig up the dirt again."

I start out the door.

"Mrs. Gold?" This is a softer tone of voice.

I turn.

"My father mentioned he met you recently...." Obviously he's trying to lighten my black mood. I see the beginnings of a smile on his face as he watches mine looking for a reaction.

He's caught me off guard. I think I am blushing. I hope I'm not. "Nice man," I mumble. And I rush out.

I have murder on my mind. How can I think of men? Especially a sexy, good-looking older gent with a twinkle in his eyes. Then again, I must be a fool not to. I need all this aggravation like I need the heartbreak of psoriasis.

28

Where Did Everybody Go?

I am so wound up from my visit with Langford that it takes me three tries 'til I can get my car parked properly.

I am beyond depressed. I was so sure there'd be an autopsy. How could they look at that poor body and not know something was very wrong? Just to look into those dead, tortured eyes. The terror, the knowledge that she was about to be killed. Couldn't they see that?! We were so close to finding out the truth....

I decide to stop at the mailbox. I never did get my mail while waiting for the phone to ring.

"Gladdy, hold up."

I reluctantly turn, knowing the owner of the voice. Sure enough Leo, the Sleaze, is rapidly bearing down at me.

"Do you know where Evvie is?"

My answer is snotty. "Am I my sister's keeper?"

Truthfully, I am, but I'm not about to tell that to Slezak. "Anyway, isn't she in her apartment?"

"No, I just came down. No answer. Then I figured she was in with one of the other girls, but no soap."

It annoys me Leo Slezak is so informed about our lives, who we pal around with, our whereabouts. Another yenta living in our midst.

"She wasn't at Bella's?" Bella being her next-door neighbor made it a fair guess. The two of them were forever visiting back and forth.

"Not Bella. Not Sophie. Not Ida. I didn't see your car so I guessed you drove them somewhere, but here you are and where are they?"

I hide my own surprise. This is atypical. "What's the big rush to talk to my sister anyway?"

He at least has the decency to blush. "Well, since it don't look like Greta Kronk has relatives, I thought Evvie, being on the condo committee, would know who has the right to sell her apartment...."

Why did I bother to ask? As Sophie might say, vultures don't change their feathers. "While we are on the subject of real estate, Mr. Slezak—"

"Leo, please," he interrupts.

"Leo. What's the news on Francie's place? I haven't seen any action around there."

"Well, business is slow...."

"And Selma?"

"Equally slow."

"The Canadians are here. I don't see you hustling."

"The Canadians are not buying. I thought I explained to you about that."

"Something's rotten and it's not in Canada, Slezak."

Slezak makes a gesture with his hand to say he is through with this discussion and walks away from me. Without turning, he calls back. "Tell her to call me. I'll make it worth her while." He gets into his car and drives off. I stick my tongue out after him, knowing how childish I'm being and glad of it.

Tessie Hoffman passes me. I have to ask. "Tessie, have you seen the girls?"

She starts toward the elevator. "No, but there's some function in the clubhouse. Maybe they're there."

"What is it, a lecture?"

"You know—that klezmer group from Israel. It started forty minutes ago. Me, I personally hate klezmer." With that she disappears into the elevator. Tessie doesn't like much of anything. Except food.

What have I got to lose? I might as well check it out. I walk down the brick path. It is starting to get dark, but the overhead lights illuminate my way. The ducks, as usual, have dirtied the path, so I have to watch my step. Out of the corner of my eye, I sense movement. Sure enough, there's Denny in his garden. I can tell by his posture that he is digging hard at something. I wonder how he is able to see in the failing light. Walking over to him I call out, so as not to startle him.

"Denny. Hello."

His back springs up and he turns toward my voice. I am close enough to see his face now. He's sweating and he looks angry. "Who's there?"

"It's only me. Gladdy."

"Waddya want?"

So unlike Denny, my mind is telling me. I don't want to hear this. Where is our gentle giant? Who is this angry man?

"I'm just on my way to the clubhouse and I saw you digging. Just came to say hello."

He stands very still, waiting. I want to ask what's wrong, but I don't dare.

"Have you seen my sister, Denny?"

"No." Abrupt. Cold.

The garden glitters in the near darkness. There is a profusion of a beautiful white flower I do not recognize, not that I know much about plants anyway. I suddenly realize I have not seen this garden in a very long time.

When Denny started out, he began with a very few little beginner shoots. We encouraged him by buying him a variety of different kinds of seedlings, and his confidence grew. He planted simple little rows of pretty colored foliage and shared this beauty with all of us. Now the garden is overgrown. And no longer orderly. It's wild, almost haphazard, and out of control. *Like Denny himself?* I wonder. Is he going through some kind of personality change and his garden reflects this?

"It's getting pretty dark," I comment mildly, trying to hint that perhaps he should go home.

"I don't care! I don't want to go inside."

I am startled. Is this why he stays outdoors most of the time? He no longer feels comfortable in his apartment? Something is wrong with him and I must stop pretending there isn't.

"Why not?" I ask carefully.

"They wanna get me. If I stay out they won't get me."

"Who, Denny? Who wants to get you?"

But he is shoveling again, ferociously, his thick hair falling over his face, covering the rage and fear. I walk away quietly, wondering what to do about this.

The klezmer concert is ending and the residents are exiting, many humming the catchy tunes. But there is no Evvie. Or Bella. Or Ida. Or Sophie.

Just as I reach our building, Harriet's van pulls up and all the lost ladies pile out. I see from their shining, excited faces, they've had a big adventure and they are dying to tell me. Believe me, I'm dying to hear it.

Everyone starts talking at once.

29

My Worst Nightmare

Since they are all chattering at once I have to extricate their words as I would unravel a tangled line of knitting.

Ida: "You wouldn't believe the day we had!"

Sophie: "Oy, I'm starving. We haven't had a bite."

Harriet: "I have to leave you girls. I must get Mom her dinner. Fill Gladdy in." With that she gaily waves and leaves us.

Evvie: "Where *were* you? You should have gone with us! You missed such a day!"

Sophie and Bella slap high fives.

Bella: "Are we good or are we good?"

Evvie: "You wouldn't believe what we found."

Ida: "Or what we got done. What a team!"

"Stop!" I say. "Start at the beginning."

Evvie grabs my arm. "Right. We got to do this in order. First come up with us to the Kronk's apartment."

"You're not going to believe," says Bella, eyes glittering, as she pulls on my other arm.

"I got to eat or I'll perish," cries Sophie.

"So go eat," says Bella. "We'll go without you."

Sophie considers this for a moment, but hell would freeze over before she'd miss anything. "I'll eat a cookie at Greta's. She wouldn't mind."

I must admit I am curious about the condition in which they found Greta's apartment. Ten or more years of all of us speculating on the mystery of Greta's existence, never able to get into her apartment, never invited, blinds always shut, no way to snoop. Ten or more years of Greta never speaking to anyone except on the phone to order in supplies. Undoubtedly going to her mailbox in the middle of the night to get her Social Security checks.

I remember how many times we wondered if we should call the Board of Health. God knows what was crawling around in there. Even when we sicced the police on her, she never let them in. She stood inside her doorway to talk to them. When we got the social worker to visit, she did get in, but afterwards told us Greta's file was confidential. Then turned down our request to remove her from the premises to some kind of health care facility, without saying why. Am I dying of curiosity? You bet!

Evvie unlocks the door, reaching in to turn on the lights. And wonder of wonders—I walk around inside taking it all in—the place is immaculate.

Evvie looks at me and grins. "Surprise!"

So, Greta prowled all night and scrubbed all day. Wow! The furniture was as I remembered it; she'd bought nothing new. But it was polished to a shine. Every surface gleaming. The windows spotless. A condition worthy of *House & Garden*.

Again the girls are grabbing and pushing me.

"The best is yet to come," says Ida. And I am pulled into the sunporch where a small table lamp is lit.

Here it is: testimony and only witness to the result of Greta's late night wanderings. Newspapers are carefully spread all over the floor and covered end to end with an astonishing collection of... things. In awe, I examine what Greta Kronk was able to create out of garbage. There must be nearly a hundred of these objects, these remarkable sculptures. Every size and shape imaginable. Everything we threw out as useless, Greta reinvented. Dancing costumes made from paper doilies, tissue, and wrapping paper. Dolls from wire, wooden sticks, and bits of metal like silverware and such. Damaged lamps, chairs, torn books, pots, and pans all recreated into other forms. Broken dishes and tiles had been reglued into vases of her own design. There was some craziness in the designs, but mostly they were unique and highly imaginative. And touching. How lonely she must have been.

Sophie is jumping up and down from excitement. "Look at the walls!" She turns on the overhead fixture and the entire room lights up. Bella and Ida join Sophie in crowding me to watch the expression on my face. "You coulda knocked us down with a feather bed when we saw!"

I stare incredulously at the collection of picnic paper plates lining the walls. Sketches in pastel, crayon, and acrylics of the residents of Lanai Gardens. Primitive as they are, they are each pretty good likenesses of us. If there was any doubt who they were, you only needed to read the poems she wrote beneath them. The same poems she matched to the doors. And there they are, all twenty-seven of them! I have to call Barney and Conchetta at the library tomorrow. They must see this.

The women are babbling behind me. "How about this!" "Look at that!" But I tune them out. I have to think.

Suddenly I am getting excited. Did she . . . did she paint one of the murderer? A picture to identify, a poem to accuse? I race my eyes up and down the rows, reading and recalling each and every one. No such luck. Except . . . except . . . the very last row. There's a nail hole. I glance down. The nail is lying on the floor behind a chair. I pick it up and hold it up to the light. I can see the tiniest trace of white cardboard still stuck to it. Again! Damn it! The killer is always one step ahead of us.

"What are you looking for, Glad?"

"The killer was here before us. He took his poem."

Bella looks around fearfully. "*Oy gevalt!* Maybe he's still here!"

"I doubt it," I say. Bella calms down.

Amazing. All of it amazing.

We go back into the dining area and the girls press me into sitting down. Sophie is hovering. I can tell she wants to raid the pantry and find something to eat, but she is having second thoughts about touching what belonged to the dead.

"Wait 'til you hear the rest," Evvie says.

"You have my undivided attention," I say.

"You have to admit, it was my duty to come up here. After all, with no relatives, we had to find out if she left a will."

"Absolutely," I tell her.

"And sure enough she had papers—"

Sophie interrupts, cutting to the chase. "Boy, were we surprised. She made Evvie her executor!"

Evvie beams and nods. "She had a paper she wrote by hand saying if anything happened to her, I should be in charge."

Sophie pouts. "I still don't see why she picked you."

Evvie puts her hands on her hips. "Why not me? I was always nice to her and besides, I'm on the board."

"No heirs?" I ask.

"Nobody. All her stuff goes to any charity we pick. Her bankbook has a few hundred dollars in it. That goes to some starving actors' fund. And she left a letter authorizing me to dispose of her remains as she asked."

Bella pipes up. "So that's what we were doing today."

Ida continues. "We called the coroner and they wanted to know what mortuary to send the body to, but first we had to prove Evvie had the right to say so."

"We needed you, but we looked everywhere for you, and you were gone," Sophie adds.

"Thank God we had Harriet. She did the driving."

"Lucky for you," I mutter. What turncoats.

"She knew just what to do about everything," Ida says. "We were already over the twenty-four-hour period for burial, so were we ever rushing."

Sophie continues. "We had to go to the bank and get it notarized who Evvie was, and make copies of Kronk's final instructions, then we had to run it over to the morgue and then we had to arrange it with the mortuary."

Bella grins, fanning herself. "I don't know how we ever got it all done in one day, but we did it!"

"Thank God for Feinberg's," continues Sophie. "Since everyone we know goes to Feinberg's when they die and they know us there, when we rushed them a copy of the death certificate they ran to pick up the body."

"And the cremation is," Evvie looks at her watch, "just about over now."

Everyone looks up at me, smiling, waiting for my words of congratulation for an impossible job well done. Instead, I scream, "*What cremation?!*"

"That's what the Kronk wanted."

I am hyperventilating now. I sputter. "Jews don't get cremated. It's against Jewish law."

Evvie grins. "Guess what. That's the joke. We did all that running around just to get everything done today because we thought the Kronk was Jewish."

Ida laughs. "We always think everyone is Jewish."

"Feinberg, of course, won't have anything to do with a cremation," Evvie continues. "He insists there must be some mistake. So we reread the papers again, and there it is. Turns out, after all that, that the Kronk was Catholic, so Feinstein ships her to O'Brien's right down the street on Sunrise."

I get up. My face must be purple. If I had high blood pressure I'd be having a stroke right now. I smash my fist down on the kitchen table so hard they all jump. *"Do you idiots know what you've done!!"*

I see the bright eyes dim and the smiles turn to frowns of resentment.

"Do you know why you couldn't find me?" I shriek. "Because I was at the police station demanding an autopsy on Greta so we could find poison in her body! You cannot find poison in a charred hamburger! You cannot find poison in a jar full of ashes! You knew the only way we'd ever prove Francie and Selma were murdered was if we could find poison in a body!!! And we had Greta's body! *What the hell were you thinking!*"

It slowly sinks in, and one by one they realize what I am saying. And what they have done. They cringe.

"Whose idea was it to do all this today! Who!"

"Well, we thought we had to hurry because of Jewish law..." Bella whimpers.

"Well, Harriet said since she had the car and she wasn't busy..." Sophie adds.

"Quick," I say, going over to Evvie and shaking her, "give me O'Brien's number."

Evvie fumbles though all the papers in her purse, then she looks at me, stricken. "I don't have it. Feinstein made the call."

I look through Greta's kitchen drawers until I find her phone book. "Maybe Jews have to hurry, but what was O'Brien's rush? Why would O'Brien need to cremate her so fast? Don't they go through their own kind of funeral service, like a viewing of the body or a wake or whatever Catholics do?"

Evvie's voice was practically whimpering. "Since

there were no relatives...And...the crematorium had a cancellation...."

With my back deliberately turned away from them, I find the number and dial. I get voice mail which I hate the most of all these so-called modern improvements. I wade through all the instructions to press all the right numbers and after an endless wait on hold I finally get an operator who has to find someone who knows the phone number of the crematorium. The crematorium also puts me on hold, and an electronic voice tells me someone will answer in (pause) four minutes, and then I have to listen to an advertisement about the Neptune Society and be reminded to stop in their gift shop to see their large assortment of attractive urns. Finally I get a receptionist who makes me wait some more until she can find someone with an update on the disposition of the deceased. After too long, I hear what I prayed not to hear. The cremation is over. But if I'd like to come over and light a candle...and don't forget to stop at the gift shop....

Through it all, the girls haven't moved. They sit rigidly, practically holding their breath. When I hang up they can tell by my face that the news is not good.

I walk stiffly to the door, turn, and face them.

I know I'm being melodramatic, but I can't help myself. "On behalf of the murderer of Selma, Francie, and Greta, I thank you." With that I walk out on them.

The way I feel right now, I may never speak to any of them again.

30

Nobody's Talking

Even though the weather continues its monotonous daily routine—heat and more heat—the song lyric running through my head is from "Stormy Weather." "Gloom and misery everywhere..." It might as well be raining. The grapevine, true to form, is spreading the word: The sisters aren't talking. And Gladdy's not talking to the rest of the girls, either. Buzz, buzz, buzz, but no one knows the reason. The girls, probably out of guilt, are keeping mum, and no one dares ask me. The condo board held a memorial service yesterday for Greta in the clubhouse. The girls attended when they were sure I wouldn't. I suppose everybody said kind words for the deceased and nobody mentioned insulting poems and garbage left smeared on doors.

It is too quiet these days, as if everyone is tiptoeing around us. Waiting for it to blow over or get worse. People still gossip about the murders, but there is much heated dissension as to whether they really were murders or just figments of my imagination. There are no more morning walks, and none of us go to the pool. From my window, I see the girls pile into a cab on Publix day.

I spend much of my time doing heavy thinking. Or else I am at the library commiserating with Conchetta and Barney. They share my consternation about the cremation of Greta. I do take them up to Greta's apartment at a time I knew the girls have gone somewhere, again by taxi. They are bowled over by Greta's artifacts, as I knew they would be. Dear friends—they try to get me out of my depression by saying I mustn't give up my detecting. But what is there to detect? No clues. No body. I really don't expect the killer to drop in on me and confess.

If you made a bet about it you would have won. Detective Morrie Langford calls me the next day and agrees to set up an autopsy. I briefly explain what happened, and I can tell from his voice he is genuinely sorry.

An afternoon shower hits hard, and the air seems almost cool for a few minutes. I decide to walk through the grounds just because I need to move around a little. I miss our exercise time, such as it is.

I find a bench in a quiet area, and I wipe the rainwater off and sit down. A few minutes later I hear two voices, coming toward me, singing happily, although off-key, in Spanish. Millie is awkwardly trying to stroll in her walker and Yolanda is with her, one arm keeping the walker steady. Millie seems genuinely happy. That sight finally makes me smile.

"Hi, Millie . . . hi, Yolanda."

Like twins they answer, *"Buenos días, Señora Gladdy."*

"And *buenos días* to you, too. Where's Irving?"

Millie answers. *"Mi esposo esta jugando cartes."*

"Cartas," Yolanda gently corrects.

"Yolie is giving me *lecciónes* in *Español.*"

"That's wonderful."

Millie giggles. "And I'm giving her lessons in snooping." Now Yolanda puts her hand over her mouth and giggles, too.

Getting into the spirit of it, I ask, "Why are you snooping?"

"Because the children like it. They like to see the dirties. . . ."

"The what?" I ask, curious.

"Hy Binder watches porno movies when Lola takes her nap." Another round of giggles.

"We *vemos* through *las ventanas.*" More giggles. "And Señora Feder, she walks when nobody looks."

"I don't understand. Harriet walks?"

"No, *la vieja,* the old one," says Yolanda.

Millie imitates it. "She gets out of that old wheelchair and she just sashays around." Millie lets go of the walker to show how and loses her balance. Yolanda and I both grab for her.

Millie starts singing again, *"La cucaracha . . . la cucaracha . . ."* and Yolanda joins in. Together they continue down the path happily singing about a cockroach.

Is it possible? Esther is faking being crippled? It would explain how she managed to see what Greta wrote on John and Mary's door three floors up. And why? To keep Harriet imprisoned? If she can get around, what else has she been up to? Wait 'til I tell

Evvie—I stop myself. And remember there is no telling Evvie...

I go back upstairs. I try to read, but can't concentrate. The hours drag by. The phone never rings. I guess I never realized how much of my days were dominated by the girls and their unending activities. I try to watch TV. Everything seems stupid to me. Now I am pacing and wondering what I can do to get out of this rotten mood.

The phone finally rings. I jump, so unaccustomed am I to hearing it. What a surprise. It's Langford, Sr. Why do I have the feeling the son called his father and told him I am feeling blue?

"I hope you don't mind my calling?"

"Of course not, Jack." I blush and I'm glad he can't see it. It must be genetic. Both father and son seem to be able to make me turn red. "Sorry. I've been terribly distracted."

"Things not going well?"

As if Morrie hadn't told him. "At the moment, my investigation has come to a full stop."

"Then the timing may work to my advantage. May I take you to dinner this evening?"

Suddenly that seems like a wonderful idea. "Yes, thank you."

"May I pick you up at six?"

"No!" I surprise myself at how fast I say that.

"What time would you prefer?"

"It's not the time, it's the place. I don't think it's such a good idea for you to come here."

"*You* want to pick *me* up?" I can hear laughter in his voice.

I am getting frustrated. "No, that's not what I mean, either."

"What have you got in mind?"

"Maybe we can meet somewhere else?"

"How's this: We can meet halfway between Phases Three and Four. Or how about that palm tree next to the mailbox. You can hide behind it and jump into my car as I speed by."

"Stop laughing at me," I say, laughing myself. "You know what busybodies we have in this place. People talk about me enough behind my back. Why should I add fuel to the fire? I'll meet you off campus, so to speak."

"Is ten miles far enough away? Or perhaps we can meet in Miami? Key Largo? Cuba?"

He got me at last. We are both laughing hard now. I play along. "Well, we can't go to Chinese. Or Italian. Definitely not a deli. We're bound to run into somebody we know. I've got it. Nobody here eats Greek. Do you like Greek food?"

"Mention moussaka and I'll follow you anywhere."

"You're on. Athenian Kitchen. Sunrise Boulevard, six P.M."

"I'll wear dark glasses and a fez."

"And I a babushka and a veil."

"Code names, Boris and Natasha. Which one do you want to be—the moose or the squirrel?"

"Wrong country. Try Irena and Nico."

"Whatever."

When I hang up I am grinning like a fifteen-year-old. A little ouzo, a little feta, a lot of laughter—just what the doctor ordered. Or was it the detective?

But first, I have a million decisions to make. What am I going to wear?

31

The Dating Game

Look at me! I'm wearing a bra for the first time since I can't remember when. And a smidgen of makeup. Did a little something to my hair. I keep changing my outfit, unable to make up my mind. What image am I trying to project? Am I dressing up or dressing down? I'm making myself crazy. Finally I end up with the first thing I had on. Which I now hate. But I'm exhausted, so this is it. Glancing at the mirror, I'm startled. I don't look like me, the me that's gotten used to living single in these so-called golden years. The me that does nothing more than run a comb through my hair when we go out, just us girls. None of us bother anymore, in terms of attempting beauty. It's comfort that counts. Except for Sophie, of course, but she doesn't know any better.

It's only a dinner, I keep reassuring myself. It's a date, admit it! And if you're spending so much time getting gorgeous, that means you want to impress him. You want him to think you still look good. That you are interested. It means you're actually contemplating—oh, gasp—the possibility of a relationship!

Shut up, I tell myself, and move it already or you'll be late. How much longer are you going to attempt to turn not much into something more? Go, already.

When I enter the restaurant I see Jack talking to the owner. He waves me over.

"You look lovely," he says, then, "There's a complication. A nice one." He smiles.

"What's the name again?" Mr. Thomopolis asks. I know that's his name because his picture is over the cash register, smiling with a group of Little Leaguers.

"Jack Langford."

"No problem. The very minute you get your call." With that he shows us to a table and hands us gigantic menus.

"What's that all about?"

"Right after I spoke to you, my daughter called to tell me she was on the way to the hospital to give birth. Morrie's sister Lisa."

"That is exciting. But don't you want to be there with her?"

"Not too manageable. She lives in New York. It's their third child. I just want to get the news hot off the griddle, so to speak."

Now that that's taken care of, we are facing each other for the first time since Fuddruckers. And yes, he still looks great to me. And he's smiling, so I guess I pass muster.

We make a big to-do about picking from such a

huge menu, but finally the drinks are taken care of, white wine for me, beer for him. Moussaka for him, dolmas and a Greek salad for me. That took up a little time, but here we are again looking at each other.

He seems very content with the silence. And I remember that feeling. Belonging to someone. Feeling you fit and all's right with your world. My Jack used to call it the "aha" factor. Meet the right person and you breathe a sigh of relief and your mind says, *Aha, at last. The search is over. You're home.*

"Well," he says, "I don't have anything to report. My life has been status quo. But you—clearly much has been going on. Want to talk about it, or do you want this evening to be your respite from the real world?"

"The latter. Desperately. My world has become too much for me."

"OK, then," he says, smiling. "Read any good books lately?"

And we talk about the kind of books we like (me, good fiction and, of course, mysteries; he, nonfiction, especially history); movies (me, sophisticated comedies and good drama; he, spy thrillers); music (me, opera and Beethoven and swing; he, Mahler, Britten); theater (both agreeing that the last great musicals were in the era of *West Side Story* and *Fiddler on the Roof* and in drama, Arthur Miller and Tennessee Williams); and both of us, crossword puzzles and travel, which we don't do much anymore, and our children (extreme prejudice on both sides).

We laugh and talk and laugh and talk. It's wonderful.

Mr. Thomopolis comes over, smiling. "The phone, Mr. Langford."

Jack excuses himself and follows Mr. T.

I sit there bathing in the glow of happiness. God, how much I've missed this. Someone to share ideas with. Being a couple.

And suddenly I get anxious. What am I thinking! Too late for this. Haven't I spent my widow years assuming I would never love again? Redefining myself as single. Learning to adjust to that life.

I sip my wine as negative thoughts start tumbling about. At my age, it's too late to start over. Give up the known for the unknown? And think of what's involved. Readjusting to a new, unfamiliar man living with you. What's he going to expect? Here's a woman who has all the trappings of old age, from varicose veins to the dire results of gravity on down. This body is gonna turn a man on? Part of the agreement being never to turn on a light at night again? It's one thing for couples to live together fifty years, when the changes are gradual as opposed to shocking.

What about no longer just planning for myself but having to always consider another? The subtle battles. Who will have control. Having to compromise. No more being comfortable alone with one's own self.

And will the apartment need to be kept neater? Will I have to be the housewife again, with the man's wants more important than mine? Will I not be able to read in bed 'til dawn or eat standing in front of the open fridge at midnight? Remember what you've forgotten, Glad, old girl. Living with a man is work. You've got to please him, dress for him, cook for him. Bother. And sex. How much effort will it take to do what used to come easily and naturally? Will it work at all at this age?

You've got your own baggage, now you'd have to take on his as well. A whole new load of relatives to deal with and have to make room for. How much energy is left for this? And let's not forget the downhill countdown, the body's deterioration and potential illnesses. The possibility of having to care for an invalid. And what if that invalid is you? Would you be able to dump that on a stranger? And dealing with death again. One or the other left bereft again. So much risk. So much easier to do nothing. Live the easier life. Without love.

Best to leave well enough alone.

"It's a girl!" Jack appears at the table, beaming. "Six pounds, eight ounces."

I try to recover quickly from my shambling thoughts. "Congratulations, Grandpa." A weak retort.

He looks at me, eyes seeming to pierce into mine. He sits down, reaches over and takes my hands in his.

"I leave you alone for five minutes and you start to think! Stop it immediately! You imagine I don't know what's going on in that beautiful head of yours? That I haven't had every one of those same thoughts?"

I try sarcasm to cover my feelings. "What are you, a mind reader?"

"No, I'm just a person of the same age having all the same doubts and fears and giving myself all the same rationales to run as fast and as far as I can."

My voice sounds shaky to me. "So why don't you?"

"Because hopefully we're wise enough by now not to make the same mistakes we made when we were young. We no longer need to fight those foolish battles anymore. There are different ways to live with someone at this age. A way to make life easier and simpler for both. A way to cherish whatever is left for as long as it lasts, and to have someone at your side to share it."

"But what if ... what if ..." I can't say it.

"What if it's only a few years or a year or a month or even a day? Isn't one perfect day worth it?"

I am speechless. Then I start to cry.

32

Back to Reality

I guess I drove home. My car must have made it back on autopilot. Oh, wonderful world of limitless possibilities. Jack Langford. All these years so near and yet so far. We might never have met again had it not been for—murder. Francie, why aren't you here? You would have enjoyed the irony.

Suddenly, out of the corner of my eye, I am aware of something flickering. It's coming from across the parking lot, a ground-floor apartment. Denny's apartment. There is only the barest sliver of dull light shining through the louvers on the front door, but it seems to be moving. Is it a fire? Oh, please, God, no! I quickly park my car and hurry over. The kitchen blinds are shut tight and I can't see anything. I knock, but he doesn't answer. I keep knocking. Finally he speaks to me through the door.

"Who is it?" A mean, unfriendly voice.

"It's me, Gladdy."

"Go away."

"I thought I saw a fire—"

"There's no fire."

I'm relieved, but to my own surprise, I suddenly say, "Denny, may I come in? I'd like to talk to you."

"No. Not now."

"Promise we'll talk soon. All right?"

"Yeah. Some other time."

"All right then. Good night."

I start back across the parking area again and head for my place, my mind wanting to return to pleasant thoughts of Jack. But the sound of Denny's voice has pulled me into the here and now. His behavior in the garden was odd. Now this. It's obvious he's avoiding everyone. One of these days, I am going to make him talk to me and tell me what's wrong. Though I don't want to admit it to myself, I don't want to know. I'm afraid to know. . . .

33

The Living Dead

Denny peered out the peephole and waited until he was sure Gladdy stepped into the elevator.

Moving lethargically through his cramped apartment, he was no longer aware of the putrid smells around him. Of his own body odor from too few baths. Of the clothing he no longer washed. Of the garbage piled up in the kitchen and the filthy dishes in the sink. All he knew was that he was tired all the time. All he wanted to do was sleep. And he couldn't sleep. Life was only bearable when he was in his garden.

He placed a flickering black candle under his mother's portrait and straightened the black crepe he had wrapped around it. He did that every evening before the phone call. It was a ritual he dared not stop.

It was stifling in the apartment. He knew he should fix the air conditioner, but he didn't care that

*he could hardly breathe. He didn't care about any-
thing anymore. He only wanted it to stop.*

*Everything was wrong in his life now. He'd even
lost his keys. He never lost keys before!*

He had been so happy. Without her. *He had his
garden and his jobs for all the ladies. Everyone was
so good to him. They gave him presents and food.
Nobody ever made him feel bad. Like* she *always
did. Why did she have to come back and ruin everything?*

*For seven wonderful years he'd thought he was
rid of his mother forever. But then on the night
before her birthday, she'd called him. How was it
possible? And she sounded so strange. It didn't
sound like her. But she knew everything about him
and reminded him that it was because of him she'd
died on this very date, the night before her birthday.
He had killed her. Because he was a bad boy.
He deserved to be punished. Then he knew it had to
be her.*

*He didn't understand how she could phone him
from heaven. She laughed and said they had all the
modern conveniences. But he would never know
that because he would never go to heaven. Because
he was bad.* •

*But why? What did she want from him? She told
him, but he didn't really understand. How? he had
cried out in anguish. She said she was lonely in
heaven and she wanted her friends to join her. She
couldn't wait until God was ready to send them.
Oh, no, she had to have it her way, like she always
did when she was alive. But it was confusing. It
made his head hurt to try to understand. His mother
never liked those ladies. She didn't have any friends.*

Denny kept looking at the clock, waiting for it to be ten. Afterwards, he wouldn't be able to sleep. No wonder nothing got done around here anymore.

He sat on the couch, hands clenched, staring at the clock, praying for it to be over. He didn't want to do this every night, but he didn't dare disobey her. He had tried once. He left the house, so he wouldn't be there at ten when the phone rang. The next day he found a dead rat in his bed. Strangled. He threw up when he saw it. And that night when she called she warned him: The next time it would be his *neck.*

The second hand was nearing the end of the hour. He suddenly realized he had to pee, but it was too late. He had to answer on time. He didn't dare be late.

The old grandfather clock chimed the hours. Six ... seven ... eight ... nine ... ten. Ten o'clock. And the phone rang. Denny, staring at the phone, felt paralyzed. Pick up, Denny, now!

With sweating, shaking hands he lifted the receiver.

"Mama?"

He listened with the growing awareness that he should have gone to the bathroom first. He jiggled his body up and down, trying to control his bladder.

"But I did pick it right up. I did."

"No, the clock isn't wrong, I swear."

"Oh, no, Mama, not another one. Please."

"But, why? Don't you have enough friends up there?"

"No, I don't want to. Why do you say that? I don't want them dead."

"But I don't remember doing that." He shivered

with fear. "I can't sleep, so how can I do that in my sleep?"

"Mama, no, I'm not fighting with you. I'm not..."

He couldn't help himself and Denny, mortified, could feel the pee running down the inside of his pant legs. He was sure she could see it. She saw everything he did.

His voice was dead now. Dead as he was feeling. "Who is it this time, Mama?"

"Yes, Mama, whatever you say."

Denny hung up the phone and sank to the floor. It was over. For tonight anyway. He stared at the damp spot on his pants and began to sob.

34

Back in Business Again

What a night! When I finally do fall asleep—
nightmares galore. Denny was in my tortured
night visions. Crying and standing over a grave,
waving white flowers and whispering "Not me, not
me." When the grave looked like it was opening
up—well, that sure woke me up, covered in sweat
and absolutely terrified. I shudder to think what the
dream was trying to tell me.

That keeps me up a few more hours, pacing,
thinking, attempting to read, until I can finally fall
back to sleep again.

Around eight A.M. I'm awake again, feeling like I
just drove a ten-ton truck to Tallahassee and back. I
drag myself into the kitchen and make my morning
coffee.

While carrying my cup and my toast to the dining room table where my crossword puzzles await,
my eye catches something white on the floor, half

hidden under the front door. I retrieve it after setting the coffee down.

And at the same moment the phone rings. As I answer it, I'm aware that the note is from Evvie. I feel terrible. We've come to this. To talk to me she has to leave a note under my door. *Mea culpa,* as my pal Conchetta would say.

"Good morning," says Jack Langford cheerfully. "Hope I'm not calling too early."

"No, not at all," I say, still preoccupied by the note.

"I just wanted to tell you how much I enjoyed our evening together."

"Thank you. I did, too."

"You sound distracted."

"I'm sorry. I am. I had a fight with my sister and I'm feeling overwhelmed with guilt."

"Not good. Guilt is something we should not have to suffer at our advanced age."

"Easily said..."

"I know. Well you do what you have to do to repair the damage and call me when your mind is clear."

"Thanks for understanding, Jack."

After I hang up I read Evvie's note. *Glad. We're still on the job. We have important news about Leo the Sleaze and his real-estate company. They are up to no good. Evvie.*

This is so stupid! What am I supposed to do—never forgive them? Live here and never talk to them again? Sneak around so that we don't ever run into one another? So Evvie reached out first, attempting to make up. I can guess how much it cost her. I have to let them off the hook even though I'd still like to wring all their necks.

I put on my sweats and walk outside to begin peace negotiations. This is my way of announcing to them that I am willing to begin our daily walks again, and channels are now open for further communication. Immediately, I can feel eyes peering out at me from behind louvered windows.

Sure enough, Evvie is out her door in a flash. Playing it cool, she does her warm-ups without facing me. She calls out to me across the parking area. "So, how did you sleep last night, Glad?"

If she only knew. This isn't the time or place to tell her about my nightmares. I call back. "Pretty good. Only got up twice."

And here comes Bella, peeping out her door to make sure it's safe to make an appearance. Evvie must be nodding at her, because she, too, is now out and moving at her usual snail pace.

"Hi, Gladdy," she calls tentatively at me.

"Hi, Bella," I answer. I can see her grin clear across the way.

Here comes Ida, doing her warm-ups. Head up, nose in the air, and definitely not looking at me. She is not going to say hello. Never one to accept blame for anything, in her mind she did nothing wrong; I'm to blame.

Sophie pokes her nose out the kitchen window. "I'm coming. I'm coming!"

"I think we need to have a meeting," I announce.

"When?" Bella asks eagerly.

"As soon as we can."

"I have a full pot of coffee on." This from Evvie.

Ida finally speaks. Grudgingly. "I'm not in a walking mood anyway. Might as well do it now."

Evvie chimes in. "Sounds good to me. Come on over."

With that, Ida walks right past me to the elevator. Sophie calls out from inside her door. "I'm almost ready!"

I catch up with Ida at the elevator. From the expression on her face, I can tell she was hoping not to ride with me. We descend without speaking.

Finally, I sigh. "Truce?" I ask her.

"You hurt my feelings. We were only trying to help."

"I know," I say. "Let's get past it."

A pause. Ida isn't about to give me any easy satisfaction. "Well. We'll see how it goes."

But she is still not looking at me as we cross over to Evvie and Bella's building.

As usual it takes a while to get the coffee, cut the bagels, spread the cream cheese, exchange some quick gossip, get settled around the dining room table. The only difference is that everyone is uncomfortable. Ida's body is still turned away from me. Bella is looking nervously from one of us to the other and Evvie can't quite look me in the eye.

Finally everyone runs out of unimportant things to do or say. Evvie, seeing silence as dangerous, taps on the table with her teaspoon. "The meeting of the Gladiators will now come to order." She looks around, "Where's—"

The door bursts open and there's Sophie, half-dressed, looking frazzled, breathless and hyperventilating. She stares at us, just sitting there, puts her hands on her hips, and fires away. "Well, this is a fine kettle of fish and chips! I see you all out on the walkway, so I hurry into my sweats. I come out and you're all gone. So, I figure you went downstairs, but I can't find you on the path, so I figure it was time to go swimming, so I run back in and put on my suit, then I don't see you near the pool—"

Ida puts her hand over Sophie's mouth. "Shah, still! Close your mouth or you'll catch flies."

Sophie jerks her hand away. "Nobody ever thinks about me! You know I'm not good at rushing, and what am I, a mind reader, to know you're all up here at Evvie's? I knocked on everybody's doors!! Is this a way to treat a person?"

Bella jumps up and gets her a cup of coffee as Ida pushes an onion bagel at her. "It's all right. It's over. Sit. Eat. Listen."

"As I was saying," Evvie continues as Sophie noisily accepts the bribes, "the meeting has come to order. We all know all the old business, so we better go straight to what's new . . . ."

Bella gets excited. "Tell Glad what we found out about Leo."

"I was just getting to it."

Ida jumps in. "I was there, too. I'm a witness."

"Anyway, we were heading to the pool when we ran into Tessie. Tessie had news. Selma's apartment finally sold. She heard this from Selma's kids."

"Well, that's good," I say.

"No, it's bad."

Ida can't stand being left out. "So we naturally asked, who did they sell to? And when are they moving in?"

Evvie fairly pushes her. "Will you let me tell it already? Tessie says no one is moving in. A company

202 • Rita Lakin

bought the place. And they got it dirt cheap because it was on the market so long."

"Uh-oh, that's bad," I say. "When that news gets out, the property values will drop and they're plenty low now."

Evvie says, "You know, other people can be a detective, too. I go into the office and look through the condo records and I call up the families of all the people who died in the last six months in all the phases. And guess what?"

Ida bursts in again. "All bought by different companies. With no people moving in anywhere!"

"With one family after another taking cheaper prices after these companies told them what the one before sold for."

Sophie is sitting on the edge of her chair. "So what does it mean? Are they waiting 'til real estate prices go up and they'll sell at higher prices?"

"Hah!" says Evvie. "We bought our units over twenty years ago, and our dumb luck—everywhere around us condos are worth a hundred thousand and up and we got the only price that never budged! This place always stayed cheap—" She stops suddenly, getting it, eyes wide. "But the real estate it's sitting on must be worth a fortune. . . ."

"So," I say, nodding at her, coming to the same conclusion. "They intend to buy us all out and tear this place down and build something much more valuable."

"Like a fancy high-rise," says Bella.

"Or, God forbid, a shopping mall!" says Ida.

"What's so bad about a shopping mall?" Sophie muses.

Ida swats her with a napkin. "Dummy, so where would you live?"

"Bad, very bad." Now I'm worried, too. "You said 'companies.' More than one?"

"Yes, about a half dozen different companies, but our accountant, Lou, is smart. He starts looking up the companies for me and surprise, surprise, there is one mother company who owns them all, by the name of Sunrise-Sunset, and that takes us squarely back to Leo Slezak."

"That gonif," says Sophie indignantly. "They're out to get all our apartments, one way or the other."

Bella picks up her coffee cup and her hand is shaking so hard the cup rattles. "But would they kill us to get them?"

I say, "Sleaze and his gang may be crooks, but cold-blooded murderers?!"

Ida says, "Makes sense to me. It would explain why they were trying to make us believe they were heart attacks."

"Counting all the phases, he'd have to kill off approximately a hundred and fifty of us," I say.

Ida still likes her theory. "Instead of serial killers we have mass murderers."

"Oh, well, another theory shot," Evvie says, ignoring Ida. She folds her arms, looking determined. "We'll get to the bottom of this mess, don't you worry."

"I have something else to report, though it might not mean anything." With that, I tell them of my funny little conversation with Millie and Yolanda.

Bella is truly shocked. "Esther Feder is not a cripple?!"

Sophie is grinning from ear to ear. "I knew it. I knew something was phony with that old broad!"

"She could be sneaking around when she knows no one is looking, like at night, when Harriet is also sleeping." Bella looks worriedly from one to the other. Then she brightens. "Maybe she and the Kronk hung out by the Dumpsters together?"

"But what could it mean?" Evvie asks, ignoring Bella. "It couldn't mean...it couldn't..."

"I doubt that," I say, "and besides, look at who told me. Millie? Yolanda? Maybe they made it up."

"I can believe it," Ida says. "She's plenty strong enough. Think of the muscles she has from wheeling that chair around."

"Should we say something to Harriet?" Evvie says.

"I personally am amazed. Someone as smart as Harriet wouldn't catch on?" Sophie is not convinced.

Bella says, "I don't think we should say anything. Not 'til we're sure."

"We could let a mouse run loose in the house and watch her get up and run," Sophie offers.

"Where would we get a mouse?" Bella asks, already contemplating this as a plan.

"Oh, my God," says Evvie excitedly. She quickly looks through her purse-size calendar of events. "That reminds me. I've been keeping track of everybody's birthday in our phase. Esther's birthday is in three days!"

Bella ponders that aloud. "Well, if Esther was the killer, she wouldn't kill herself on the night before her birthday. That would be suicide."

Sophie jumps in, liking this scenario. "So, if she

is killed then it would mean she isn't the killer. And she's cleared herself of the crime. Then she wouldn't have to go to jail."

Evvie is excited. "I think we better have a meeting with Harriet, and fast."

35

Warning the Victim-to-Be

The girls and I crowd in to the Feder apartment, a place we hardly ever visit. For a number of reasons. We are rarely invited. And if we are, we are intensely uncomfortable. So much furniture. Very large, ugly, heavy—totally wrong for Florida. The pieces were undoubtedly expensive in their day, but who would want them? There is only one narrow aisle for Esther's wheelchair to traverse from room to room, and it must be difficult for her to manage. No wonder she usually parks it at the front screen door and stays there most of the time. I can't imagine living in a place so claustrophobic. I don't know how Harriet stands it.

As the girls try to get comfortable, I start to work my way up to why we are here. "I'm glad we caught you before you went to work," I say to Harriet.

"You would have caught me all day. I've been switched to the night shift."

Bella groans at that and Harriet eyes her curiously.

Ida looks at Harriet sadly. "Talk about bad timing."

"It's about your birthday," I say to Esther.

"What about it? You gonna make me a party?" She cackles.

Harriet gets it. "You're worried," she says quietly, trying to downplay it.

I nod, as do the girls.

"What about?" Esther demands to know. She wheels her chair deftly about to face us. Bella stares down at her legs. Evvie pokes her for staring. Ida fingers her sharp Hadassah lapel pin meaningfully. Bella sees it and giggles.

"Can't you change your shift back to day?" Evvie asks Harriet, at the same time glaring warningly at the girls.

"No chance," she says. "I made a lot of people switch schedules so I could take my vacation last week. I don't dare ask for another favor."

"What are you talking about?" Esther says, her voice strident now. She looks from one to another of us. Then she gets it. "The night before my birthday. You think—" and with that she makes a cutting gesture across her throat. "Eh, what a crock!"

"We don't want to take any chances," Evvie says. "Selma and Francie were killed—"

But Esther interrupts. "Who says they were killed? Only you girls, spreading rumors. I don't see any cops around investigating."

"Mom, be nice. The girls are only trying to help you."

"Who needs their help? I don't. And besides, Greta didn't die just before her birthday."

"Mom," Harriet intercedes. "We all think Greta was killed because she knew the killer."

"We? We all think? Suddenly these crackpots are your new best friends? Ha!"

Harriet looks at us, extending her hands, helplessly. I can see Ida getting red hot under the collar, just itching to say something. I shake my head at her.

Esther keeps jabbering. "Then what about Eileen O'Connor? Her birthday passed and she's still around. Too bad. She's such a big mouth, getting rid of her would be a blessing."

"Can't you behave!" Harriet exclaims, embarrassed.

"Frankly, I think her leaving and going to stay with her sister in Boca probably saved her life," I say quietly, trying to ignore Esther's rotten remarks.

Esther folds her arms. "OK by me. Send me to Miami Beach. I wouldn't mind a nice cabana for a week. You could also throw in a Cuban beach boy while you're at it."

Harriet smiles wryly. "That's a great idea. If only we could afford it."

"You would say that," Esther says sarcastically. "You don't let me spend a dime on anything."

Bella is again staring at Esther's feet, but they stay perfectly still under her blanket. Evvie pokes Bella. Sophie snickers.

"At least ask if you can have that one night off?" Evvie is determined to ignore Esther's rudeness.

"I'll try, but you don't know my supervisor."

"Then we have to set up some kind of plan," I say.

"I agree," Evvie says. "We can all sit here with Esther until you get home."

Ida wants to know what time her shift is over.

Harriet tells her it's four A.M.

Sophie groans at that.

"Hello? Don't I have any say in this matter? I don't need you. I don't want you," Esther says. "Don't do me any favors."

"Mom. This is no time to get stubborn."

"The whole thing's stupid anyway. Who'd want to kill me?"

From the looks on the girls' faces, I'd say, right now, four people.

Harriet is exasperated. "Foolish old lady. Why would anybody want to kill Selma or Francie? But they did!"

"Even if I believed all their *chozzerai,* you think I'd be afraid? Just let that guy come. I'll be ready." Esther makes boxing jabs with her hands as if to show what she would do.

Sophie laughs out loud.

"You think I couldn't?" Esther says, annoyed that they are laughing at her show of bravado.

"Mom, please. Don't be ridiculous," Harriet says.

Bella tries appeasement. "What have you got to lose? We could keep you company, play a little cards."

"Big shots! Nosy old biddies. Mind your own business."

Ida is up in a shot. "That does it. Let's go."

Sophie and Bella jump up with her.

Esther smirks and steers herself out of the cluttered living room and heads down the hall to her bedroom, muttering to herself. "As if I'd eat any food from some stranger! You have to be a moron!" Now she is shouting. "Like the TV show, that's my final answer!"

Harriet shrugs. What else can we say? As we start out the door, she whispers to us. "We'll talk later."

From the bedroom, Esther calls out again, "Don't forget to send me a present. Just don't send food!"

We can still hear her cackling when we step outside.

Back to square one. What's that funny saying? No good deed goes unpunished? We're going to have to find a way to save her in spite of herself. From the looks on the faces of my angry cohorts, I'd say I'll have a hard time convincing them.

Under her breath I hear Sophie mutter, "We shoulda let Ida jab her."

36

Double Feature

How can I describe this day? Everyone is on
shpilkes. *Shpilkes*—an untranslatable word.
It's like going crazy without going crazy. A high
state of nervous anxiety. Or—as Ida calls it—ants in
your pants.

Today is the day before Esther's birthday and
our hands are tied. She won't let us help her. I
thought about calling Detective Langford, but what
would he say? What the police always say: We can't
do anything unless something happens. So, it's up to
us without Esther's permission.

The girls are driving me nuts. They are calling
every hour on the hour. Do you see anything? Do
you hear anything?

At three o'clock, there are multiple knocks on
my door. I can see four anxious faces through my
kitchen window. Reluctantly, I let them in.

Evvie takes the floor. "We've made a decision.
We're going to the movies."

"But first dinner," says Bella.

"There's a great double feature at the Reprise Theater. Harriet read about it in the papers and called me," says Evvie.

"You'll really love it," says Sophie. "Two murder miseries."

"That's 'mysteries,'" Ida corrects her.

"Whatever."

I look at them in horror. "Are you trying to say we shouldn't stay home and guard Esther? Have you all lost your minds? Who's going to be able to concentrate on a movie!"

"Me!" A unanimous chorus.

"I can't do that!"

"Yes, you can," says Ida.

Sophie throws it to first. "We picked a deli right in the same minimall as the theater."

Bella takes it to second. "We do the early bird at four-fifteen."

Ida makes it to third. "The double feature is from four-thirty to seven-thirty. We'll be home before Harriet has to leave for the night shift."

And Evvie brings it to the plate. "We'll be home before dark. Well, anyway, it won't be too dark."

"Is that the movie?" I ask. *"Wait Until Dark?"*

"No, that's the plan," she informs me.

"So, tell me already." I can't believe I'm even asking. "What's playing?"

"Sorry, Wrong Number," Evvie says. "With Barbara Stanwyck."

"I love Barbara *Sandwich*," Sophie coos. "Is she dead?"

Bella says, "I think so."

"Such a pity, so young," says Sophie.

"And *No Way to Treat a Lady* with Rod Steiger," Evvie adds. "Perfect for this week's movie review on golden oldies. Waddaya think? What with all the murders getting in the way, I haven't had time to write one single review. My fans miss me!"

I am fairly salivating. Two great classics. What am I thinking? This is crazy!

Evvie pokes me playfully. "Admit it, you want to go."

I am pacing now. Torn, and ashamed of myself. "We have a responsibility here!"

"To Miss Ungrateful?" Ida says. "Why should we care?"

"And how will you live with yourselves tomorrow if she's dead?"

That stops them for about a minute.

"The killer won't do anything until it gets really dark," says Evvie.

"You know that for a fact?" I say icily. "He killed Selma around five in the afternoon and Greta early in the morning."

Evvie smiles knowingly. "With all the noise we've been making, he knows we're watching. He'll have to wait 'til he thinks we're all asleep."

"Some watching. He'll watch us take off for the movies."

"Exactly. That'll fool him. But then he'll think we're trying to trick him. See?"

See? That's about as clear as mud.

Bella and Sophie jump up and down, grabbing my arms, pulling at me, like a couple of spoiled five-year-olds. "Please! Pretty please! Let's go."

"All right," I say reluctantly.

They are all out the door. Ida has to have the last

word. "Downstairs in ten minutes, not a second later!"

I can't believe I am sitting in this theater. Those lunatics I live with dragged me so fast, my head is spinning. Rushed to the theater, rushed around looking for a parking spot, fairly dragged me out of the car and raced us all to the deli, so we'd have a whole ten minutes to choke down a dry pastrami on rye. I'm amazed I don't have indigestion.

Why did I go? Because Harriet reassures me she won't have to leave for work until we get home. Because I'm so edgy and the girls so crazed, the movies will relax us. Believe me, I hedged my bet. I called Langford's office and left him a message. What a world. Even cops have voice mail. Whatever happened to some gum-chewing tough guy saying, "Yeah, waddaya want him for?" My message was to the point. "This is the night before Esther Feder's birthday. If I'm right, she'll die tonight. I hope I'm wrong."

I also intend to phone in between features.

Stanwyck is as wonderful as I remember, as the bedridden invalid who overhears two men plot a murder, and I relax into supreme enjoyment. Then that delicious chilling moment when she realizes she is the target!

Now I find myself staring at the screen. Barbara dials everyone she can think of to get help and I stare, hypnotized, at her hand as it keeps reaching for the phone. What does it remind me of? I think of Selma and Francie and someone else so long ago...

but who?? It's been nagging at me since all of this started.

I lean over to Evvie. "Who was it who died in Lanai Gardens years ago holding a phone?"

"Wait a minute, this is the good part. Barbara hears someone breaking into the house."

"Evvie, this is important."

"What?"

"Someone died a long time ago—"

"In this movie?"

"No. Pay attention. In our phase."

"Someone we know?"

"Yes, of course. She died trying to get help."

"Shhhhh!" I hear from behind us.

"Sorry," I whisper. I talk lower. "Think!"

"I'm thinking," she hisses at me.

"Be quiet!" someone yells at us.

"Mind your own business," Evvie yells back. "There's a film critic sitting here, you know!"

Someone throws popcorn at us. Ida jumps up, hands on hips. "Who did that!" she shrieks. In a moment, the manager is running down the aisle.

"If you wanna talk, go home and watch TV!" someone heckles.

But it all calms down quickly. This isn't our usual neighborhood theater where everyone talks incessantly throughout every movie. We must be in a theater with real movie buffs.

I call Harriet at intermission. All quiet, she tells me. Have fun, she says.

My mind is not on the opening credits for the next feature. I am suddenly starting to remember what I cannot believe I'd forgotten.

And as if someone on the screen is helping direct

my thoughts even further, there's Rod Steiger, a serial killer, standing in front of the portrait of the mother he hates, the reason he kills older women one after another. Putting on disguises to fool old ladies into letting him in. Leaving his trademark, lips painted on the forehead of the dead women with their own lipstick.

We are three quarters of the way through the picture when it finally hits me. Maureen Ryan! Denny's mother. Ohmygod!!!

The pieces are falling into place.

I hit Evvie on her shoulder. "Tell the girls we're leaving!"

"But we're at the thrilling part. Steiger is going after George Segal's girlfriend, Lee Remick!"

"Now! Meet me in the lobby."

I race out to the lobby bank of phones and I dial Harriet's number as fast as I can. The line is busy. Come on, Harriet, get off the line! Or is the phone off the hook because Esther knocked it down as she tried calling for help? I try to calm my hysteria.

The girls tumble out into the lobby, grumbling. This is unheard of. They never leave a movie in the middle. I ignore their complaining. I'm out the door, so they follow.

"We've got to get back now. We've got to stop him."

"Who?" Evvie asks.

"Denny," I say, choking on my traitorous words. There's no more denying what's been staring me in the face all along. Denny's gone bad. "He's going to kill Esther!"

They stop dead in their tracks, but I'm still moving.

"Come on," I yell. "We haven't a minute to waste!"

Quickly, panting with exertion, they run to catch up with me. They are incredulous and frightened now.

We reach my car as I am groping in my purse for my keys. I can't find them. I always put them in the outer pocket. Otherwise I'd go nuts digging for them every time. They have to be in there!

Evvie shoves me nervously. "Open the door already!"

I hiss at her. "I can't open the door because I can't find my damn keys!"

They are not where they should be, and now I grope anxiously all through my purse. Nowhere! And then I see them. Dangling from the ignition. In all that hurry I locked my keys in! The girls look where I am looking, then back at me, sheepishly.

God keep me from committing murder, as well.

37

Stuck in the Minimall

By now we have quite a crowd of kibitzers around us. Testimony to boring lives, that everyone in the Hollywood minimall has stopped whatever they were doing to witness these little old ladies' embarrassment at being locked out of their car. I am not embarrassed, I am livid. With passersby either jeering catcalls or giving us bad advice, the scene is only adding to my aggravation.

Advice like get a piece of gum and stick it on a stick and drop it down the window. Gum, hard to come by in a group heavily into dentures. A stick, equally hard to find in a concrete shopping area. And the so-called window opening? Merely a sliver of air space.

A reedy voice calls out to us, "How come you don't carry an extra key? I do."

"Gimme permission to smack her," Ida says under her breath.

The girls hover close to me, waving their hands helplessly.

"But how do you know it's Denny?" Bella whispers behind my head. The girls can't get over the bombshell I threw at them. I can't get over that we are trapped here in this stupid minimall.

"Remember how Maureen died?" I answer, unable to hide my irritation at them.

"Maureen?" Sophie asks, befuddled. "She's been dead, what—six, seven years? What's she got to do with this?"

"Maybe everything."

I have sent Evvie back to the theater to call the auto club. I'm waiting anxiously for her to report back.

Everyone's favorite suggestion is to get a hanger, bend it and push it through. So where do we get a hanger at this time of night? I gaze longingly at Betty's Better Dresses, which is five feet from where I'm standing, and count all the hangers through the locked store windows.

I am desperately trying to control my temper, impatience, and anxiety, but I'm not doing too well.

"I knew we shoulda listened to Hy. He told us to get a car phone," Sophie says, hitting me on my back. "Single women need a car phone to be safe."

"And where would the car phone be right now?" I say icily. "In the *locked car*, that's where!"

"Then we shoulda got a cell phone," Bella whines. "But no, you have to hate progress. And besides, my feet are hurting."

Evvie returns, looking dejected. "Auto Club said forty-five minutes, give or take."

"Then maybe we should call a policeman," says Bella.

"Yeah," Ida says bitterly, "I can just hear us on the nine-one-one. Emergency. Send a cop quick. Tell him to bring a hanger."

Bella continues worriedly, "Maureen died of a heart attack, didn't she?"

"But don't you remember," I say, "she was eating a piece of steak and they thought maybe she choked on it?"

"So?"

"God. I can't believe we didn't remember this before. Food. Isn't this all about food?"

And another, "So?" This from Ida.

But Sophie is finally starting to get it. "Wait a minute...she was holding the phone when they found her. *Oy vay!*"

"Do you remember the date?"

"Who can remember that far back?" Bella says.

"I don't mean the actual date. I mean the event."

Evvie makes the connection. "Oh, my God, it was the night before her birthday!"

"Yes! I'm so stupid! Why didn't I remember?"

"Cause your memory is shot, that's why," adds Evvie helpfully.

Every minute that passes frightens me. I need to know what's happening back at Lanai Gardens!

38

No Way to Treat a Mother

Denny stands in the middle of the living room, unable to catch his breath.

No matter how hard he tries not to look at it, he can't help himself. Slowly, he turns to face his mother's portrait. He feels her eyes following him everywhere. He wants to get out of there, but he can't get his feet to move. It's like those dreams he has when his mother is chasing him with the clothesline that she used to use to tie him to his bed. His feet would go numb and she would always catch him and do all those terrible things to him.

The phone rings. Denny jumps, terrified. Sweating freely now, he stares at the phone hypnotically. Stop ringing, he begs. Make it stop ringing. He puts his hands over his ears but he can still hear the ringing. Save me, he mutters under his breath. Someone save me. Finally, unable to stand it anymore, he answers.

"Hello..." He is shaking so hard he can barely stand. "But it's not ten o'clock...."

"I know I'm a bad boy.... I know...."

"In the kitchen? When did you put them there?"

"Please, no, don't make me..."

"I can't.... I can't...."

"Yes, Mama. Right now."

Denny hangs the phone up and walks into the kitchen where a small basket, prettily decorated with a lace cloth, sits there just where she said it would be. And right next to it are his keys, the ones he lost.

Slowly, sickly, he moves back into the living room. He can feel his anger and his impotence rising up in him like bile in his throat. His hand reaches for his toolbox nearby. He opens it and grabs for a screwdriver. In rage he leaps for the portrait and gouges out his mother's face. "No more... no more..." he sobs.

39

Death by Poppy Seed

I keep looking at my watch as if that will make any difference. The cab we called still hasn't arrived. Neither has the auto club. By now we've lost our audience, and the minimall is nearly deserted. The girls are huddled in a doorway, shivering in the cool night air.

I am beside myself. There is still no answer at the Feders, only the same busy signal. Why can't I reach Harriet? Something is very wrong.

I've called Irving. No answer. He is already asleep, early as usual. With the phone locked away from Millie. I tried Tessie. Not home. I better call Hy...

A trio of teenagers walk by. They clank from all the metallic piercings they have hanging from various body parts. Their boom box is booming some ugly-sounding rap.

"Hey, old ladies," one of them calls sarcastically, "waitin' for some action?"

They are very big and scary, but I am at my wit's end. "Yes," I say, ignoring the innuendo. "Do you know how to break into a car?"

"Are you crazy?" Ida shrieks.

"No, desperate," I tell her.

The boys stop, amused. You can see it in their faces. This ought to be fun. "It'll cost ya," says a huge lump of lard with black and white zebra stripes painted across his bald head.

"How much?" I ask, trying to keep cool while my legs are shaking.

Ida hides behind me. "Don't talk to them. Maybe they'll go away."

"Twenty large," the purple-haired one says, sneering.

I attempt a sneer myself. "How about five small?"

The girls are gasping, all of them now crowding behind me.

Zebra Stripes erupts into laughter.

What few people are still around quickly move as far away as they can.

Bella tugs at me, terrified. "Tell them we don't need them," she whimpers.

I shrug her off. "But we do."

The third one, with dreadlocks and a lime green crocheted skullcap, walks over and surveys the car with a most professional air. I think he's the leader. "Give the ladies a senior discount, Horse," he says, and that starts another outburst of hilarity.

"Fifteen," says Purple Hair, aka Horse.

"Shame on you," says Dreadlocks. "Ain't you got no old grandma?"

With that, he whips out a very thin strip of metal

and instantly snakes it through the narrow window opening. Within two seconds I hear the door locks unlatch. And just as fast, the metal is back in his pocket and his hand is outstretched. Even though my own hands are shaking, I get a ten and a five out of my wallet and hand it to him.

They walk off, laughing. "You are one hella hip granny," Dreadlocks calls back.

"Thanks for your help," I answer as I notice both the taxi and the auto club driving into the minimall.

Bella waves her little fingers at the boys and gaily calls out, "Thanks for not killing us."

As he walks out the door and starts to cross the parking area, Denny can smell the sweetness of the poppy-seed rolls he carries.

At Esther's door, he stops. He opens it with his master key and walks inside.

The nighttime silence at Lanai Gardens is abruptly shattered by agonizing screams. Doors and windows are flung open or, in most cases, cautiously cracked, and faces peer out. The braver ones come out and lean over the balconies to see what's happening.

Esther Feder is running, falling, then crawling down the middle of the street. Esther can walk!? is the first shocked response. But what's wrong with her? She is gagging, clutching her stomach and grabbing onto cars for support.

"Help me," she cries.

Half walking, half running behind her is Denny,

crying. And oddly, he seems to be carrying a basket of rolls.

She falls down as her legs no longer support her.

"Poison," she screams as Denny reaches her. "Denny...you...? Why, why?"

He stands over her helplessly, sobbing now. "She made me do it," he says as he drops to his knees beside her.

"I am a dead woman," Esther Feder cries and then falls silent as paralysis sets in and she can no longer move. Only her eyes stare in horror at Denny as her life slowly drains from her body.

And it is just at that moment that the girls and I arrive home.

40

The Cop and the Private Eye

I walk downstairs, exhausted and depressed from lack of sleep, to where Detective Langford is waiting for me in front of the Feder apartment. He called half an hour ago to tell me he was on his way over, saying he wanted to "touch base" with me.

It is chilling to see the yellow crime scene tape across their door. Poor Harriet. She's gone to work because she can't stand being in the house. I can still see her agonized face when she was called home from the hospital three nights ago. I can still hear her shriek as she threw herself down over her mother's dead body lying on the concrete.

"My fault," she kept sobbing.

My fault. I think bitterly. *My fault. God help me.* Had I stayed home, Esther would still be alive. I would have stopped Denny in time. *Woulda, coulda, shoulda,* as Sophie would say.

The girls are hovering on the second-floor balcony of my building. They are itching to come down and talk to Langford, but too shy to do it on their own. When they see me, the scampering downstairs begins.

Pretending not to see them, I greet Morrie Langford.

"How's Denny?" I need to ask.

"He's still being evaluated at the hospital."

The girls all titter their hellos and Langford politely acknowledges them. I wave them away. They ignore me. Evvie moves in closer. "He must be so frightened," she says.

"I'm sure they have him on meds to keep him calm."

Ida is appalled. "Why is everyone so worried about him? He's a killer."

Morrie starts to walk toward the pool area. "I want to show you something," he says.

We follow him down the path, past the duck pond, and over the bridge that takes us to Denny's garden. The girls follow behind us, keeping their distance.

"With their families' permission we've exhumed the bodies of your friends Selma and Francie. And you were right. Poisoned, both of them." The news hits me hard in the pit of my stomach. Even though I've always suspected it, finally knowing the truth is a jolt. I hear the girls gasp.

We reach Denny's garden.

"And here's where he got his poison." Langford leans over and plucks one of those beautiful white flowers I'd noticed only recently. "Right in front of everyone's eyes."

Evvie can't stand being left out anymore. She

moves in right next to us. "A pretty flower? How is that possible?"

"A deadly poisonous one, Mrs. Markowitz."

Sophie now closes the gap and is breathing down Langford's neck. "You mean, he made them eat a flower?" She is incredulous. "Francie wouldn't eat a flower."

Bella, scampering over, is in tears. "How could he do it? He loved Francie!" Sophie puts her arms around Bella to comfort her.

"How could a flower turn into poison?" Ida closing in fast, so as not to be left out, demands to know.

"I won't go into details," Langford answers, "but it isn't too difficult to crush the leaves and boil them down into a substance he could put in their food."

Sophie stares at the blossoms that have overwhelmed the garden and caused such tragedy. "Who even knows what they are. I've never seen such things before."

Langford answers her. "They're called oleander."

"I just don't get it," Evvie says. "Denny was a happy man. He had a good life here. He was kind to everyone and everyone liked him. What set him off?"

"Hopefully the doctors will figure it out." Langford starts walking back. "There's something else I want to show you. Maybe it will help you see how disturbed Denny was."

We walk back to our buildings and, with our backs to the Feder apartment, now stand in front of Denny's place, where the other crime scene tape is draped.

Langford moves the tape and unlocks the door. "I have to warn you—" he starts to say, but we've already hurried inside.

At first we can't see anything because all the blinds are drawn, but we can smell something, and the smell is awful. We quickly cover our mouths and noses with our hands.

"Gott im Himmel!" Ida is gagging. "What died in here?"

Langford turns on the lights and we look around, horrified. At the garbage, the filthy dishes, the overwhelming clutter, the candles and the black crepe around Maureen's portrait. And in the center of the portrait, Maureen's face, mutilated beyond recognition.

If I were Catholic, I would cross myself. Instead I utter a silent prayer for poor, sick Denny. Sophie and Bella are crying and holding onto each other. Evvie and Ida are trying hard to be brave.

Langford faces us. "You all knew him, and I assume you've been in his apartment. Was it always like this?"

Everyone is shaking their heads. "Never!" Evvie says vehemently. "He was always proud of how well he kept it up and how neat he was. Even his garden tools and his repair kits were always in good order."

Ida continues, "But we haven't been in here in a very long time."

After a lengthy silence, I ask if we can get a cleaning crew in. That is, if they're through searching.

"We'll be finished after tomorrow," he says. "The doctors will be here to see this, and it will be part of Denny's evaluation."

"He went crazy, that poor boy," Bella whispers. "And nobody knew."

I feel defeated. I look at this abomination. I don't want to believe Denny is a killer. How can I deny his guilt now?

41

M Is for Mothers
and Murder

It's a fairly nice memorial service and a very large turnout at the clubhouse considering that Esther Feder did not have any friends. Oh, everyone manages to find some kind words to say for Harriet's sake, but you can sense the strain.

Residents of all six phases of Lanai Gardens show up and no wonder, considering all the excitement. They are still reeling from the information that is slowly trickling out day by day. They really were murders! And Denny Ryan, the killer! That such a thing could happen here ...

All of us from Phase Two are attending the service. Enya is seated by herself as always. I can see her lips moving, saying Kaddish for the dead. Irving brought Millie with Yolanda's help. Millie is going though a bad stage and Yolanda is becoming indispensable to Irving. He adores her now, and she truly has become a member of his family.

Tessie is greatly subdued now that she realizes

her beloved friend Selma had indeed been murdered. And everyone loved Francie, so that realization is a bombshell. It was bad enough thinking of losing her to a heart attack, but cold-blooded murder . . .

All in all, it's a solemn ceremony and it's not just Esther being mourned here today.

I am ashamed to say I am sitting in the back row, not wanting Harriet to see me. How can I face her feeling all this guilt?

The service is over, and as we all leave the clubhouse, I hear my name being called. Twice.

I hadn't even realized he was there, but it's Jack Langford calling as he walks toward me.

At the same time Harriet speaks my name as well. Alas, she reaches me before Jack does. Jack backs away. I shrug, indicating to him that I am trapped. He pantomimes phoning me. I nod and he leaves.

I look around for the girls, needing a buffer, but they are here and there chatting with neighbors, busily filling in the blanks for those who came in late to our tragedy.

"Can we talk, Gladdy?" Harriet asks in a plaintive tone. I'd rather not, but how can I say no?

"Of course," I say.

We stroll along the path leading back toward our building. We pass Denny's garden, and I quickly avert my eyes from the sight of those beautiful, deadly flowers. Harriet stiffens, so I assume Detective Langford has told her the results of the autopsy.

We find a bench under a palm and sit down. We are silent for a few moments.

Finally she says, "I desperately need to talk to somebody, and you are the one I thought of."

"I'm here and I'm listening."

"I am so angry at myself," Harriet says. "God help me, it's all my fault Mom is dead. And I'm going to have to live with that the rest of my life."

I stare at her in amazement. Here I'm bracing myself for her condemnation of me and she says *she's* at fault? "*You?* It's me. I failed you terribly. It's *my* fault your mother died," I blurt out. "If only I'd been there ..."

She takes my hand in hers. "Oh, no, don't blame yourself. You tried to warn us. It was one thing to talk about the others getting killed just before their birthdays, but I never believed it would happen to Mom. Never. How could I have been so blind?"

"No one wants to believe the worst. It's only human."

"But I sat in meetings with you, and we even talked about the coincidences with Denny. Then I just denied it all. I'll never forgive myself."

Poor Harriet. She was saying all the things I'd been saying to myself. We both made so many mistakes.

"I hope in time we can forgive ourselves," I say.

"Dear God. I hope so." She turns to me and I can see the anguish in her eyes. "You know what's the saddest part of all? That she pretended to be crippled so I'd stay with her. And I had to find out this way—the way she died—running down the street. Oh, my poor mama, didn't she know? I would never have abandoned her!"

"I'm so sorry, Harriet."

Again we sit silently, then Harriet speaks once

more. "I've made a decision, Gladdy. I'm putting the apartment up for sale. Ring up another victory for Mr. Sleaze." Harriet chokes on a laugh at her sorrowful attempt at a joke.

"I'm sorry to hear that."

"I can't live here anymore. Everywhere I turn I see Mom's face. I feel haunted."

"Listen. You don't need to convince me. Of course you should move. And to someplace cheerful, where there are younger people and especially younger men..." I attempt a smile at that. "You've given up all these good years for your mother; now it's time to live your own life."

I hear these tired old clichés coming out of my mouth, but that's what clichés are—truths retold.

Harriet reaches over and kisses my cheek. "I knew you'd understand. I just didn't want to hurt everyone's feelings. You've all been so good to me. And oh, how I'll miss all of you."

We shed a few tears and we both feel better.

We continue our walk, hearts lightened, and Harriet asks my advice about condos and where to live and is open to my suggestions, and I am more than happy to try to help her.

Harriet has forgiven me, but I'm not sure I can forgive myself.

42

Feeling the Blues

The girls are cranky. I won't take them anywhere.
Sophie insists her cupboard is empty. Ida must
get to the bank. Evvie needs to get to the newspaper
office. I just want everyone to leave me alone.

Sophie humphs at that with, "Who do you think
you are, Garbo?"

Ida snaps, "Just because you're a big shot,
you're too good for us now?"

And Evvie adds her bit. "What's eating you?"

I don't know. Yesterday I felt fine. Today I feel
terrible and I don't know why. I have no patience for
the girls. I take my phone off the hook. The designated driver, wallowing deep in depression, is not
available.

I need to think. I sneak out and go to my sanctu-
ary, the library.

No easy getaway. The celebrity must be waved
at and yoo-hooed at and smiled at by one and all, in
homage paid to the smart person who realized there

was a killer in our midst. Just what I need when I am feeling so confused. I try to avoid everyone, but good old Hy grabs me by the arm as I reach my car. Needless to say Lola is her usual five steps behind.

"My fedora's off to you, Glad. You got some kind of balls. Who knows how many more of you old broads he would have iced."

"Gee, thanks, Hy. I'm glad I lived long enough for such a glowing compliment."

"Lola and me, we knew there was something hinky about old Denny. We would have said something but we didn't want to get the kid in trouble."

"I commend your sensitivity." I sidle past him and get into my car.

"Didja hear the latest dumb blonde joke?"

"Some other time." I rev up the engine, hard, and Hy nervously moves out of the way. Taking my opportunity, I quickly drive off.

At the library, my two buddies greet me warmly. I almost relax in their comforting demeanor. They, of course, have heard the news—the grapevine is working overtime. They want to know what they can do to help. But there is nothing. I confess my agony over avoiding dealing with Denny when I knew he was emotionally in trouble.

"All the symptoms of a breakdown were there right in front of me. Why didn't I act? I have no excuse."

Conchetta pours me the inevitable coffee. "Hey, maybe it's because you're only human. Or maybe you can't take care of the whole world all by yourself. The girls are enough of a handful for one person, don't you think?"

"Or maybe it's because I'm getting old and

careless. The damn synapses work slower now. It takes forever to react in time."

Barney hands me a doughnut. "Don't go there. It's not true. You made an error in judgment."

"Esther is dead. Harriet's lost her only relative. And Denny's life is over. I don't call that an error. I call that a tragedy."

"I don't mean to belittle your pain," Conchetta says, "but can't you take this to the next level and maybe you'll feel better? It's over. The killings are stopped."

"I've tried to tell myself the same thing, but it doesn't work. Something still feels out of whack."

I pace agitatedly up and down along the shelves of books as Conchetta and Barney watch me with concern. Books, my old friends, are of no comfort to me now.

"What's bothering you?" Conchetta asks.

"Something. But I don't know what."

"Quick! What pops into your head?" Barney asks. "Don't think, just say it!"

I wheel around and face the both of them.

"It's too damn pat!"

I surprise myself at my intensity and at the words that jump out of my mouth so totally unexpectedly.

My friends watch me, waiting, as in my mind I feel a settling.

"It's not over," I say quietly, and I feel the tight muscles in my back begin to loosen.

43

To Sleep, Perchance to Dream

What a nightmare! It jolts me up from a deep sleep. It's so strong that I find myself sitting bolt upright in bed, heart pounding, body sweating.

I was dreaming about two people dressed as ninja assassins, standing in the middle of Oakland Park Boulevard. Having a tug-of-war. And what a tug-of-war it was! I recognized Denny holding the rope at one end, but his opponent's face was fuzzy and unrecognizable. The rope was made of a daisy chain of white oleander flowers. I remember thinking *How pretty,* until I realized that they were entwined around dead bodies! Selma was there. And Francie and Greta and Esther. But then there was Maureen, and Enya's husband and children who were killed in the Holocaust. And there was Enya on her knees, praying. I could hear her whisper. Injustice, she was crying. Injustice.

It is when the dead bodies all turn to me and

240 • Rita Lakin

open their eyes accusingly that I catapult into wake-fulness, and fast. Wow!

Someone once told me that if I had a problem I wanted solved, all I had to do was state it before I fell asleep. And by next morning I'd have my answer. Well, last night I went to bed and framed my question, and asked my subconscious to tell me the answer.

I got my answer; now all I have to do is inter-pret it.

Forget about falling back to sleep. I am wide awake and my mind is going a hundred miles an hour. I make a pot of coffee, but it takes two pots to keep me going. Another night of hardly any sleep. I'll be a wreck tomorrow, but who cares.

So I pace and think and pace and think and talk to myself out loud. I can feel the pieces falling into place. Click. Click. Click. And then I make notes and I'm still at it when it gets light.

I remember my grandchildren, when they were small, loving Bugs Bunny and that funny thing he always said when he made a huge mistake. Well, Bugs, so did I. Boy, did I make a left turn at Albuquerque.

I go over and over my conclusions, and now all I have to do is prove them. Not easy, that. But I know I'm right. Everything fits. I have to tip an imaginary hat to my opponent, tugging at the other end of Denny's oleander rope. I have to give the devil its due.

Plain and simple, *I've been had!* All of us have.

First things first. I have to be patient until Detective Langford gets to his office. I need to ask him one question.

Then I need to get permission to visit Denny. He has all the answers. Only he doesn't know it.

Look out, world. Here comes Gladdy Gold, Private Eye. On track at last!

44

Poor Denny

I'll bet Detective Morgan Langford hadn't had time for his first bitter cup of police department coffee before my call came in. I guessed right and he tells me so.

"How come you're calling and how come this early?"

I'm still rattling around in my bathrobe. I'm too wired to bother getting dressed. "I couldn't sleep. There's an important question I have to ask."

"Not to worry. Everything's moving along smoothly. I told you I'd call and keep you in touch."

I can tell from his voice he is giving me only half his attention. He's probably looking through his day's workload. "That's not the question. Did Denny actually confess to killing Esther and the others?"

"Sort of."

"What kind of answer is that?"

"He admitted his dead mother made him do it, but he doesn't remember doing it."

"Doesn't that answer bother you?"

"Not really. Many psychotics admit to hearing voices."

"Yes, but don't they usually remember doing the killing as well?"

"Maybe it's too traumatic to remember. So he shuts that part out."

"Believe me, if you had known Maureen Ryan, *she's* what he'd want to shut out."

"Why is this suddenly so important?"

"I need a favor, Morrie. Excuse me—Detective. I need to see Denny. As soon as possible."

Now I have his full attention. "That's not a good idea. He isn't in very good shape."

"Why? Didn't the marks from the rubber hoses fade away yet?"

"Very funny, Mrs. Gold."

"*I* thought so." I feel like I'm losing him again. He's covering the phone and talking to someone who's come in and I can hear him rattling through papers. "As your possible future stepmother, I'm asking you to do this for me."

"What did you say?"

I knew that would grab him. "This may change everything. I can't tell you any more right now."

"No, not that. Go back to what you said before that."

I play dumb. "What did I say? I forgot."

Langford sighs, and I know I nagged him into giving in. Besides, he owes me. And he knows it. "Maybe you could help. All we got out of him was gibberish. Maybe he'll tell *you* the truth."

"He's already told you the truth, Morrie. At least the truth as he understands it. Denny Ryan has never uttered a lie in his life."

"All right. All right. I'm a busy man here. I'll arrange it and let you know when."

The sight of Denny makes me want to cry. This big man, in such a small, narrow hospital room with bars. He looks like a big bear with all the stuffing knocked out of him, frightened and confused.

"Did you come to take me home, Mrs. Gold?" he asks plaintively.

"I can't do that right now, Denny, but I do want to help you." Carefully I put my hand in my purse and turn on my tape recorder. I have a feeling I'm going to need it later. Forgive me, Denny.

"I don't like it here."

I look around at the plainness and the coldness. "I don't blame you."

"There's no window. How can I see the sunshine? I need the sunshine."

"I know you do."

"Why am I here?"

"Don't you know?"

"Because of Mama, isn't it?"

Denny is seated on his narrow cot, his legs spread wide, his hands splayed across his knees. How does this poor man sleep at night in that tiny bed? I sit down opposite him on the edge of the one small chair in the room. Our knees are almost touching.

"Is that why you've been so upset lately? Because of your mother?"

He hangs his head, ashamed. "Yes. I'm sorry I've been so mean to you."

"It's all right. I know you didn't mean it. Tell me about your mother."

"That's what those policemen kept asking me, and I told them but they wouldn't believe me. They got me all mixed up. Why did she have to come back? Everything was so good."

"I believe you, Denny. When did she come back?"

"The night before her birthday."

Bingo! I'm excited but I don't show it. I make a quick calculation in my head. Two weeks before Selma died. "How did she come back?"

"She called me on the phone. Ten o'clock in the night."

"The phone? Just like that?" I keep my chatter nonthreatening and interested.

"Yeah. I just finished watching the wrestling show. I like that show and they really don't hurt each other, it's just for pretend." He smiles, then remembers where he is. "And the phone rang and I answered thinking maybe one of the ladies had a problem. Like last week Mrs. Fox thought she had a cricket in the bedroom but it was only the smoke alarm. She was so funny. When I came in she was standing on a chair and hitting the alarm box on the ceiling with a broom and trying to kill the cricket." He laughs hard at that and I join him.

His face turns ashen. "But it wasn't one of my ladies. It was *her*!" He reaches for a cup of water and his hand is shaking. "At first I didn't believe it, she sounded so funny. I could hardly understand her. I thought somebody was playing a joke, like Mr. Hy

Binder likes to fool me. But she said it was her and what did I expect, she was calling from a billion miles away. I said yeah, yeah, like they got phones in heaven. Then she got mad and yelled at me and called me Dennis like she used to when she was mad, and said I better pay attention because she came back for a reason."

My God, I think to myself. This is not of heaven, but of hell.

"And she tells me the names of the CDs on my shelf over my bed and the plants I got in my garden. I didn't have CDs or a garden seven years ago. How does she know all this stuff I ask her? She tells me she can see me plain from up there. She sees everything I do and hears everything I say." He lowers his head in misery. "She always could. Know everything I did."

"Why did she come back, Denny?"

"Because I killed her, that's why."

Oh, no, I think. Not that. "Why do you say you killed her?"

"Because I had this fight with her. I got mad because she wouldn't let me go to the movies, so I ran out. Then Mama ate that steak and choked on it. It was all my fault, because I wasn't there."

"But you didn't kill her. It was an accident." Such guilt this boy suffered all these years.

"She said I had to pay."

"How?"

"By killing all the nice ladies. Every night she called me. Every single night 'til it made me sick and she just kept calling me and she wouldn't let me alone. And then she left that rat in my bed. I didn't want to do those bad things, but she made me. I loved Miss Francie." Denny starts to cry.

"Did you kill them, Denny?" I can hardly breathe waiting for his answer.

"She said I did it when I was sleeping, but I don't remember. But I must have, 'cause they're dead, aren't they?"

"The night Mrs. Feder died, tell me about it."

"Mama called and told me I had to go over there right now and carry some rolls she left in the kitchen. I didn't even know there were rolls in the kitchen, but there they were in a little basket."

Denny puts his head in his hands, shaking hard, as if to rid himself of the demon mother inside.

I take his hands in mine and hold them. "It's all right, Denny. Tell me what you did then."

He looks at me with tormented eyes. "I didn't do nothing. I just stood there in the kitchen. I didn't want to hurt Mrs. Feder. But if I didn't..." His eyes tear.

"How long did you stay there?"

"Maybe an hour. But I had to do what Mama said. So I went outside. I looked careful each way— she said make sure nobody saw me—so I went across the street and went inside, and just then Mrs. Feder started screaming she was dying and she ran in the street and I ran out after her."

"Did she eat any of the rolls you brought?"

"No. Like I told you, I just got there."

"The garden, Denny. I need you to tell me something."

Denny frowns, worried. "Everything's gonna die if nobody waters."

"I promise your garden will be taken care of.

The white flowers, Denny, where did you buy them?"

He smiles. "Aren't they pretty, those whacha-macallits? I always like to read the little tag that comes on them, but those flowers never got a tag."

"They're called oleander."

I watch his face for a reaction and there is none. He doesn't have a clue. "They didn't have a tag when you bought them? That's unusual."

When he answers me, my heart skips a beat.

"I didn't buy them. They were a present."

"From whom, Denny?" I know the answer, but I need to hear him say it. When he does, I send a silent prayer to God to thank Him.

I promise Denny he'll be home soon, and that's a promise I intend to keep.

45

Scavenger Hunt

I call an emergency meeting of the Gladiators and they march promptly up to my apartment where the coffee and bagels are already waiting. Why is it nothing can be done without food as part of the proceedings? The girls are all atwitter. Anything out of the ordinary is met with eagerness.

I tell them we are going on a scavenger hunt.

"You mean like when we were kids?" Evvie asks me.

"Something like that." I don't dare tell them about my visit to Denny and its result. It would blow them away, and within five minutes, since they are incapable of keeping a secret, everyone in the building would hear about it. That mustn't happen. What we accomplish today is crucial.

I'm encouraging their nosiness. As Sherlock would say, the game is afoot. I dramatically announce that by the end of today they will be amazed and dumbfounded. It will be a day they will never forget. I can sense them fairly drooling with anticipation. You want to know the secret of staying alive? Stay curious.

Well, that sure got their juices going and they started a barrage of questions, like what are we doing and why and where and when, which I immediately nip in the bud.

"Listen, dear friends and sister. Later for questions and answers. Now we have work to do."

I hand them each a sheet of paper and they read what's written with puzzled looks.

"But what does it mean? . . ." starts Bella, and I shush her.

"Just do everything it says to do, and over dinner tonight you'll find out. I know it doesn't make sense right now. It will later."

"But—" says Sophie.

"No buts."

"I really, really need to ask this question," Sophie says pleadingly. "Where are we eating?"

"No place you've ever eaten before."

They are all so excited they can hardly contain themselves. "At least give us a name," says Bella.

I smile. I am on such a high today that I feel silly. So, I improvise. *"Dinner at the Homesick Restaurant."*

"Huh," says Ida. "I never heard of it."

"Or you can join me at *My Dinner With André.*"

"Who's he? You're bringing a stranger?" asks Sophie.

"You might like the *Fried Green Tomatoes at the Whistle Stop Cafe.*"

"That sounds awful," says Ida.

"Or how about *Dinner at Eight*?"

"But you said five," Bella wails in confusion.

I stop. This is cruel, since they haven't a clue to what I'm talking about. Except for Evvie, who's beginning to catch on and is watching me as if I've got a screw loose. "I'm only teasing. You'll learn the name of where we're eating when we get there. Come on, get in the spirit of the game."

The girls study their sheets of paper.

"I need the applesauce crumb cake in an hour," I say to Ida. It's her finest creation. "Can you do it?"

"Of course," she says proudly.

"But we already talked to Meals on Wheels," Evvie reminds me.

"Go in person. That might jog their memories," I say.

"How are we supposed to get around? Are you driving us?" Ida demands to know.

"No, I have my own errands to run. Take taxis."

"Taxis?" Sophie, the cheapskate, asks in horror. "Spend our own money?"

"All right," I say wearily. "I'll pay you back."

"I see a lot of walking on this one," Ida points at her paper.

"A little real exercise won't kill you."

"Every phone booth?"

"Every single one."

"So, what's the prize?" Sophie asks. "For winning the scavenger hunt."

Evvie shakes her head. "We're all doing this together, Soph. There's no winner."

"Oh."

"Believe me," I tell them, "you'll all be winners. Now the most important thing of all: Tell nobody anything! Talk to no one. And I mean *no one*. Not one person! Can you do that?"

I get a chorus of yeah, sures.

"This is a matter of life and death. No mistakes this time." This is my only reference to the Kronk cremation catastrophe and they hear me loud and clear. Now I get steady nods of assent.

"Promise. Swear to me on your children's heads."

This is the most serious of all promises, and one by one they swear.

And we are off and running.

Book Soup

The girls haven't stopped talking about food the whole drive over here. Visions of pot roasts and chicken livers dance in their heads, so naturally when I stop the car at the Lauderdale Lakes public library they are puzzled. Especially since the library is closed.

I give no explanations. I walk to the back entrance, I knock three times for dramatic effect, and it is unlocked for us by Conchetta. With Barney right alongside. I do the introductions. Conchetta Aguilar and Barney Schwartz meet my girls. They all shake hands, most bewildered. And even more so when Barney identifies them by the books they read that I take out for them.

"Bella," he says. "The lady of the romance novels. Large print. And Evvie and her Hollywood biographies and Ida who likes best-sellers and Sophie who likes *Reader's Digest*."

Evvie beams. She's getting into the spirit of this.

"So that's what you meant when you called off the names of restaurants. They were book titles. And a few movies, too."

I wink at her, but Ida is not pleased. "OK," Ida says, hands on hips. "Just what is going on here?"

"Yeah," says Sophie, whose mind is never far from the subject of food, glaring at me, "I thought we were going out for dinner."

"We *are* out. And we *are* going to have dinner. What we have to do tonight is very private, and this is as private as we can get."

"I brought in food that I cooked at home," Conchetta says cheerfully, leading us into the main reading room. There along the checkout counter are hot plates with an assortment of covered dishes. "I hope you'll like Cuban food."

There is much consternation at this.

"What's Cuban food?" Bella asks nervously.

"Hot and spicy," Barney says mischievously.

Conchetta jabs him. "You know I kept the spices down."

The girls peer suspiciously into each pot as Conchetta lifts the lids and identifies them. "*Potaje de frijoles negros, masa de puerco fritas* with mango sauce, fried plantains and rice, with *boniato* and chimichurri." She opens all but the last.

"I never eat beans," says Ida, recognizing only one word. "They give me the gas."

I grab a plate. "Well, I'm excited here. I can hardly wait to try these."

The girls continue to hang back, except for Evvie who also takes a plate. "Hey, I'm game to try anything. What's a plantain, Conchetta?"

"Like bananas."

"And chimi . . . whatever?"

"That's a green sauce with garlic and lime juice you can dip your bread in. I'll finish translating. The *masa de puerco* is a pork dish. *Boniato* is sweet potatoes. *Mojo* is another sauce. And the *potaje* is a wonderful black bean soup."

So Conchetta, Evvie, Barney, and I pile up our plates, but there is no forward movement from the others.

Barney breaks into laughter first. "Let's put the girls out of their misery," he says as he unveils the contents of the last pot. "Stuffed cabbage, for the less adventurous of the Jewish delegation. Compliments of my mom."

Needless to say there is a rush on the stuffed cabbage.

"Save room for the apple strudel afterwards," he adds, grinning.

As we spread out at the library tables, which Conchetta has set prettily for us with tablecloths and linen napkins, I glance over the pages Barney hands me: their research on oleander. I nod vigorously. "I knew it!" I say victoriously.

"You were right on target. From the time the victims ingest, they go through severe abdominal pain and heart palpitations, paralysis, then death."

"But it takes an hour or so before they die, and that's the big issue here," I say.

The girls look at me, befuddled.

"Isn't it about time you filled us in, Glad?" Evvie asks. "Why are we getting phone numbers of telephone booths and visiting Meals on Wheels?"

"In a moment, the big picture." I smile as I see Bella and Sophie, one by one, taking tiny portions of

Conchetta's food, liking what they taste and coming back for more. Not so Ida, of course. "Did anyone at Meals remember anything?"

"You were right about going to see them," Evvie says. "One volunteer remembered that on the date that Selma died, someone ordered a meal, then at the last minute came in and insisted they better deliver it themselves to a frightened elderly aunt. He remembered it because it never, ever happens that way."

"Good. Good. Could he identify the person?"

Evvie shakes her head. "He didn't think so. All he remembers was someone in a baseball cap and sunglasses."

"But at least we know it happened. And the phone booths? How many did you find?"

"Five of them, between Lanai Gardens and across the street at the Florida Medical Center," reports Sophie.

"Excellent."

"And what about my applesauce crumb cake?" Ida asks. "What on earth was that for?"

"To bribe a chubby bank teller, who loves to eat, to do the unthinkable—give me confidential information. Which she did."

"So, all right already, I'm about to bust from not knowing," Sophie says. "So, tell us already!"

"Since we're in a library, let me tell you all about it—in a story."

47

The Very Sad Story of a
Very Foolish Mother

Six pairs of eyes are riveted on my face. Six sets of ears are listening to my every word. Dinner is forgotten. Even dessert is forgotten. Not a chair is allowed to squeak. Since the earliest campfire, the storyteller has held his audience enthralled as he spun out tales that made the dark a little lighter and life a little clearer. And so I, a storyteller, begin my tale.

"Once upon a time there lived a very foolish old woman. After her husband died the old woman was afraid of being alone. Since she had no one in the world but her daughter, she was determined to make her daughter live with her and take care of her. The daughter didn't want to, so the old lady pretended to be crippled and tricked the daughter into moving in."

I already hear the whispers starting.

"The old woman happened to be quite rich."

"Shush," Evvie hisses.

"But she wouldn't share any of her money with her daughter. This turned out to be her biggest mistake. So what little money the daughter had was what she earned at her job, or what her mother doled out to her. This made the daughter very angry. She couldn't stand her mother, but she pretended to everyone that she loved her. All the while she kept waiting for her mother to die. Her mother boasted how long people in her family lived, and she just kept on living."

There's more whispering and plenty of speculating.

"Be quiet!" Evvie says.

"The daughter finally got tired of waiting." And here I stop for a very long attention-getting pause. Then softly, "So Harriet Feder decided to kill her mother."

Suddenly all movement comes to an abrupt halt. Dead silence. Then all hell breaks loose.

"What!" Evvie cries out.

"Say that again!" Ida says.

"What are you talking?" Sophie asks.

"Why didn't I bring my hearing aid?" Bella whines. "What did she just say?"

"Harriet wanted to kill her mother!" Evvie exclaims.

Ida is about to explode. "Harriet!? But what about Denny? I thought yesterday he admitted killing Esther!"

Sophie is benign about change. "So, today he didn't."

"Oy, could we start all over again?" Bella whines, leaning her good ear in.

"Then who killed the other girls?" Sophie asks.

"She killed them all."

I promised them they would be amazed. And dumbfounded.

"Glad, are you sure?" Evvie asks.

"All the pieces fit. It's the only thing that makes sense."

The uproar and general carrying-on stops abruptly because I start talking again, and they aren't about to miss one single breath of the rest of *this* story.

"But Harriet knew if she killed Esther, no matter how cleverly she did it, she would still be the prime suspect, especially when it would come out eventually that her mother was worth nearly four hundred thousand dollars."

Another round of sputtering.

"Oy gevalt," Bella cries.

"You found that out at the bank, with my applesauce crumb cake!" Ida shrills triumphantly.

I smile. She's got it.

"That's a lot of money, four thousand dollars," Bella says.

"Not four thousand, forty thousand," says Sophie in amazement.

"Everybody needs hearing aids around here," Ida says impatiently. "That was *four hundred thousand*!"

Sophie reaches nervously for her strudel. "Who could have so much money besides a Donald Trump?"

"I am going to smack the next one who opens her mouth!" says Evvie angrily. *"I am trying to hear this!"*

Everyone quiets down. For the moment. I continue.

"So she came up with this idea. What if there was a serial killer loose who was murdering old women, and poor Esther just happened to be one of them? But Harriet decided a phantom serial killer was too risky. It had to be someone who could be caught so that she'd never be suspected. And she found the perfect patsy: simpleminded Denny."

Bella gets so agitated, she falls off her chair. Barney and Conchetta help her back on.

I'm determined not to let anything sidetrack me, and I just keep talking.

"So she did some snooping and found out exactly how Maureen Ryan died. Maureen died while eating food. Died reaching for the phone. Died on the night before her birthday. So Harriet recreated the pattern. The food our unlucky friends would eat would be poisoned. And where would she get the poison? Why, from the oleander that happens to grow in Denny's garden, a plant Harriet gave Denny as a present."

"I still don't know how Francie would eat a flower," Sophie insists.

"My very clever friends, Conchetta and Barney, did some research. Guess what they learned from Harriet's hospital résumé?"

"She used to work in a lab?" Evvie guesses.

"Right on," Barney says. "Toxicology is one of her specialties."

"So the die was cast as to who would be the victims: the next birthdays to come up in Phase Two before Esther's. If you recall, Harriet managed to point out to us how nice it was that Denny made a birthday calendar of everyone in our Phase. Calling our attention to Denny knowing everyone's birthday."

This time Evvie interrupts. "That was when we were clearing out Francie's apartment. She just showed up. And said she was too sad about Francie to go to work."

I nod. "She planted the hint so that I would figure out that it was too coincidental that these women would die in order of their birth dates. Three birthdays came up before her mother's. Selma, then Francie. However, lucky Eileen O'Connor became rightfully nervous, and saved her life by going to her sister in Boca Raton."

"And she doesn't even like her sister," Sophie has to add.

"Greta Kronk, who prowled around at night, probably saw Harriet going in and out of Francie's apartment, so she had to die, too. Then everything was set up for the one murder she was waiting for: her mother."

I am aware that it's very quiet now. I think they're all in shock. I take Denny's tape out of my purse and put it on the table.

"Now she had another problem to solve. How to pin it on Denny. Happy-go-lucky Denny. Who would believe he'd kill anyone? She had to make it look like Denny was having a breakdown. She had to drive him crazy. How? She brought back his awful mother from the grave to haunt him."

"*Jesucristo*," Conchetta says, crossing herself. "The woman is a devil!"

"Maureen is back?" Sophie asks in amazement.

"I never did like that woman," Ida says.

"I went to see Denny yesterday and he told me all about it."

"Wait a minute," Evvie interrupts. "You went to jail without me?" Then she stops, chagrined. "Sorry."

"You can hear it on this tape. Denny, who had been terrified of his mother when she was alive, actually believed she had returned from the dead to frighten him again. Calling him up on the phone every single night and tormenting him."

"Wait a minute," Bella asks. "She could call from heaven?"

Ida snorts. "How do you know it wasn't from hell?"

"Whatever," Bella says, "they're both long-distance. Maybe it was only from the cemetery. That's local. Do you think she used an eight-hundred number?"

"Will you silly twits stop it!" Evvie says. "Maureen is dead. Harriet was making the calls!"

"Oh, so how was I supposed to know that?" Bella says, feeling put upon.

I continue relentlessly. "Harriet called Denny from different phone booths, either near the apartment when she was home so she could sneak in and out quickly, or near the hospital when she was on night shift. She didn't use her home phone because that could be traced."

"The phone booths you sent us to today," Sophie says, finally getting it.

"And so, pretending to be Maureen, she told Denny he had to kill Selma first, then the others. She really did a job gaslighting him."

"I remember that movie," Evvie says, "with

Charles Boyer and Ingrid Bergman. It was named after a light fixture."

"She actually got Denny to believe he did the killings, even though he kept saying he didn't remember. She told him he did it in a trance. Since Esther was going to be the last murder, he had to be caught."

I stop to take a drink. My mouth is dry. The girls are itching to ask questions, but I motion them to wait until I'm finished.

"She had it timed perfectly. She cold-bloodedly fed her mother dinner with poisoned poppy-seed rolls."

Sophie can't stand it. She has to interrupt. "Esther told us she'd never eat food from a stranger!"

"Well, she didn't," says Bella.

"Better she lived with a stranger than that daughter from hell," Ida adds.

"Then later she tells us she had to leave early for the hospital, thus establishing her alibi. She calls Denny, as Maureen, and tells him he must go to Esther's house immediately with the other rolls she left in his kitchen. By that time the poison would have taken effect, Denny would be at the scene of the crime, and we'd be home from the movies in time to catch him."

"But we got home late from the movies—" Evvie starts.

"And let's remember whose idea it was for us to go to that movie," Ida says, arms crossed, brimming with outrage. She mimics Harriet. 'You girls go out and relax. You'll be home just when I'm going to work. We're covered. So have a good time.' That *farbissener*!"

"She needed us to be away from Esther's apartment," Evvie says, feeling awful. "She knew us all too well. I feel so ashamed."

"She conned everybody, Ev. But it turns out this time Denny didn't obey his 'mother.' He stayed home for an hour before he could bring himself to leave. And we were delayed that long getting home. It didn't matter. Denny was caught red-handed leaving her apartment anyway."

Barney pours us all another round of sangria. Bella is fanning herself; the wine is getting to her.

He says, "I'll bet she was in some sweat when the call didn't come in at the hospital at the time she expected, with the sad news about her poor, dear, dead mother."

I continue. "She needed one more element for this vile crime to work. She had to make sure the first deaths were seen as murders and not heart attacks. She certainly couldn't be the one to point that out, and that's where yours truly came in. The next perfect sucker. I began to suspect on my own, but she had to make sure I went down the trail she pointed out, and that explains why Harriet Feder, who never seemed to be able to escape her mother, suddenly was always available. Wherever we were, she turned up. I kept looking for someone whose behavior had changed, and it took me a long time to realize it was Harriet's."

Evvie says, "So that's why she was able to show up in the clubhouse when we had our big meeting."

"And I bet she took her vacation just so she

could keep an eye on us." Ida sniffs with righteous indignation.

"That's how she found out everything we knew," Evvie says.

"She really did have Esther spying on us for her!" says Ida.

"She didn't make any mistakes, did she?" Conchetta asks.

"But she did. She left a piece of the Meals on Wheels package in Selma's apartment," says Evvie.

"No mistake," I say. "That was her way of leading us away from heart attack to someone who came to Selma's apartment to poison her. Someone delivering Meals on Wheels."

"Aha," says Sophie, now seeing it. "She picked up the food, poisoned it, and then delivered it to poor Selma, may she rest in peace."

"I get it," says Ida. "She also left the cake crumbs in Francie's sink. But the cleaning lady cleaned up before you figured that out."

"You can bet she arranged it so that poor Denny would find the bodies, further freaking him out," I add. "Then she points it out to us, the 'coincidence' of Denny having a master key and finding the bodies."

Barney is puzzled. "But why so elaborate a plan? Why not murder the women outright, rather than go to such lengths to make it seem like heart attacks at first?"

Evvie is so excited, she's fairly jumping out of her chair. "Wait a minute. She knew you wanted a body to autopsy, a body that would prove it was murder, yet Harriet's the one who got us to get Greta cremated."

"It was all about timing," I say. "That would have the cops investigating too soon, and that might have gotten in the way of killing her mother. And she couldn't wait until after her mother had died to get us to think about the earlier murders. Suspicion would immediately fall on her. She couldn't take that chance."

Barney is incredulous. "She makes Lizzie Borden seem like an angel."

"Four hundred thousand is a lot of incentive," I say. "Can you imagine her frustration? Year after year knowing she was rich and not being able to get at the money."

We're all exhausted, especially me. We drink our wine and nibble at our dessert, lost in our troubled thoughts.

"What put you on to her, Glad?" Barney wants to know. "I mean I have to hand it to her, it was a perfect plan."

"It was almost perfect. My realizing that Greta Kronk didn't write the last poem, and Denny arriving too late with the rolls, got me thinking. I just could not believe, no how, that Denny could kill anyone. Nor could Denny have written that poem or managed the sophisticated ways she got the poison to each of them. If she hadn't tried to set him up, I might never have figured it out."

"She outsmarted herself. We've got to call Detective Langford," Evvie says, tugging at me. "Right now. Tell him everything."

"Yeah," says Sophie, "put that *kurveh* in jail and let poor Denny out!"

"So why are you waiting?" asks Bella.

Barney says, "I think I know. Everything we've heard tonight—it's all circumstantial."

"What's that mean?" Sophie asks.

"It means even if Langford agrees with us, we can't prove a thing."

"But you said she made a mistake with the poppy-seed rolls," says Evvie.

"Still not proof. It could be argued that Denny made her eat the rolls earlier as well."

"So how is your story going to end?" Bella asks worriedly.

"You aren't going to let her get away with it?" Ida demands.

All eyes look to me for a solution. I've already given this a lot of thought and I share it with all my helpers.

"If we want a happy ending, we're gonna have to do the impossible. We're going to have to make Harriet Feder confess."

My coconspirators look at me as if I'm crazy.

"Why would she do a stupid thing like that?" Evvie wants to know.

"I think I have an idea," I tell them.

48

Now What Do We Do?

Detective Langford and I have been talking for a very long while. He's actually told his switchboard not to interrupt us, although a number of police personnel have looked in the door to get a glimpse of me. Who knows what he's told them, but it can't be too bad, because they're smiling.

He's read my summary of why I know Harriet is the murderer. And listened to Denny's tape. He's questioned me on every single point until I'm hoarse from talking. Finally he stops.

"Gladdy Gold, you are an amazing woman."

"So," I say impatiently, "does that mean you think I'm right or not?"

"I'll tell you what makes me sure you're right. Something you don't even know yet."

"What's that?" I smile. Justified at last.

"Something very odd came up in Esther's autopsy. There were bruises all over her body that were unexplained. The medical examiner wondered if they were self-inflicted, since all the contusions were in places she could get to. Thanks to your very thorough analysis, we know now that Harriet abused her mother."

I gasp, then shake my head and feel such overwhelming sorrow for Esther. "Oh, God, that, too?"

"And for a long time. There were very old bruises as well."

I jump up, agitated. Morrie looks at me, surprised. "Sorry," I say, "you really threw me with that."

I walk around the room to calm myself. There's a wall of black-and-white photos. Morrie at his cop graduation. Morrie posing with a huge marlin that he caught. Morrie and his dad, Jack, and his mom, Faye, circa 1970, arms around one another. Jack with dark curly hair. Yes, I think, I do remember Faye.

"Gladdy, you still with me?"

I turn back to Morrie. "Esther joked to us about being beaten, but of course, we didn't believe her. We thought it was her pathetic attempt to get attention, but it was a cry for help, wasn't it? And Harriet probably beat her even more every time she did that."

"Sad, but probably true."

"Why didn't Esther just give her the damn money?" I cry out, frustrated.

"Probably because she knew Harriet would leave her, and being alone seemed worse to her. We'll never know."

"So what do we do now?"

"You're right. It is circumstantial. We could bring her in for questioning, and what we would get is a poor, grieving daughter, highly insulted and how dare we say such things? She will deny, deny, deny. This kind of woman won't crack because she knows we don't have any proof."

"But what if we do a lineup—the man in Meals on Wheels might identify her."

"But you said that the guy *thinks* he remembers someone in a baseball cap. And he wasn't very sure at that."

"She could have been seen at one of the phone booths."

"We can try asking around, but I'll bet she was very careful. Probably disguised herself there as well."

"What about at the lab? Maybe someone saw her boiling the oleander—" I stop myself. Harriet was never careless. I'm dejected. "We can't let her get away with it."

"Don't give up. Even though the evidence is purely circumstantial, people have been convicted on it. We won't let her walk."

"What can you do?"

"Start a full investigation. We'll follow through on every single piece of information you've given us. Hopefully, we'll get her in time."

"Can you stop the bank from giving her Esther's money?"

"Unfortunately, no. Had it been insurance money, it would have been a different story."

"Unless Esther didn't leave it to her." I know I'm kidding myself. "I'm sure she did."

"We'll find out."

"An investigation could take a long time and she might still get away with it, couldn't she?"

"It's possible."

I shrug. "I may have an idea. I think I could get her to confess."

He takes a long look at me. "And what miracle are you thinking of performing, Gladdy Gold?"

"Think about it. We have a real advantage right now. She has no idea we're on to her. She's happy. She's packing. She's shopping for a new place to live. She's smug. She thinks she fooled us all. Maybe we can catch her off guard."

"How?"

"I may know a way to trap her."

Morrie Langford leans back in his chair, puts his feet up on the desk, and grins at me. "You solved the case and now you're gonna trap the killer. I am very impressed. This I gotta hear."

So I told him.

49

Poor Harriet

"Doesn't it seem like a lot of people are at the pool today?" Harriet asks me as we walk toward the clubhouse.

I answer her in this perky mode I've affected for the occasion. I'm hoping it hides my stark terror. I'm also wearing my brightest orange-peel sundress, hoping color will give me courage. "Just another beautiful day in sunny Florida, and the natives are taking advantage."

I fling a casual wave toward the sunbathers, and a few casually wave back. But most of them ignore us.

"How funny," Harriet says. I glance over to where she's looking, and there are my girls dressed for swimming. Then I realize what she's commenting on. Next to each of their lounge chairs is a peculiar object—a bathroom plunger, a fly swatter, a rolling pin. I groan inwardly. I told them to bring weapons. That's what they brought!

I move along quickly. I don't want her lingering. "You never know when you'll need a fly swatter," I toss back at her.

She catches up to me. "Your friends are so quaint."

Needless to say the usual Muzak is playing over the loudspeaker at full volume.

We pass the pool, make a right at the palm tree, and arrive at the clubhouse.

"Oooh, how sweet," says Harriet, feigning delight, as she sees the huge, garish sign over the door. The girls and their helpers really put their all into it, using lots of Day-Glo colors. It reads, for my taste, low on subtlety:

"Farewell Harriet,
We Hope You Get All You Deserve!"

"We really shouldn't be here 'til everyone arrives for the party; we'll spoil the surprise," I say, all sugary, "but I wanted to give you my gift in private."

"And I can't wait to see it. I really always thought of you as my favorite person."

"Why, thank you. I'm honored."

"It's because you're the only smart one around here."

Or so gullible, Harriet? "No, you're really the smart one."

We go inside, and the girls have done a great job. Multicolored streamers everywhere. Lots of balloons. All kinds of photos. And a great big sign reading, "Good-bye Harriet, So You'll Never Forget Us," and signed by just about everyone in Phase Two.

Harriet puts her hand over her heart. "I am so touched."

She wanders around the room looking at the photos and the pretty little flower baskets made for the tables, while I move around fiddling with this and that.

Finally she turns back to me, eyes wide in anticipation, and I smile with equal brightness.

"So what's this wonderful mysterious gift you're giving me?"

I take a deep breath and plunge in. "Me."

She looks puzzled, and rightly so. "Me, what?"

"Just me. I am giving you the gift of me. Since you've lost that dear, sweet woman, your mother, I am offering to take her place in your heart."

Her voice is getting this teeny-tiny edge. "Gladdy, what are you talking about?"

"Well, you're about to blow this joint and have a wonderful life, and I want to share it with you."

Her eyes are like slits now. "I'm afraid I'm still not following you."

"No, it's *me* wanting to follow *you*. I see us taking trips around the world. I always did want to see Paris. And maybe after that, buying a gorgeous mansion somewhere. I'd like to suggest the Bahamas. That's always been another dream of mine. With four hundred thousand dollars you can buy anything!"

Her hand grips a chair now, very tightly, I notice. She forces out a phony laugh. "Wherever did you get an idea like that?"

"A little birdy told me." I giggle nervously. "A chubby little bird at the bank."

"How dare anyone discuss my personal finances!"

Harriet knows exactly who I mean. "I'll have that fat pig fired!"

Chalk one up for the home team. She isn't denying it. And it's nice to see her temper has a short fuse.

Then she realizes what she's admitted, and pulls up short. "I hope you'll keep my little secret," she says coyly.

"Why on earth would your mother live here if she had all that do-re-mi?" I ask in all innocence.

"My mother was very eccentric. I didn't want anyone to know. It was very embarrassing for me to be here, when we could have gone anywhere. You can see that."

"I certainly can, and now that you are free to do anything you want, I want to share in your fun."

"Will you stop saying that!" She actually stamps her foot.

I smile. She's starting to lose it.

She pulls herself back under control. "You're acting very strangely today, Glad. It's not like you."

"That's 'cause I'm giddy with excitement. I see a chance for me to get out of this dump and live in the manner to which I'd like to get accustomed. After all I did for you, I deserve it."

Harriet is having trouble holding still. She moves erratically around the tables, her fingers beating little tattoos on their surfaces. I can sense she'd like to walk out right now, but she has to find out what I know.

"Just exactly what did you do for me?"

"I helped you get away with murdering your mother." I say it very calmly and I'm proud of myself. Considering my heart is pounding and my stomach is in a knot the size of Chicago. I want out of here myself. It's the memory of Francie, who died for nothing, that keeps me going.

She stops moving and stands very still. I can almost hear the wheels clicking.

"I mean I didn't know I was doing that, but you so cleverly led me down that garden path, and little old me just did everything you wanted me to."

I can't take my eyes off her because I'm scared to death of what she might do. And believe me, she can't take her eyes off me. So I babble on.

"That's just it, you see. You wanted me smart and you wanted me dumb. You can't have it both ways. I needed to be smart enough to pick up all the clues you left for me, so I would come to the conclusion that Selma and Francie had been murdered. It wouldn't do for the medical reports to remain heart attacks. Then you wouldn't be able to kill your mother, who was really the intended victim. You needed a serial killer to take the heat away, because otherwise you'd be the prime suspect."

"You're crazy!" she says, low and ominously.

"No, but speaking about crazy—that was brilliant, the way you brought back good old dead Maureen to drive Denny nuts."

"Denny!" she says, almost snarling. "Who gives a shit about that retard! They should have drowned him when he was born!"

I am shaken by the force of her hatred, but I know I mustn't show it. "Poor, sweet Denny who couldn't kill a mosquito, let alone someone like Francie whom he worshipped! So that's how I finally figured it out—if he didn't do it, you did it. For the money."

Harriet starts toward the door. "I'm walking out of here, you lunatic."

"So, go. What's holding you?"

She stops as I knew she would. "Why are you making this up? What did I ever do to you?"

Now she moves very close to me. I can feel her breath on my skin. She grabs me by the shoulders and shakes me. I hold very still and don't try to resist, though every instinct in me wants to fight her. Or, at least, scream.

"You silly cow!" she hisses in my ear. "Who would ever believe a story like that!" Then she stares into my eyes to see if I'm telling the truth. "Who did you tell?"

I manage to keep my eyes steady. Please, God, let her believe me. "Nobody, yet," I say. "Nobody *ever*—if you take me with you when you leave."

She relaxes her grip and slowly backs away from me. She actually smiles. "So you want to blackmail me, you greedy old fool."

"Something like that," I say, as casually as I can, considering that my jellied knees are about to give way.

"But what about your dear friends, those ugly, stupid women you spend all your time with? How could you bear to leave them?" The fangs are really out now, and her voice is dripping acid.

"Try me. See how fast I pack."

I can feel her analyzing her options. Can she kill me here and now and get away with it? Or should she promise me anything until she can find another Dumpster?

"I don't think so," she says icily. "It's your word against mine. Nobody would believe a senile old fool like you who has nothing to do but read too many murder mysteries."

"They'd believe my proof." I whip out of my pocket a sheet of paper and read: "Five five five-six two four three, five five five-seven seven six three, five five five-five two two eight—need I go on?"

"What the hell's that supposed to be?"

"The phone numbers in the phone booths you used here and next to the hospital to call poor, pathetic Denny every night at ten o'clock. There will be a record of his number being called when I hand it to the police to check."

"That does it!" she shouts, lunging for me. "I've taken enough of your crap!" She knocks me against the wall. I grab at her hair and pull.

"Stop it!" I scream at the top of my lungs, holding on for dear life. "You might have gotten away with beating your mother up all these years, but you won't get away with hurting me!" Instinctively, my eyes look toward the door.

The twisted expression on Harriet's face is terrifying. "Bitch! You're too smart for your own good! Watch me!" She smashes her hand against my mouth and, although I'm in agony, I instinctively bite as hard as I can. She pulls away, shrieking.

"Murderer! Why did you have to kill them that way? Why!?" I shout at her, now crying bitter tears. "They died in such pain!"

Her voice hisses back at me. "Maybe I liked seeing them suffer! Maybe it was *fun* getting rid of you old miserable pieces of garbage! Maybe I was doing society a big favor! Wasting space, still living when you should have died long ago. Who needs you, you pathetic, brain-dead losers. With your goddamn wheelchairs and walkers. With your shriveled-up, useless bodies. Even your families have deserted you. Even they wish you were dead!"

With what little strength I have left, I butt my head into her stomach and ram as hard as I can. With ease, she lifts me away from her and knocks me down on the floor.

"Damn you! You're dead, old lady, you're finished!" she shouts at the top of her lungs.

If ever I heard an exit line, that was it. Practically crawling, I manage to get out the front door as fast as my arthritic knees let me.

And fall into Evvie's arms.

"Come back here, you bitch," Harriet screams, rushing out the door. "I'm not through with you—"

Harriet stops dead in her tracks as she is aware of two things at once. Everyone who was around the pool is now standing in front of the clubhouse. And her voice is reverberating over the loudspeaker: "...through with you..."

I manage to smile, though every bone in my body is hurting. Harriet stares, thunderstruck. Hostile faces stare back at her, and then she sees Detective Langford, off to one side, grimly looking at her. And next to him is Denny Ryan.

"Hey, Harriet," I say.

Harriet whips around to glare at me.

"I'm sure glad Hy finally taught me how to use the PA system."

50

The New Old
(Not an Oxymoron)

Picture this. Time seems to be standing still. Nobody is moving.

I am reminded of a game we used to play when I was a child, called Statues. (Do kids still play that?) The leader would yell "Freeze!" and everyone would stop immediately, caught in some dramatic pose or another. The leader would turn around and there we'd be, statues frozen in time. Who would move first?

Today it will be Evvie.

She turns toward Langford, terribly upset. "Why didn't you go in to help my sister! Harriet could have killed her!"

"No," I interject. "He was right not to. You know I had to go all the way."

"You did a hell of a job," Langford says to me, slowly starting to walk forward, his eyes never leaving Harriet.

And Harriet's eyes never leave him.

"It was too dangerous. It was crazy to try it!" Evvie says.

"But it was the only way, dear Evvie."

"With a lot of help from my acting lessons," she adds, finally relaxing, wanting her due.

"You bet," I say, kissing her cheek.

"Do you need a doctor, Gladdy?" Langford asks me as he continues his move toward Harriet.

"I'm fine, really," say I, the stoic, but boy, will I be black and blue tomorrow morning.

"But did you have to call this place a dump?" Ida whispers.

"Yeah," says Sophie, "and couldn't you put in a nice word for us?"

The crowd parts for Langford as if they are the Red Sea, and he, our Moses. Everyone watches him intently.

"I want a lawyer," Harriet says.

"Why do they always say that?" Bella wants to know.

"Harriet Feder," Langford says, "you are under arrest for the murders of Selma Beller, Francine Charles, Greta Kronk, and Esther Feder..."

There is much murmuring and sighing at these names. Sophie is practically jumping up and down from the drama of it all.

Bella says, "Again like in the movies."

Sophie pokes her. "This is better than the movies. Come on, let's move closer."

Ida, queen of grudges, is enjoying the sight of payback at last. She announces, "I knew it was her all along."

The other three give her a dirty look.

As Langford continues to recite the Miranda

282 · Rita Lakin

warning, the three girls, holding hands and
weapons, move sideways and forward for a better
angle. "I hope he pulls out his gun," Bella says, shivering with anticipation.

"Nazi!"

Everyone looks around.

And there is Enya, eyes wild, rushing toward
Harriet, hands fashioned into claws. "Nazi!" she is
moaning and sobbing. "My *shayner kindlach*, my
Jacov . . . They put my beautiful babies to die. Put
them out of their misery, they said, pushing them
into the ovens. The world would be better off without them, they said. Oh, *Gott im Himmel*! God,
where was God?? Why didn't God stop them! Why
didn't God stop *you*!" The clawed hands stretch to
Harriet's face as if to scratch and tear at it. "*You* are
one of them! *Nazi!*"

But the hands go limp, trembling, impotent.
Harriet looks down on her, pitiless. Enya, finding a
last bit of strength somehow, spits in her face.

With that, she runs off sobbing.

Silence. Everyone is transfixed by what has just
happened. Then someone calls out. "Yes, Nazi!"
And a chorus of people echo the vile word, reaching
for one another for comfort.

"My God!" Ida says. "She never cried. Never!
Not in fifty years!"

Harriet takes a few steps back, wiping at her
face, as the group rage builds.

And suddenly there's Tessie pushing past
Langford, through the crowd to Harriet, who cringes
at the sight of her. Tessie, all two hundred fifty pounds
of her, lifts her arm, opens her hand, and smacks
Harriet's face with a sound as loud as a gunshot.

"This is for my Selma!" she cries.

The crowd, now caught up in the hysteria, goes wild, moving erratically, yelling and calling her names. Harriet, forgetting caution, begins to run across the lawn away from them. I suddenly find myself thinking of a famous story of long ago, Shirley Jackson's "The Lottery," about a public stoning. Is it turning into that?

"Stop!" Langford shouts at the crowd. Frustrated, because he can't push through the mass of elderly folks, he is stuck.

Utter chaos. "Somebody do something!" A voice in the crowd yells. "Don't let her get away!"

The crowd is now speeding up in Harriet's direction.

"And they're off!" Sol Spankowitz shouts, elbowing Irving as if they were at the starting gate at their beloved Hialeah.

The three Gladiators go rigid in shock as Harriet heads right for where they are standing.

Ida punches Sophie. "Spread out! Block her! Move!"

"*A klog iz mi!*" Sophie cries. "And me in my flip-flops!"

Puffing away on short, stubby legs, disregarding osteoporosis and every other ailment, the girls spread out and take blockade positions. With weapons aloft, they prepare to attack. Sophie wields her toilet plunger. Bella, her fly swatter. Ida, her rolling pin. Ida, in her usual choler, shouts, "So we're ugly and stupid, are we, you ... you ugly, revolting ..."

But they are no match for Harriet, who lifts hundred-pound weights at the gym. She plows through them, knocking them away as if they were bowling pins. Bella is down, still gripping her swatter. The other "weapons" go flying, but amazingly Sophie and Ida manage to cling to Harriet like a couple of swamp leeches. Harriet keeps running, unable to shake them, dragging them behind her as Sophie hangs on to the tail of her blouse and Ida clutches the belt of her pants suit.

Langford is trying to find an opening, but by this time the Red Sea has closed and he is falling farther behind. "Stop! Everyone stop!" he calls. "Let me through!"

Exhausted, Sophie can no longer hold on, and she falls by the wayside, plopping down like a rag doll. Evvie reaches her and, without breaking stride, gets her to her feet and pulls her along.

The crowd of seniors, giving it their all, is still trying to catch up, but at their ages, and physical conditions, and those old legs—not to mention the metal walkers—they don't stand a chance.

Ida, the bulldog, is still clutching the back of the belt of Harriet's pants suit. Her feet are being dragged along, her body almost scraping the lawn, as Harriet tries to shake her off. But she's gamely hanging on, working like an emergency brake and slowing Harriet down a little.

I look for Langford, but he's now on the ground under Tessie, who accidentally tripped over him, God help him.

Sol, still at the track, announces, "Harriet, carrying a one-hundred-ten-pound handicap, is four lengths ahead. Langford is blocked at the far turn. The rest of the pack is losing ground. What a race for a trifecta!" Sol is jumping up and down in excitement. "Whadda ya know—Harriet's now passing the long shot, Denny, who is the only one not running after her!"

That's not quite accurate. Denny and I are the only ones standing still. Evvie left me long ago to join the fray. My body hurts too much to move. But the muscles of my mouth still work. "Denny!" I shout. "Go get her!"

Denny, who has been watching it all, befuddled, reacts to the sound of my voice.

"It's all up to you now!"

His slow mind is processing what I am telling him.

"After all she did to you, don't let her get away!"

Denny may not be swift of mind, but he sure is swift of foot. Like a greyhound after the rabbit, he takes off after Harriet, who is now right in front of him, still lumbered with the stubborn Ida.

And just in time. Ida has finally lost her grip and has tumbled down next to the duck pond. "Shit!" she cries out in disgust, as she realizes what she's landed in. Poor Ida. The ducks quack at her, having had the last laugh.

Denny is breathing down Harriet's neck. She sees him coming and panics. She turns quickly trying to avoid him, but in her confusion she's now running back toward the crowd. Seeing her mistake, she tries to turn again, but Denny is on her. He grabs her by the arm and with the other hand hammerlocks her around the neck, holding fast. The two of them stand there, panting.

Sol catches up to them and starts gesturing with his fists. Now Hy is there, joining Sol, dancing up and down, jabbing along with him. "Hit her. Knock the broad out!"

"Don't lose her!" Irving yells, and he puffs up to them, his hands punching air.

Denny studies the three excited, jabbing men. Harriet is about to break loose.

"You're not my mama!" he yells, and with a neat left uppercut, he knocks Harriet out cold.

Sol grabs Denny's arm and pulls it up high. "The winner and new 'champeen,' Denny Ryan!"

The crowd cheers.

The running stops.

The kvetching begins. "I lost my glasses." "I need my nitroglycerin." "My bathing suit is ruined." "Does somebody have a seltzer? I have such a thirst."

My girls and Evvie come back to where I'm leaning. They are panting and disheveled. Sophie's lost both of her pool sandals. Ida's French twist has come undone. I won't even describe her clothes. Bella is hyperventilating. I hug them all. "I told you to bring weapons. That's all you could come up with?"

Bella holds up her fly swatter proudly. "There's a lot of flies who wouldn't agree with you."

"You were brave and wonderful and I love you all." We all hug and kiss again.

I'm surrounded by all the well-wishers congratulating me. I thank them profusely for their gallantry. And boy, am I glad no one dropped dead of a heart attack from all that exertion!

"Best entertainment we ever had at the clubhouse," says Mrs. Nettie Fein from Phase Three, tugging at her support hose that came flopping down in the chase.

Yolanda leads Millie to me. They are both giggling. With a terrible Spanish accent Millie says, "*Basura, malo, hasta la vista, bueno.*"

"What, in the name of heaven," Evvie asks, "does that mean?"

Yolanda answers in equally bad English. "I teach Millie, she teach me. Means good riddance, bad rubbish."

Leo, the Sleaze, is smiling. "Gotta hand it to ya, Glad. You took a fixer-upper and turned it into a fast seller!"

"Good show!" chorus the Canadians.

My heart swells with pride that word of mouth brought out nearly fifty "extras" from the other five phases, who turned up to give me moral support and bear witness.

As the accolades keep coming, I glance toward the lawn and watch someone familiar reach down to help Langford up. Morrie balefully looks up into his father's eyes. "You look like hell, boy," I hear Jack Langford saying as he grins. "Wait 'til the guys at the station hear about this. Done in by a bunch of old fogies!"

"Dad!" Morrie says, horrified. "You wouldn't!"

Jack sees me looking. He waves at me and I wave back.

We all watch Detective Morgan Langford (who is not only disheveled, but limping) take the handcuffed, and still groggy, Harriet away.

"I hope she gets the chair," Hy says cheerfully.

"God forbid," Ida retorts. "Life in prison without parole. I wanna see how she likes it when *she* gets old!"

"Like you're gonna be around to find out?" Evvie asks, sarcastically.

I put my arms around Hy and hug him. "No, but Hy will be here. He can tell us."

We all have a great big laugh at that. And it feels wonderful to laugh again.

Do I feel good. Considering how bad I hurt. At last the forgotten ones have had their day. We senior citizens fought back. We reserve our right to live.

We are the new old.

51

All's Well . . .

What a celebration we had last night! All six phases attended. The Manischevitz Malaga kept flowing, the klezmer band kept playing, the deli platters never ran out. I even sneaked in a dance with Jack and the girls never saw us. Which made me face the fact that I haven't gotten around to telling them about him. And wait until Evvie hears. . . . Well, they're going to find out today, heaven help me.

It's ten A.M. and no sign of the troops yet. Probably hungover like everyone else and slept late. Oops, I spoke too soon. Four bleary-eyed faces peer in at me through the open louvers.

"Coffee," a desperate Evvie begs.

"Bagels, or I'll perish," adds Sophie.

"With a schmear," continues Bella.

Ida, as usual, has to be different. "I could go for some scrambled with a little lox. And maybe a slice of Bermuda onion."

"Come on in, the kitchen is open. The cook is up."

In they march. "I'm so tired I could sleep for a month," Sophie announces cheerfully.

"But wasn't it wonderful?" Bella says, sighing. "A day and a night to remember."

Ida says, "My favorite moment was when Denny floored Harriet."

"Mine was seeing you on the grass with the ducks." Sophie chuckles at the memory.

Ida scowls. "You would. My best pool lounging outfit is ruined!"

"Did you see that Enya came to the party?" I comment. "She was actually talking to people."

"And even smiling," comments Sophie.

"So out of killing came a mitzvah. Enya joined the living again." Evvie's eyes tear up.

"And Denny," I say, and this time it's my eyes tearing. "Just sitting there shyly as everyone came up and said how glad they were that he came out all right."

"Wasn't it nice of the Haddassah women in Phase Four to clean up Denny's apartment for him?" Bella says happily.

Ida comments, "I hope they got rid of that battle-ax's portrait. Right smack into the Dumpster!"

"You know what Tessie told me?" Sophie says. "She's thinking of moving. After knowing what really happened to Selma, she says she can't bear living here next door to her apartment anymore."

"And speaking of moving," Evvie says proudly, "I cornered the Sleaze and told him we're on to him.

Don't be surprised if there's a 'for sale' sign on *his* place soon."

"Yeah, that was some party," Sophie says contentedly. "Even the Canadians had fun after a few belts of the Manischevitz."

"But," says Ida, "what I really want to know is who gets Esther's four hundred thousand dollars?"

"Good question." Evvie turns to me. "Glad, maybe you can ask Langford."

"Poor Morrie," I say, laughing. "We totally demoralized him."

"Do we get a reward for catching Harriet?" Bella asks eagerly. "Maybe they'll give *us* the money."

Ida sniffs. "In your dreams."

Bella keeps shaking her head. "I just can't get over it. How could it be?"

"How could what be?" asks Ida.

"Harriet, a killer." Bella reaches for an onion bagel for comfort. "And she was such a nice Jewish girl."

As they pile around the kitchen table, digging into the basket of bagels, they plan the day. Ida must go to the bank, Bella to the cleaners. Sophie looks at me, with my head full of curlers. "Looking at you reminds me. I could use a trip to the beauty parlor. I'm thinking, maybe, of dyeing again. I'm fed up with Champagne Pink. What do you think about Strawberry Blonde?"

"Now that you mention it," says Evvie, eyeing me suspiciously, "what's with the curlers?"

"I'm setting my hair. What does it look like?" It's starting, I think to myself. I am reminded of

Bette Davis's famous line in *All About Eve*: "Fasten your seatbelts, it's gonna be a bumpy night."

"Since when?"

"Since today."

Now everybody stops to study me. Ida picks up my hand as if I had leprosy. "Is that nail polish?"

"Curlers? Nail polish? What's going on?" Evvie wants to know.

"I'm giving myself a makeover."

"Since when are you a fashionable plate?" Sophie asks.

"Hey," I throw at them, "you're all big-shot detectives now, so detect."

With time only to grab a macaroon or two for dessert, they have at it.

"You're maybe going somewhere tonight?" Sophie ventures.

"Yes. Out," I answer.

"To the library?" Bella adds.

"Who wears pink polish to a library?" Ida argues.

Sophie is now sniffing about the apartment for clues. Evvie is standing with her arms folded. I can tell she doesn't like this one bit. It feels like it won't be good news for her. And she's right.

Sophie shrieks from the bathroom. "There's a bottle of Chanel Number Five on the sink!"

Evvie glares at me. "You haven't worn perfume since your daughter's wedding eighteen years ago!"

By now Ida and Bella have dashed into the bedroom in time to hear Sophie say, "And take a gander at this!"

Ida calls out. "It's her best silk shantung."

Evvie's voice is ominous now. "Ditto worn at the same wedding."

"Not really," I correct her. "That was blue. This one's green. It's only seven years old."

"And her good fake pearls," Bella now calls. "With the matching teardrop earrings."

The girls all converge back in the dining area. Now everyone is staring at me.

"I detect," says Ida officiously, "since you're getting so gussied up, you are going someplace nice."

"I also detect," says Bella, "since you didn't tell us about it, you're going by yourself."

"Where would you go alone?" Evvie demands to know. "You take me everywhere."

I take a deep breath and plunge in. "Who said I was going alone?"

Silence. Finally, "So...who are you taking?" Ida demands.

"Actually, I'm going on a date."

Shock. Surprise. Consternation.

"Waddaya talking?" Sophie says, irritated. "You haven't had a date in a hundred years!"

I smile. "Not quite. It only seems like it."

"A date?" Evvie asks, genuinely startled.

"Really? A date?" Bella asks, grinning.

"Don't I speak English? A. Date. With. A. Man!"

"Impossible," Evvie says. "What man?!"

"A man I met a short while ago." I'm really not trying to torture them. I'm just afraid to tell them.

"Oy," Sophie says. "Say it already. This is like

having a mammogram from a nurse with icy fingers."

Evvie is flabbergasted. "How can you meet anybody? You're never out of my sight for a minute."

I grin impishly. "Well, obviously I was out of your sight for more than a minute. I met him the day Greta soaped my car and flattened my tire. When I went to that bookstore party near the garage."

"That was weeks ago. How come you didn't tell me?" Evvie is now indignant.

"I was going to, but then Greta got killed and it went right out of my mind."

"Oh. So it's a first date," says interrogator Evvie.

"Actually, a second."

Evvie is speechless. Ida picks up the grilling. "That slipped your mind, too?"

"Actually, I was mad at you guys then. You just had Greta cremated."

"That's no excuse!" Evvie says sharply.

"Excuses, excuses," singsongs Sophie.

"Yeah, you just didn't want to tell us," Ida says. "Why? Is he ugly?"

"Actually, he's very handsome and actually, he lives in Lanai Gardens and actually, you all know him."

"Enough with the actuallys already," says Ida. "So actually, what's his name already?"

I take a deep breath. "Jack Langford."

Click. Click. Click. Click. Four minds are data-processing.

"Phase Six," says Ida.

"His wife, Faye, passed a few years ago," remembers Sophie.

Evvie is stunned. "Langford? You said Langford?"

Bella claps her hands gleefully. "Morrie's father!"

"I can't believe you didn't tell me," Evvie says, unable to let it go.

"I guessed," Bella says proudly. "I saw them dancing last night. Making goo-goo eyes at each other." She giggles.

They turn to her, amazed.

"And you didn't say a word?" says Evvie, wanting to choke her.

Bella shrugs. "I forgot."

Ida glares at her.

"So, kill me," Bella says in a huff.

Sophie moves in closer to me, conspiratorially. "So, are you having an affair?"

"Sex?!" Ida spits out the loathsome word. "That's disgusting! You're too old!"

I can't take anymore. This is torture. "Well, girls, I'm removing the curlers. Five minutes and we go on our errands." With that I start to leave them in the dining room to stew.

As I pass them, I try to ignore their expressions. Bella grinning. Ida horrified. Sophie intrigued. And my beloved sister, just plain flummoxed.

Whew. I'm glad that's over.

This evening, as we drive away from the building in Jack's Cadillac, I look back to see the girls leaning over the third-floor balcony watching us. Boy, do I feel guilty.

"Don't look back," Jack says, smiling. "You'll turn into a pillar of salt."

"I knew we should have met at the Greek restaurant."

"No more Greek odysseys. We're out in the open now. Let the chips fall where they may. You only live once."

I poke him in the shoulder. "Any more clichés you want to throw at me?"

"Just testing to make sure you're paying attention."

"So now what do we do?" I move closer. His aftershave smells so good. He actually dressed in a suit and tie for me. Oh, my, it's been such a long time. He puts his arm around my shoulder.

"We negotiate."

"I'm not giving up my apartment."

"Who asked you to?"

"Maybe we'll only get together on weekends."

"If that's what you really want."

"Don't ask me to give up my new profession. The phone is ringing off the hook with people needing private eyes."

"I have no problem with you supporting me."

"I'm not cooking."

"Fine. I'll cook."

"Ha-ha. You're English. No, thanks."

"I am a good cook. Ask Morrie."

"Right. And for breakfast you'll serve bangers and bacon and fried eggs and fried tomatoes and blood sausage. With enough cholesterol to kill a horse."

"Who needs breakfast? We're gonna live on love."

We are both laughing by now. He pulls over,

turns off the ignition, takes me in his arms, and kisses me.

And inside my head I hear aha, aha, aha.

THE END

Acknowledgments

MY EVERLASTING THANKS

To the women of Hawaiian Gardens, who shared their laughter and their tears: Helen, Arlene, Eva & Snookie

IN MEMORIAM
Family at Hawaiian Gardens

My beloved dad, David, Aunt Rose and Uncle Hy, Aunt Bronia

THESE TWO I OWE REALLY BIG

Caitlin Alexander
Lynn Vannucci

THIS GANG I ALSO OWE

My sons, Howard and Gavin, and daughter-in-law, Leslie. Always on my side.

My wonderful grandchilden, Alison, Megan, James & Amara. For just being themselves.

Sister Judy and adopted sister Rose. Who tried hard (and failed) to make a bingo player of me.

Margaret Sampson & the Women Who Walk On Water Book Club of Green Bay & Dykesville, Wisconsin. My first readers and supporters.

MY SPECIAL READERS—FAMILY & FRIENDS

Ginger Leibovitz, Harriet Rochlin, Dick Katz, Doug Unger, Dolores Raimist, Jack & Ruth Kay, Guiamar Sandler, Adrienne Goldberg, Sandy Carp, Joan Cohen.

All characters, though inspired by knowing the women at Hawaiian Gardens, are fictitious. Fort Lauderdale is, of course, real, but I have changed many of the locations for the sake of plot. Continental Restaurant, everybody's all-time early-bird favorite, is closed, but it remains alive forever here.

About the Author

Fate (aka, marriage) took Rita Lakin from New York to Los Angeles, where she was seduced by palm trees and movie studios. Over the next twenty years she wrote for television and had every possible job from freelance writer to story editor to staff writer and finally, producer. She worked on shows such as *Dr. Kildare, Peyton Place, Mod Squad,* and *Dynasty,* and created her own shows, including *The Rookies, Flamingo Road,* and *Nightingales.* She wrote many movies-of-the-week and miniseries such as *Death Takes a Holiday, Women in Chains, Strong Medicine,* and *Voices of the Heart.* She has also written the theatrical play *No Language but a Cry* and is the co-author of *Saturday Night at Grossinger's,* both of which are still being produced across the country. Rita has won many awards from the Writers Guild of America, as well as the Mystery Writers of America's Edgar Allan Poe Award and the coveted Avery Hopwood Award from the University of Michigan. She lives in Marin County, California, where she is currently at work on her next mystery starring the indomitable Gladdy Gold.

If you enjoyed
GETTING OLD IS MURDER
you won't want to miss
Gladdy Gold's return in

Getting Old Is the
Best Revenge

by

Rita Lakin

Available from Dell Books
in April 2006

Read on for an exclusive sneak peek—
and look for your copy at your favorite
bookseller.

Getting Old Is the

Best Revenge

On sale April 2006

Margaret Ramona Sampson, fifty-four,
always said the seventeenth hole
would be the death of her and she was
right.

Let's not mince words. Margaret cheated
at golf. After all, being wealthy (inherited,
not earned) meant being entitled. It meant
always getting what she wanted. And what
she wanted was to break the women's
record for the course. Always so close. She
had a feeling today would be the day.

Wrong.

She was with her usual perfectly coiffed
and outfitted foursome. Rich women who
played every Friday at the exclusive West
Palm Beach Waterside Country Club. It
was a beautiful, perfect Florida day. The
lawns glistened in the sunlight. The weather

not too muggy. She was playing brilliantly. All was right in her world.

One of Margaret's techniques for enjoying the game was to golf only with women who played less skillfully than she did, and were easily intimidated.

She knew her caddy saw through her, but didn't care. He was the caddy everyone wanted, so she paid triple in order to get him at her convenience. He was worth it. The money bought his loyalty. When things went wrong, she would blame him. He played his role very well, looking sheepish and admitting his "errors."

So here was the dreaded seventeenth hole and all she needed was a bogey. Unfortunately, here too was a troublesome serpentine water hazard. She routinely selected her best balls for this hole, but that never helped. Invariably she'd hook the ball before it cleared the water, and it would land in the trees. Today was no different. With angry, imperious strides, she marched into the foliage, leaving behind her the timid catcalls of the gals. "Meggie's done it again!"

As her caddy began to follow, she waved him off.

Yes, Margaret thought, I'll get out of it! No way would she take a penalty.

Dismayed, she discovered her ball wedged hopelessly in a clump of decaying turf. Without hesitation, she kneeled to pick it up.

"Naughty, naughty," a strong baritone voice chastised.

Startled, Margaret turned her head to find a pair of snappy argyle socks at her eye level. She got up slowly, preparing her defense. When she saw all of this other golfer, her expression turned to happy surprise.

"Well, look who's here. I didn't know you belonged to our club—"

Abruptly, he grabbed her, pulling her against him with one hand as he shoved a hypodermic needle in her arm with the other. Moments later, she stopped struggling and sank down onto the dark and mossy rough.

Her last dying thought was that she should have used the three iron instead of a wood....

One parting shot was irresistible. "Sorry I'm about to ruin your day, Meggie, old thing. You shouldn't toy with a man's game."

Heigh-ho, heigh-ho, it's off to the pool we go. As soon as they get past the swimming part of the morning, my little ragtag bunch of adventurers will be primed for another mission improbable. Towels at the ready, we cross the parking area, head down the winding brick path, through the small grove of palm trees, over three little bridges, past the clubhouse and the shuffleboard court, all the while avoiding those pesky ducks coming out of the ponds to leave their little droppings.

And here we are. And there they are—the other early morning so-called swimming enthusiasts. Their lounge chairs parked in their usual spots on the grassy perimeter of the pool, guarding their tiny turf jealously.

Plump Tessie Hoffman, the only real swimmer among us, is energetically doing her laps.

Enya Slovak, our concentration camp survivor, has her nose buried in the inevitable book. Always the loner.

The Canadian snowbirds are gathered together in their familiar clique. They are doing what they love most, lapping up the sun, and reading their hometown newspapers and comparing the weather. Thirty degrees in Manitoba...fifteen in Montreal. They chuckle smugly.

We have new tenants, Karen Wright and Beth Bailey. Bella shudders, still unable to believe anyone would want to live in an apartment where there'd been a murder, but the price was so low these gals found it irresistible. They've only recently moved in and it's nice to have young people around. They're cousins, in their thirties, originally from San Francisco. They don't look the least bit alike. Karen is kind of chunky and wears her dark, curly hair very short. Beth is a tall, skinny blonde, and very cute. Karen seems to live in blue jeans, but Beth loves frilly sundresses.

Next up, our beloved eighty-year-old Bobbsey twins, Hyman and Lola Binder (aka Hy and Lo), bobbing up and down in the shallow water, holding onto each other like chubby teenagers in love. They've been married over fifty years. Amazing.

Hy sees us and greets us as usual with the same inane comment. "Ta-da, enter the murder mavens. Caught any killers lately?"

Evvie glares at him. "You're just jealous."

Mary Mueller now joins us every morning. She's living alone since her husband, John, left her. It caused quite a stir, I can tell you, when he was "outed," (a new modern term we've learned). He recently met a guy in a Miami gay bar and fell in love. Boy, that was a first in Lanai Gardens. But Mary is holding up nicely, I'm glad to say.

Dropping our towels, we kick off our sandals and step carefully into the pool.

The girls walk back and forth across the shallow end splashing a lot. I do two laps and I'm done. Such is swimming exercise.

Pretty Beth addresses Evvie. "So, what movie are you seeing this week? I can hardly wait for the review."

Evvie, our in-house critic for our weekly free newspaper, is on a mystery kick since we've gotten into the P.I. biz. Last week she did a hilarious review of *Hannibal*. She was deadly serious; I couldn't stop laughing. This week she'll be reviewing a French mystery. Who knows what she'll do with that.

"Wait and see," she chirps. "But I promise it'll be gory."

"Hey, girls, didja hear this one?" And Hy is on us like schmaltz on chopped liver. God help us, he has a new joke off his e-mail. Prepare to be offended.

"So, Becky and Sam are having an affair in the old age home. Every night for three years, Becky sneaks into Sam's room and she takes off her clothes and climbs up on top of him. They lay there like two wooden boards for a couple of minutes, then she gets off and goes back to her room. And that's that. One night Becky doesn't show up. Not the next night either. Sam is upset. He finally tails her and, waddya know, she's about to sneak into Moishe's room. Sam stops her in the hall. He's really hurt. 'So, what's Moishe got that I ain't got?' Becky smirks and says, 'Palsy!' "

Hy grins at us, thrilled with himself. Affronted as usual, we turn our backs on him and paddle away.

"What? What'd I do? What?"

"Schlemiel!" Ida hisses under her breath.

"Hey, did you read this?" Tessie asks. She's now drying off on her chaise, her nose deep in today's Miami paper. She half reads, half condenses: " 'Mrs. Margaret Ramona Sampson, fifty-four, of West Palm Beach, died early yesterday morning on the seventeenth hole at the Waterside Country Club where she was golfing with three friends. Mrs. Sampson, "Meg" as she was known to all who loved her, died suddenly of a massive heart attack.' "

The group reacts with shocked surprise. The heiress is well-known, because reading the society news around the pool is a daily ritual. I only half listen as I work on my crossword. Tessie continues. " 'Mrs. Sampson, listed as one of the twenty-five richest women in the state, was a noted member of Florida society, known for her charitable works. She is survived by her husband, Richard "Dickie" Sampson.' "

"What a pity," says Evvie. "All that money she didn't get to spend."

"But she left a nice, rich widower," says Sophie. She picks up a tube of sunblock off the ledge of the pool and lathers her face and shoulders. "Maybe he'd like to meet a nice, poor widow. Like me."

Ida takes the sunblock from her as Sophie turns to let Ida do her back. "Dream on."

Sophie twists around to stare at Ida. "What? I'm not good enough for him?" She pushes Ida's hand away. "You're making me into a greaseball."

Ida slaps the cream into her hand. "Do it yourself. As if a rich guy like that would even look at a nobody like you."

Sophie hands the cream to Evvie. "And you know what? If he's old and ugly I wouldn't want him anyway."

Evvie continues working on Sophie's back. "What's old anyway? Look at us."

I look up from my puzzle. "Barnard Baruch, the famous statesman, said, 'Old is always fifteen years older than you are.' "

"Yoo-hoo...?" It is a wobbly little voice and the Canadians, who still have all their hearing, are the first to glance up.

"Over here." The voice manages to raise a decibel or two.

Now everyone looks up. A tiny elderly wisp of a woman stands at the pool gate, seeming almost too fragile to hold on to her metal walker. Her back is humped slightly. She looks as if a strong wind would carry her away. She's dressed completely in black, including the kerchief on her head. She must be sweltering in that outfit. "I'm look-ing for Gladdy Gold."

All eyes automatically turn to me as I make my way out of the pool and reach for my towel. "I'm Gladdy."

Needless to say the girls get out, follow-ing right behind me, my little ducklings all in a row.

"Your neighbors told me where I could find you."

"They would," Ida mutters into my back. "Ask them when we go to the toilet. All our neighbors know that, too. Yentas!"

I ignore Ida. "What can I do for you?"

"I am looking for a detective," the woman says, and then adds worriedly, "if the price is right."

In a flash, Hy is at our side, dragging one of the plastic pool chairs. "Here, mis-sus, have a seat," he offers, helping the woman into the chair, and then positioning himself right next to her. A minute later, here comes Lola, gluing herself onto her husband, leaning in.

Everyone around the pool shifts slightly to the left. My unofficial staff. Unwanted. Uncalled for. The other inhabitants of Phase Two, determined to get into the act, whenever they can. Tessie, ever so casually, moves her chaise a little closer. Mary puts down her crocheting. Beth and Karen openly stare. Even the Canadians have folded their newspapers. They all gape and listen intently.

The little woman puffs out her chest and grips the arms of the chair. She shouts, "I'm eighty-two years old and I don't need this *agita* in my life! My old man, maybe he's cheating on me! And I want to know who the *puta* is!"

Ahhh...I hear a collective sigh of happiness behind me. A problem they can all relate to after years of watching Oprah, Sally, Geraldo, and the rest.

"Hah!" says Hy with great delight. "The old man is dipping his wick somewheres else!"

The woman stares up at him. What did this fool say?

"Hy! Butt out," I say.

He shrugs, feigning hurt. "I'm trying to lend a hand here."

"Maybe he's lonely," Lola contributes.

"Maybe he's not with a *woman*," says Mary darkly. She's still pretty traumatized over John.

I have to nip this group intrusion right in the bud. Now.

"Shall we go to my office?" I say to the woman in black. Quickly helping her out of the patio chair, I reposition her behind her walker and firmly start moving her out the pool gate.

As we leave, my cohorts scampering to keep up, I hear another sigh in the background. This one of disappointment. Followed by a buzz of complaints.

I hear Tessie whining. "Didn't I ruin my best bathing costume chasing after our murderer? Where's the gratitude?"

"Wait awhile," says Hy complacently. "She'll figure out she can't do without us."

"Right," adds Mary. "She owes us. Big time."

I tell you, it's not easy being a star.